MEET THE PEOPLE OF
NIGHTMARE COUNTY!

ELIZA WEBSTER—she got tired of bearing children, so she fixed her man so he couldn't make any more . . .

MORGAN HUFF—he killed a man in broad daylight by beating his head into a jelly on the courthouse steps . . .

THE FLETCHER BROTHERS—they ran Nightmare County like it was a kingdom; they raped the land like it was a voiceless slave woman . . .

DOC CALLAHAN—he figured life's made up of good and bad minutes, and everybody should have as many good ones as he can get . . . and to hell with the fancy reasons . . .

JUDGE FLOYD COOPER—he was owned by the Fletchers just like they owned their coal mines and timber stands; they spoke and the Judge jumped . . .

AND Lucy Hammond, and little Dickie Huff, Anse Webb, Sheriff McCabe, Ward Thomas, Marie Wingate, and dozens of others—all in this big, shattering novel about the shame and sin of

NIGHTMARE COUNTY

Also by Frank Harvey

THE LION PIT

Published by Bantam Books

NIGHTMARE COUNTY
A NOVEL BY FRANK HARVEY

YOUR ASSURANCE OF QUALITY · BANTAM BOOKS · NEW YORK

NIGHTMARE COUNTY
A Bantam Book / published July 1964

Library of Congress Catalog Card Number: 64-19576
All rights reserved.
Copyright © 1964 by Frank Harvey.
Published simultaneously in the United States and Canada.

To my wife, Christine Holzer Harvey, whose editorial advice on this book was crucial—as it is in anything I ever write.

With all my love.

CONTENTS

This book is written as fiction, but it is based on fact. There is no Knight County in Kentucky. There is no abandoned mining camp called Hammond. All of the characters in this book are made up. But there are many counties in Kentucky as bad as Knight County, many abandoned coal camps as bad as Hammond, and many characters in as desperate straits as those portrayed herein. This exists now, in 1964, and will continue to exist for the foreseeable future unless something very drastic is done, on a very large scale, to change the desperate situation in Eastern Kentucky.

Frank Harvey

BOOK ONE
1900–1920

The Curse

The land was hushed. A high white sun stared down. In one of the coves of the mountain area which is known today as Knight County, Kentucky, a dragonfly alighted upon the moist pink throat of a wild rhododendron blossom, fanning with its iridescent wings, its bulbs of eyes shimmering greenish, its thin wormlike body writhing nervously—then shot off into the darkness of the hemlocks. A stream lay in the sunlight like a sheet of absolutely clear glass. A black bass lay in the stream, still as death, and the sun caught its flanks in a bonfire glow. A moth fluttered erratically out of the grass on the bank, faltered, touched the water with a kiss. There was a burnished streak, a swirl, and the miller was gone—and a moment later the bass was back, motionless, waiting, under the glittering water.

In that cove, in other coves and hollows, on the shoulders and crests of mountains, great trees rose high into the silent sunlight. Then a breeze ruffled the treetops and set up a soft sighing and the breeze moved off into a mountain meadow and creased the grass in long green ripples. There was a smell of woods mold, of pine, of flowers, of grass—borne along softly on the wind. It was Indian country then, vast, quiet, rich in grass and leaf, animal, fish and fowl—a hunting ground . . .

But there was a secret curse upon this smiling land. Centuries upon centuries ago, giant ferns had sprouted

3

and matured and died and gradually formed a deep bed of decaying vegetable matter. Chemical changes had made that thick stratum peat, a combustible material—and then the geologic pressures had compressed the spongy peat into hard black seams—some buried deep, others cropping out through the forest floor to glitter in the sun—coal. Those seams of coal lay in wait in the hills and hollows of Knight County, Kentucky. They waited to be discovered by men—to lure men to destroy the forest, the streams, the land, and themselves. Those seams of coal, rich in heat, rich in power, have been a curse upon the mountains of Kentucky in the twentieth century . . .

ANDERSON WEBB

My daddy's name was Anderson Webb. He run a blacksmith shop down in Booneville, Kentucky. He had thick hair like Abe Lincoln and he looked a lot like Abe except he had a flowin black mustache. He stood over six feet and even though he wasn't too heavy built he could swing a twelve-pound sledge with one hand like a little old carpenter hammer. Everybody called him Big Anse. They called me Little Anse. Neither my ma nor my daddy could read or write but hit didn't matter in them days because there wasn't no time for readin and writin. You was always out choppin wood or fishin or hoein the corn or fetchin chestnuts or shootin squirrel or sloppin the hogs. My daddy had me doin them things when I was just a little feller and I used to take on terrible and feel real sorry for myself. But now, as I look back on hit, I see where I wasn't never as happy again as I was back on Mad Dog Creek before the railroads come.

When the railroads come the bad things begun to happen. None of us knowed hit at the time, but them bad things had all been studied over by the smart fellers from the East and they had been layin the groundwork for years. I can remember hearin my grandaddy tellin about sellin the mineral rights to the six hundred acres he owned on Mad Dog Creek to a feller named Hammond. John M. Hammond. He never met a nicer man in his whole life, grandaddy said. Nobody had ever said one nice word to grandaddy or grandma about their place afore this Mr. Hammond come. Mr. Hammond had a feller with him from Booneville that grandaddy knowed—the County Clerk hit was—and he told grandaddy that Mr. Hammond was a man you could count on. If Mr. Hammond said somethin, hit was true. Well, grandaddy didn't need no County Clerk to tell him that. He could tell by hisself that Mr. Hammond was a man you could trust; he never seed a man so polite and friendly and full of amazin stories about them big buildings in New York and the like of that.

Mr. Hammond told grandaddy he never seed hogs like them that was wallerin in the pen back of the house. Them was the fattest, slickest hogs Mr. Hammond ever seed in his life. And when Mr. Hammond tasted grandma's apple butter he stopped dead a-eatin and looked around like he just discovered a diamond or a big hunk of gold and everybody was quiet and Mr. Hammond says, "Mrs. Webb—I don't know if I should or not—but I'm agoin to ask you a favor."

Grandma was so out of breath she could skasely speak but she said for Mr. Hammond to ask away and he says, "Mrs. Webb, I'm about to ask you for the recipe of this delicious apple butter I'm now eating. Now if it's a secret, don't you tell me. But if it isn't a secret, I'd be real proud and honored if you'd tell me every little step you took when you made it."

Grandma was never so flattered in her whole life. She wanted to give Mr. Hammond a whole crockful of apple butter, not just tell him how she made it, but Mr. Hammond wouldn't hear of it. He was bein an imposition already, he said, what with eatin her apple butter and her squirrel stew which was better than any chicken he ever et, Mr. Hammond said—and that went for chicken he'd et in them big fancy hotels in New York—and he wouldn't think of acceptin a whole big supply of her apple butter even though it was the finest

6

in the world. Then Mr. Hammond told about this building called the Woolworth Building which was so tall that if you put hit on the banks of Otter Creek, in Booneville, and climbed to the top of hit, you could see clean over Pine Mountain into Virginia. Neither my grandaddy nor my grandma rightly believed that story but they was too polite to say so to their new friend, Mr. Hammond.

When the talkin had died down a little, grandaddy got out a jug of his best moonshine and offered Mr. Hammond a nip. Hit was stuff that had aged in a charred keg and got a nice red color to hit and grandaddy said it was smooth as honey out of a bee tree and Mr. Hammond thought so too. They both had a drink or two and then Mr. Hammond come around to the deed. They was two kinds of deeds. They was what they called the "short form" which warnt hardly no deed atall, because it left everything kinda to chance. They was a much better deed, which was called the "long form" and that was the kind Mr. Hammond had with him.

"This deed doesn't take one inch of your land, Mr. Webb," Mr. Hammond told him. "Not a single blessed inch. All it does is sells the mineral rights to any coal or oil or other minerals that might be buried under the property."

The County Clerk gets into the discussion then. He tells grandaddy that Mr. Hammond is what they call a Speculator. He's buyin them mineral rights even though he aint sure if there is coal or oil or anything under grandaddy's land—and he's also gamblin that railroads will come in through the valleys later—maybe in ten or twenty years. If no railroads come, them minerals won't be touched, the Clerk says, because there won't be no way to get em out.

Grandaddy took him a look around at the knobs and hollers and big timber and he thinks to himself that

7

Mr. Hammond is a real fine gentleman but he aint got much common sense. Nobody could put a railroad track through them hollers unless he blasted out the rock and nobody was goin to do that. Hit would take a hundred years to make one mile. So grandaddy asks how much money Mr. Hammond is goin to give for them mineral rights and he finds hit's fifty cents an acre. That's three hundred dollars for his property. Hit's more money than grandaddy ever seed at one time in his life, so he and grandma puts their mark on the deed and the County Clerk signs as a witness and Mr. Hammond tips his hat and off he goes. But not before he thanks grandaddy and grandma again for their hospitality and says how he will always recall this place with joy and pleasure.

Well, in that respect at least, I guess he wasn't lyin. He probably recalled grandaddy's six hundred acres with joy and pleasure as long as he lived. They was three seams of coal under the place. Each seam was five feet thick. When the railroads finally come in, they opened up ever one of them seams and took out an average of 5,000 tons per acre. That was about nine million tons of coal they took out from under grandaddy's land. The price in them days fluctuated all over the place. For example, the trash screenings which we called "steam coal" because hit was only good for makin steam power, sold for $22.50 a ton in 1922. In the bottom of the depression, after the crash in 1929, that trash stuff was goin for fifteen cents a ton. But by and large you could say that the top-grade coal on grandaddy's property averaged out about $5 a ton in good times and bad. So what Mr. Hammond bought for three hundred dollars brung in $45,000,000. That was a pretty stiff price for the old man to pay for them nice compliments Mr. Hammond paid grandma on her apple butter, but hit weren't all of the price, even

8

so. That "long-form" deed sure didn't leave nothin to chance, just like Mr. Hammond said. Hit give any owner the right to cut timber for mine props, run roads through a coal property any place they seen fit, fill a creek with garbage and coal dust, turn the air black with smoke from burnin slag heaps, and many years later, when them big strippin shovels come in, that old long-form deed give them the right to tear the hills themselves down and turn them into spoilbanks nine stories high. The fish died. They aint a squirrel or a coon or a rabbit in the whole six hundred acres—or in the whole county, for that matter.

Over on Rockhouse Creek they had a big cloudburst in 1963. Hit rained all night, hard. Around mornin they heered an awful sound, roarin grindin, like the hill was acomin apart. Hit was. The rain had loosened up one of them big spoilbanks and it come down on the fields. It didn't git to the houses or it would of killed a lot of people. Hit smashed a barn flat and covered a cornfield with twenty feet of rocks and shale and busted trees. Those people over at Rockhouse was peaceful but they couldn't sit by and let themselves be wiped out like that. So they took hit to court. All they was askin was damages for the losses they had. Do you know what the judge told them people when the trial was over and the coal company that done the strippin and throwed up them spoilbanks won the case?

"You people have my deepest sympathy," the judge told them. "I sincerely wish I could award you these damages. But I can't. According to the laws of the state of Kentucky, my friends, you have only two rights on your land. You can draw breath on it—and you can pay taxes on it."

That happened in the summer of 1963. So them long-form deeds that are lyin in the county courthouses all

over Kentucky, yella with age, aint dead yet. Not by a
long shot. They are still messin up the people just like
they been doin for a hundred years.

CHARLES HAMMOND

When my uncle John Hammond died in his villa
in Cannes, France, he left me the deeds to some mineral rights on properties in Knight County, Kentucky.
My family couldn't understand why. They knew Uncle
John didn't like us because they'd given him the cold
shoulder when he married an actress from New York
and tried to bring her into the house in Back Bay and
present her to the clan. I was very young at the time
but I still remember how ashamed of them I was. I
went out to the street when Uncle John took his new
bride out to get a carriage and told them both how I
felt. I said I thought she was ten times prettier than
all those old sourpusses in there put together and I said
for two cents I'd get my piggie bank and break it open
and go to New York with them to seek my fortune.
As I say, I was about nine years old at the time and
it's a little vague in my mind. But I remember that
Uncle John's new bride got out her handkerchief and
wiped her eyes and Uncle John said, "Charlie, someday
you might get those two cents, who knows?"

Well when I heard the news about the deeds in
Kentucky, I had graduated from Harvard Law School
and was getting set to go into a law office and start
from the bottom, which was how all young men did
in Boston in those days, and my father said he'd write
to the bank in Booneville and find out about my holdings and we'd decide what to do. He did write and

10

he got a nice letter from the President of the Booneville bank which said that they knew about the property covered by the deeds and it was, unfortunately, in
an inaccessible location and without any minerals to
speak of, so that it would really be a waste of time
for anybody to come clear from Boston to investigate
them. Of course we were perfectly welcome to come
if we wanted to, the letter said, but in their judgment
it would be a waste of time and money.

My father was one of those people who thought the
world was bounded on the east by Boston Harbor and
on the west by the Charles River and any sections not
included in this area were inhabited by "scrubs" as he
put it. A scrub, in my father's definition, was a person
who had not gone to Harvard and who did not live in
Back Bay and there were a great many scrubs in
Kentucky, very probably, and it would be probably not
only a waste of time but very unpleasant to go out
there and get involved over nothing. My father did
not tell me these views of his. He wrote them to the
bank in Booneville, in somewhat more polite form, but
the friendly bank did not take offense. They wrote
back and congratulated my father on his judgment
and inclosed a quit-claim deed which we could sign
and they would pay us the $300 my uncle John Ham-
mond had paid Mr. Anderson Webb for the mineral
rights, and they would close the whole matter without
further expense or trouble to us or to them.

When I found out that my father had written the
letter and had received the quit-claim deed I said that
it was my property and I preferred at least to look at
it before I let go of it. My father said I was a fool
and if I expected to go to Kentucky I could get the
train fare together myself. I did. I borrowed it from
some classmates of mine who'd graduated from Harvard with me.

I didn't go directly to the bank president when I

reached Booneville. I went there dressed in my old clothes and I walked around until I found a fellow who knew the lay of the land and he took me up to a place called Mad Dog Creek and showed me the property covered by my deeds. Halfway up one hillside he showed me a shiny black outcrop of coal. It was five feet thick and he said it went all along the hill for miles and there were probably other seams on this hill that we couldn't see. Most of the hills around these parts, he said, had two or three seams of coal running around them like layers in a cake.

I hung around there about a week. By that time I found out all about my property. There were three seams on it, each of them five feet thick. I figured it out with a pencil and paper, and being as conservative as I could, I still couldn't see how I had any less than $10,000,000 in coal from my uncle John Hammond.

Then I went in and introduced myself to the President of the Booneville bank. He was a little fat man with blue eyes and red cheeks who looked like Santa Claus. I told him I had come from Boston to look into the mineral rights on my deeds up on Mad Dog Creek. He pursed his mouth and shook his head sadly. "I am sorry you wasted your time and money coming out here, my boy," he said. "You are on a wild goose chase, I'm afraid."

"How much will you give me for the deeds?" I asked him.

"I wrote to your father and offered the original cost," he said, "but since you're a young fellow and you've come all this way at your own expense, I'll add enough to it to pay for a round-trip ticket also. Let's say, in round numbers, five hundred dollars."

"What's your name, sir?" I said.

"Guthrie, son," he said. "Harold R. Guthrie."

"I'm glad to know you, Mr. Guthrie," I said. "I'll keep your name in mind."

"You aren't accepting my offer?" he said.

"No sir," I said. "It seems to me to be a little low."

"Well I'll be reasonable," he said. "If you feel I ought to make a slight concession, I guess I can do it. How low would you say my offer is?"

I didn't crack a smile. "I'm not sure to the penny, sir," I said. "But I would say it's about nine million, nine hundred and ninety-nine thousand, five hundred dollars too low."

Then I rose and bowed to Mr. Harold R. Guthrie and walked out.

I was wrong, however, in my estimate. Before we closed the books on the property my uncle John Hammond had willed me, we'd grossed in the neighborhood of $45,000,000.

FRANK McCABE

The big boss got me in his office down in Cincinnati before I started up to the job, and he said, "Frank, I want that railroad pushed up to Booneville by the first of July. Now I don't care how it's done. But if it isn't done by the first of July, you're through. However, if it is done, there'll be five thousand dollars in cash waiting for you in this office on July one, at nine o'clock in the morning when we open for business. Do you understand?"

"Yes sir, Mr. Fletcher," I said. "I understand."

We brought gangs of niggers from all over the South and handed em sheep-nosed sledges and hand drills and shovels and we used thousands and thousands of mules and we fired dynamite by the carload and we didn't let them black sons of bitches rest from Monday mornin to Saturday night. On Saturday night we didn't give a goddam what they did. There was cocaine and morphine peddlers in the camps, of course: there was no law agin it in them days, and there was rotgut whiskey by the barrelful. A man swung a sledge all week, he was entitled to a little fun on the weekends, we figured, and we brought in carloads of black bitches from New Orleans and Memphis that'd singe a pine tree just by walkin past it, and we turned em loose. Jesus, the hootin and hollerin down in the nigger end of camp on Saturday night would make you think you was in Africa, among the cannibals. I don't know what went on down there but it got good and wild. Niggers like to fight even better than white men, and we figured it was their business what they done on their own time. There wasn't hardly a Saturday night went by without a nigger getting stabbed or razored or shot to death in any big railroad construction camp you could name. And on Sunday you'd see the drug addicts lyin in the grass out in the woods in summer, pukin and gaspin. We never let em get out of the camps with any money. We took it all from them in the commissary that they didn't use for liquor or drugs or their women. They never had a dime come Monday mornin.

I was Shotgun on the whole job, so to speak. It was up to me to keep things hummin, and I can tell you, I done it. I worked out a system which kept them boys in line—even the tough hillbillies. Come Monday mornin there was always some nigger that couldn't git up to go to work, or wouldn't. It didn't make any difference to me. I'd go in his cabin with my pistol and I'd tell him to get up, and if he gave me any lip—even the slightest grumble—I'd shoot the sonofabitch dead. I always went alone. I never had no witnesses. And when I come out I always said I done it in self defense.

14

I tell you one thing—I was the most hated and feared man that ever ramrodded a labor gang in the state of Kentucky.

And I can tell you another. When the first of July come that year I walked into the big boss's office down in Cincinnati, at nine sharp, when they opened for business and he handed me $5,000 in crisp new twenty-dollar bills.

JACK ETHERIDGE

I was General Manager for the Charles Hammond Mining Company on Mad Dog Creek in Knight County, Kentucky, from the very first. I was there when young Mr. Hammond built the camp and everybody said he was a foolish young idealist from Harvard and he would soon go broke, in spite of the rich veins of coal that ran through his holdings. Nobody in their right mind, people said, would build homes for coal miners with running water and cesspools, and also a school system, a big recreation building with bowling alleys and pool tables and a swimming pool, and refuse to jack up the prices in his commissary. They said the type of people who dug coal for a living were pretty close to animals and they couldn't appreciate that kind of treatment and Mr. Hammond would find out soon enough when they started messing up his nice houses and starting fights in his recreation building and running up big bills at his commissary that they couldn't pay.

I will admit I thought they were right, but Mr. Hammond was offering me the top job, and he was paying me top money, so I took it. I figured the little Utopia he was trying to create would run along for a year or so, no matter how foolishly he operated, and then, if he wasn't broke, he'd crack down on those ignorant hillbillies and Negroes which the railroads had imported to lay the rails and who now hung around to work in the mines. I didn't think Mr. Hammond could possibly go broke, because his coal veins were so rich —even if he built every man jack of his miners a big brick house and bought them all one of those new Model T Fords. I did figure, however, that he'd get sick of the loneliness and dirt and violence and sell his coal at a profit and go back where he came from.

Well, Mr. Charles Hammond fooled everybody, including me. He wasn't as silly as people thought. He hired all the men himself, personally, and he kept a check on them later to see how they were working out. He set up a quota system. A man had to load fifteen tons a day. That was the minimum. Mr. Hammond paid more for fifteen tons than any other operator in the field. But he did more. He paid a bonus for every ton over fifteen—a good fat bonus, worth working for, if a man had any get-up-and-go in him. If he didn't, Mr. Hammond didn't want him. Some of the top loaders put twenty-two, twenty-three tons of coal in the cars in a working day.

Of course that meant that the whole operation took a jump. If more coal was loaded, more had to be cut, shot, and hauled out to the tipple. In other words, production had to jump all along the line. Mr. Hammond knew this, and he had a system of pay figured out so that everybody in the outfit who handled coal benefited by increased production. The more the mine put out, the more the men made. You might think he'd go in the hole paying bonuses like that for extra tonnage but it didn't work that way. There was a big profit on a ton of coal in those day, bonus or no bonus, and Mr. Hammond didn't stop his efforts at the mines. He made personal trips to Detroit and Pittsburgh and elsewhere to line up the best buyers—buyers who paid on the dot for good coal, and he contracted for bigger tonnages than other operators were able to deliver. Based on this mass marketing to good outlets, Mr. Hammond made money in spite of his bonus system— or perhaps because of it.

As time went on the word got around that a miner had the best deal in Kentucky if he could get hired by Charles Hammond, and all sorts of loafers and phonies and big dealers showed up and tried to get in on the gravy. It was inevitable that some of them would make it. Mr. Hammond was a good judge of character, but he was being worked on by experts.

The thing of it was, you could maybe get by Mr. Hammond during the interview, but you still didn't have it made. You then had to produce. If you didn't, you heard about it from the other guys on your shift because you were holding up their production and hurting their pay check. They gave you the word in a hurry and usually you either shaped up or quit.

Of course there were exceptions. I recall one big hulk of a man who had a bad reputation all over the area for getting in fights, both with his fists and his .38 special pistol which he packed at all times when he wasn't actually on the job. This ape's name was Big Son Evartz. I warned Mr. Hammond about taking him on, but Mr. Hammond said any man as strong as Evartz looked would be a fine coal loader if we could straighten him out, and he hired Big Son.

That was a mistake. Big Son wasn't just a loud-mouth. He was a real dangerous man, and the men who worked with him knew it. They knew he'd kill any one of them if they crossed him bad enough. He'd done it before. He liked to drink and when he was drinking, murder stuck out all over him. So when Big

17

Son started dogging it in the mine and terrorizing the rest of the men on the shift nobody raised a peep. The men actually worked harder to cover up, so as not have any trouble. But a thing like that is bound to bust loose, sooner or later, and it did in Big Son's case. He started failing to come to work, after he'd been out on a big weekend drunk, and the men couldn't cover for him. Mr. Hammond heard of it and called Big Son in.

"I hear you've been getting drunk and missing work," he said.

"I may of missed a day or so," Big Son said. "A man got to have a little time off for hisself. He aint a machine."

"You do have time off for yourself," Mr. Hammond said. "You get every Saturday afternoon and Sunday off, just like the rest of the men."

Big Son stared at his young boss and it was obvious that he didn't have much respect for him. Big Son didn't respect anybody who wasn't big and rough and ready to kill him if they was to fight. "I aint like the rest of your men, Mr. Hammond," Big Son said. "I'm different."

Mr. Hammond met his stare and when he replied he didn't raise his voice. "Yes, Evartz," he said. "I can see that now. You are different. You are also fired. Pick up your time in the office as you go out, please."

Big Son's face got ugly. "No man talks to Big Son Evartz like that and gets away with it," he said. "You got coal and money, mister. But I'm gonna find out one of these days if you got any guts."

"You know where I live," Mr. Hammond said. "Now if you please—I've got a lot of work to attend to."

Nothing happened for several days. I was over at Mr. Hammond's house on Sunday helping him with some paper work that had fallen behind when Big Son Evartz rode up on his horse, full of whiskey and pack-

18

ing his .38 special. He reined the horse up outside and yelled for Mr. Hammond to come out.

"You go in the bedroom and lock the door," I said to Mr. Hammond. "I'll sneak out the back and run for help."

Mr. Hammond was very pale, but his voice was steady. "No Jack," he said. "If I run for help now I'll be running for help around here the rest of my life."

"Well, it's better than having that drunken no-good kill you," I said.

Mr. Hammond didn't reply. He had been expecting this, I guess, because he went directly to a cupboard across the room, opened it and took out a pistol. It was a peculiar one. It had a long barrel and a beautiful rosewood handle, and when he brought it across the room I saw it was of very small caliber—.22, it looked like.

"I don't know where you got that gun, Mr. Hammond," I said. "But it's no match for the one Big Son's got out there. He's got a thirty-eight special. If he hits you anywhere with it, even in the leg, it'll knock you down."

Mr. Hammond didn't seem to hear me. His lips were set, his face was quite white, and his eyes were very bright. He looked at the pistol carefully, checking to be sure it was loaded, and then he went to the front door. He called through it to Big Son.

"This is Charles Hammond," he said. "I'm busy working on some accounts. You are creating a disturbance and I want you to go away."

There was a short pause while Big Son took in what Mr. Hammond had said, and then a burst of laughing. I must say, it sounded kind of feeble under the circumstances, what Mr. Hammond had said. And it wasn't only Big Son who was laughing. A crowd had gathered. They were laughing too.

19

"Don't worry about your accounts," Big Son yelled. "When I'm through with you, you won't have to pay them. Now are you comin out or am I comin in and get you?"

Charles Hammond took the long-barreled pistol carefully in his right hand, opened the door with his left, and stepped out on the porch.

"All right," he said. "I'm here. What did you have in mind?"

Big Son had his .38 out. He shot from the hip, across the saddle, almost before the words were out of Charles Hammond's mouth, and he got off three shots before Mr. Hammond fired. Mr. Hammond did a strange thing. He held his little long-barreled pistol out in front of him, at arm's length, steadying his right hand by gripping his own wrist with his left hand, and locked his aim and sighted carefully along the barrel and gently squeezed off his shot. The crack of the .22 was like the sound of a boy's cap gun compared to the boom of Big Son's .38.

Mr. Hammond fired only one shot. Big Son stopped shooting and slid off his horse forward, like a sack of cornmeal, and tumbled down in a heap in the dust of the road. Nobody knew where he had been hit until they rolled him over. Then they found the bullet hole the .22 had made. It was in his right cheek, about an inch below the eye. He was dead.

Mr. Hammond called to me then. "Jack," he said, "I think you'd better go and get the Sheriff now. I want to make a report on just what happened, and I hope some of the good people who are here will bear witness to it."

Well, they did. And the Sheriff didn't do a blessed thing to Mr. Hammond. Why should he? It was a clear case of self defense.

NOAH ADAMS

When I saw those gangs of railroad men blastin their way up through our valleys and saw the mines begin to open up, I saw the handwritin on the wall.

"This is a curse, this coal," I said to my wife. "Every person who touches it will be blighted. It will ruin the people and the state of Kentucky and I am not goin to have anything to do with it."

"What are you goin to do?" my wife asked.

"You and I are goin to buy us a nice slopin hillside," I said, "and plant an apple orchard. Then we can live our lives as we see fit and not have to ask those rich slickers from the city for a blessed thing. We'll be free and clear and those fools that are rushin to the mines to get those high wages will be slaves."

So we looked around and found three hundred acres of the finest apple land you could imagine—a big long gentle slope and nice soil, and way back up at the head of a holler, about ten miles from the nearest main road. We put in about seven hundred trees—Northern Spy, Golden and Red Delicious, Rambo, Winesap, and Maiden Blush—and we tended those trees like little children, mowed around em, fertilized, pruned, killed the tent caterpillars by squeezing them into green mud with our bare hands, sprayed, mulched —and they came into bearin about five years after we started. It was a lovely sight in the fall to go out and see those big rosy apples peepin through the leaves.

21

And I was right about sellin them. Nobody else in the county had thought to have an apple orchard, and we had the only apples around, and everybody was glad to buy them from us at our price.

"We did a smart thing," I said to my wife. "We're sittin pretty."

"You are a smart man, Noah," my wife said. "I'm right proud of you."

Well, as it turned out, I wasn't as smart as I thought I was. Seven years after I planted my orchard some men came around with surveyin tools and started takin sights in my orchard. I went out and told them, in no uncertain terms, to get off and stay off.

They didn't argue with me, and there was a good reason: I was carryin my little 32-20, and they saw I meant business. But a couple of days later the High Sheriff from Booneville came ridin in and he had a lawyer with him and they had a copy of my deed that they'd got out of the courthouse somehow. They showed me a little clause in the deed that said I didn't own the mineral rights to my farm. I guess I'd read that clause when I bought my place but I had no idea there were any minerals on it, and it was so far out in the country that I didn't think there was a chance in a million that that little clause would cause any trouble. I checked my surface rights real close. I had em, sure enough, but this lawyer says the mineral rights were bought by this big coal company long ago and now they aimed to put a mine in the side of my hill, right in the middle of the Red Delicious trees.

"You can't do that," I said. "It'll mean I'll have to take out a whole row."

"I'm afraid you'll have to take out more than that," the lawyer said. "We'll need access roads and a site for the tipple and another site for the tool-repair shed, and of course we'll have to build a camp for the workers, and this hillside is the best place for that."

"Well you sonofabitch," I said. "You're talkin about tearin up my whole farm."

"There's no cause to become violent," the lawyer said. "I'm only telling you what the owner intends to do. You don't have to abuse me."

"No cause to become violent!" I yelled. "I'll bet you'd become violent, mister, if you'd spent seven years workin on a nice orchard like this and some smart sonofabitch came in and starts tellin you he's gonna put a shed here and a shed there."

"Noah," the High Sheriff said, "I'm just as sorry as I can be. We all know how hard you've worked out here. But Mr. Simmons is right. They have the law on their side. They have the mineral rights to this land and you don't."

"Well they may have the mineral rights," I said. "But if they touch one twig of one of my apple trees I'll have em in court and sue em until I've collected for every step, every drop of sweat, every pound of fertilizer and every other damned thing I put into this place."

The lawyer gave a sour little smile. I guess I had made him mad when I yelled at him. But the Sheriff felt sorry for me: I could tell by the way he hated to tell me about the way the law read. The law had been written by duly-elected Kentuckians, I guess, but it sounded as if it had been written by a bunch of big coal companies in New York. The way the High Sheriff explained it to me, I didn't have a leg to stand on if I went to court. The owners of the mineral rights were legally allowed to do anything—*anything at all*—that could be called "convenient or necessary" to get the coal out. And there was a final clause that tied everything up tight. That clause relieved the mining company of any liability to the landowner for such damages as might be caused "directly or indirectly" by mining operations on the land.

23

Well, I didn't take it lying down.

"I don't give a damn what these old laws say," I said. "I spent seven years plantin and tendin this orchard and the first stiff-assed lawyer or surveyor or mining engineer that sets foot in my orchard is going to get a thirty-two twenty bullet right up his ass!"

"That's wild talk, Noah," the High Sheriff said. "If you shoot anybody I'll have to come out here with my men and take you to jail, and the jury'll probably hang you for murder."

"Get off my land!" I yelled. "Both of you! I might as well hang as let myself be run out of business and ruined. From now on this orchard is Tombstone Territory as far as any trespassers are concerned!"

"Think it over, Noah," the Sheriff said. "When you cool down a little you'll change your mind."

"I won't change my mind in a million years," I said.

But even as I said it, I knew I would. I loved those seven hundred trees like they were my own kids. But you can always get more trees, and you can't do a thing after they put a rope around your neck and drop you through that trapdoor. I saw a man hung, once, down in the Bluegrass, and they botched the job and he flopped and tried to scream only he couldn't and his face got red and then purple before he died of suffocation. It was an awful thing to see.

Me and my wife didn't do a thing when the minin company men showed up to start work. We didn't even go outside. But I could hear the sound their axes made on my young apple trees, and if there's a hell, mister, I sure hope the smart men that wrote that smart little clause in my deed and anybody else responsible for those axes burns in that hell for the rest of eternity.

RUFUS FUGATE

All this talk about us miners and how hard we have it gives me a royal pain in the rear end. The mines are supposed to be some kind of a hell on earth, and everybody that goes to work in them is supposed to be a poor devil that hates every second he spends down there in the cold and the damp just awaitin for the roof to fall on him or a spark to set off a big explosion and blow him out of the drift mouth like a punkin ball out of a shotgun barrel. Well if it was so godawful bad as they make out, how in the world do you think you could get hundreds of thousands of men to do it every day of the week?

Well, I'll tell you. The mine is the nicest place I know of. It never gets too hot in there and it never gets too cold. It's just the same, summer and winter. Some people think a mine is lonely, but I don't. It's peaceful in a mine, particularly when you are workin a place all by yourself. You're not supposed to work without a buddy but lots of us does it, and I do it more than most. When I'm in there in the quiet and the dark, with just my carbide lamp shinin on the coal it's like I'm in a private Kingdom and I'm the King. I don't have to listen to nobody nor talk to nobody. I just bore my holes in that glitterin black face and fill em full of powder and lay my fuses and tamp em good and tight and then I sit there for a couple of minutes and don't do a thing, just listen to the silence. It makes a hummin sound, like blood runnin through a big ar-

25

tery. If Time has a sound, I reckon it's the same sound you hear in the mine when you're by yourself back in a headin and you hold your breath and listen.

Yes, people gets hurt and killed in the mines all the time, but in a way that adds to the excitement of it. You never know, when you get in the mantrip in the mornin, whether you'll be comin out again at night. If somebody was to put me at a desk in an office, addin up figures all day, I'd go nuts. I'm a coal miner. Nobody has to be sorry for me. I love those mines, and when I die I want to die in one of them—quick, under a big slate fall, with my boots on.

WILBUR UPSON

As soon as the railroads penetrated the valleys of the Cumberland Plateau, starting around 1912, there began a great building boom. Everywhere there was a big mine a coal camp would grow up. Sometimes a full-scale town would grow around it. There were no building codes in those days and the coal companies were free to put up the cheapest structures they could get away with—and did, in most cases. No paved streets, no street lights, no sewage or water system. Just shacks hammered together out of rough lumber with a room or two, set on rickety timbers or piles of field stone. The houses had a privy outside. Wells were drilled here and there, often close to and down grade from the privies. The shacks were heated with open fire-places or potbellied stoves and they were so poorly insulated and constructed that you had to keep shoveling coal from morning to night to keep warm on the cold days.

You'd think this would be a fertile field for a Labor Organizer, but it wasn't. When I went there to try to organize for my union the men would listen to me when I told them how terrible their working conditions were; they'd nod their heads in agreement. But when the time came to sign up they usually said they'd think it over and let me know later. Well, later never came. They just let it slide. That's the story of a coal miner's life. He'll lie on his side in a coal seam thirty inches high and work with a pick from morning to night—but he won't join a union and try to improve his wages and working conditions. It's childish.

One day an old man got me aside. "Listen Mr. Upson," he said. "Afore you go any further tryin to talk these here men in joinin your union, you git you a horse and ride around back in them hollers and see how the folks is livin that *don't* work in the mines."

"Why should I do that?" I asked.

"Don't ask me why," the old man said. "You just do hit."

Well, I didn't get a horse. I don't know how to ride one. But I did go back into the hollows on foot and spent a day and a night there, and when I came out I knew what the old man meant. Those miners had it rough—but they didn't have it near as rough as those hillbillies in the hollows. Those shanties in the mining camps had wood floors and coal stoves and while it's true the privies were close to the wells, it was better than the hill cabins. Those cabins had dirt floors, some of them. I saw people all eating out of the same pot with their hands. I saw them using their yard for a privy. I saw them washing out of a tub of water that was black as ink—because they had to carry it from the creek half a mile away, and they wanted to get as much use out of it as they could. Those people in the hollows

27

didn't have any money at all. They lived off the pigs they butchered and the shucky beans they strung on threads and on rotgut whiskey. There is good moonshine and bad moonshine, I discovered. I saw moonshine out there that had so much dirt and stuff in it you had to strain it through a rag before you could drink it. In some of those places, to tell you the truth, there wasn't a whole lot of difference between the house and the pigpen.

But I didn't give up. I came back and kept trying to organize the men. It didn't seem right to me that the men should have such unfair, dangerous and poorly paid working conditions—just because it was much better than the pigsty lives they'd been used to. I tried to tell them that. I talked about safety regulations and disability protection and higher wages and the right to buy from stores outside the camp, where prices were half what they were in the gyp-joints that the mine operators ran. Everything I said was true and reasonable and the men all nodded and agreed. I even managed to sign a few of them up.

Then one day I was out near a tipple talking to a miner and the owner came up with a man wearing a sheriff's badge and he pointed me out.

"That's him," the mine owner said. "That's the goddam IWW organizer that's been hanging around here plotting to dynamite my tipple."

"Wait a minute," I said. "That's not true. I'm an organizer for the mine workers. I have never had any intention of harming a single stick or stone on this property. I am here on legal and legitimate business."

"Arrest him, Sheriff," the mine owner yelled. "He's a goddam Wobbly out here poisoning my men's minds!"

"Come along with me, mister," the Sheriff said. "If you come peaceful you'll be better off."

"This is a frameup!" I yelled. "This is a travesty of

the law. I'll come with you, but you haven't heard the last of this!"

The Sheriff smiled a little. "Neither have you, mister," he said.

He was right, too. When they got me in jail down in Booneville they took turns beating me. They used a big piece of Ivory soap tied in a woman's silk stocking. You might think that a cake of Ivory soap couldn't hurt a man—but you'd be wrong. It feels just like a fist, only it doesn't leave any mark—and when you come out of jail and try to prove the police beat you up, they ask you to show where you were hit, and you can't. When I finally got out of the Booneville jail I was so sore and weak I could hardly walk. I went back to the coal camp one more time, but I found that the men who'd signed up had changed their minds while I was in jail. I guess the owner had talked to them about how I was really a Socialist. Anyhow they said they'd thought it over and come to the conclusion that they didn't need a union. They were doing all right on their own. One miner even accused me of tryin to take away their natural freedom of speech by sneakin in all those union demands—it wasn't "American," he said. I saw that the bosses were too much for me, and I used the last of my money to buy a ticket back to Cincinnati, where I went into the lumber business with my brother in law. We didn't have any labor troubles. There was just the two of us and we got along fine and I had money every weekend to pay the rent and the groceries and no dumb bastards of coal miners to try to baby along, and no big-assed sheriffs to beat me up with cakes of soap tied in a silk stocking. I figured it this way: if a man doesn't look out for himself, who is going to do it for him?

ALBERT ROYCE

Shortly after I graduated from college in upper New York State I read an advertisement in the New York *Times* describing an unusual teaching job in the hills of Kentucky. A man was wanted to organize and run a school in a new mining camp that was being built. I didn't believe I'd have a chance because I was so young and inexperienced but I wrote a letter anyhow. I have always had confidence in myself. I worked my way through school waiting on tables and doing construction work in the summer. I played football. I was an end and I held the record, when I was in high school, for the number of completed passes. I wasn't carried away by it, though. I knew that the important thing a kid learned in school wasn't football, it was his studies. It was the most important thing, bar nothing. And when I answered this letter I said so. I didn't hide my football record however, or my summer work. I wasn't ashamed of waiting on tables.

When I didn't hear for two weeks I forgot the ad. I thought some older and more experienced man had been hired. But I was wrong. A letter came to me from a Mr. Charles Hammond saying he was going to be in New York city at the Waldorf Hotel at such and such a time to interview applicants and he enclosed a check for $50 to cover my train fare and hotel bill while I was in the city, if I cared to come. I wrote immediately that I'd be there. I thought it would be a lot of fun going to New York, all expenses paid, even if I didn't get the job. I met Mr. Hammond in the lobby of the Waldorf-Astoria and he was a younger man than I had expected. He didn't seem much older than I was. The first thing he did, after he looked at me, was to ask me to go to dinner with him there in the hotel.

I'll never forget that dinner. The dining room was high-ceilinged and carpeted in red, and there were glittering chandeliers and the waiters were dressed in formal clothes and the people who sat at the other tables were obviously either wealthy or cultured or distinguished, at least compared to people I'd known. The waiter placed a menu in my hand. It was very big and fancy and the foods and drinks were printed in a fairly small block in the center of the pages. There were many unfamiliar French words connected with the items of food. Of course I had had one year of French in college but I was by no means an expert. In fact, this was the first time in my life I had ever been to New York, and the first time I had been to a big restaurant.

Mr. Hammond asked me if I saw anything I liked. I studied the menu. I couldn't make much out of it. The waiter was standing there waiting to take my order. Then I did the only thing I could think of. I looked up at the waiter, and I said, "I have never ordered from a menu like this one before. I'm going to ask you to tell me a few things on it that you know are good. I'll be grateful if you will do that."

The waiter's eyebrows went up a little, and then he smiled at me. "Certainly m'sieu," he said. "It will be a pleasure."

He pointed out four or five items which he said he could recommend personally. I thanked him and I ordered one of those things. And when I had done that he was ready to help me with my choice of soup and appetizer and vegetables. It was very easy. And with his help I was able to get a fine meal, and I could

31

see the waiter was as pleased to help me as I was to be helped. Mr. Hammond made no comment; he just ordered for himself and let me go. He let me display my table manners or lack of them. He let me offer subjects for discussion. It all took about an hour and a half. And when it was over and we were leaving the restaurant, Mr. Hammond said, "I'm paying fifty dollars a week to start. If you take the job and succeed, I'll expect to give you raises at regular intervals."

I looked at him in amazement. "You mean you're offering to hire me?"

"That's right," Mr. Hammond said.

"Without even having an interview?"

He smiled a little. "We just had it," he said.

I went to Kentucky the next week and started organizing the school program. Mr. Hammond was strictly business. He said he wanted those mountain kids educated so they could grow up to be useful citizens. That was why he had gone to all the trouble and expense of putting that ad in the *Times* and coming to New York. He said he wanted me to take charge and run the show, and not come running to him for the decisions. However, if I needed anything, I was to come to him and if in his judgment it was a legitimate request, he'd see I got it.

I went to Mr. Hammond almost as soon as I took over.

"We need a chemical laboratory," I said. "Not a big one—but at least big enough to perform certain basic experiments in."

"What sort of things do you need?" Mr. Hammond asked.

"Well I've got a list I made out," I said. "It's rough, but it will give you an idea."

I handed Mr. Hammond the list. It contained things like Bunsen burners, glass tubing stock for heating and bending to make set-ups, the standard range of beakers, test tubes and retorts, and of course a supply of all the basic chemicals. Mr. Hammond read the list and handed it back to me.

"There's nothing here we can't easily get," he said. "But how are you going to run those Bunsen burners without gas?"

Well I felt pretty silly. Where I'd come from we had all the gas we needed. It had never occurred to me that they had no gas at all in Hammond. Mr. Hammond saw my embarrassment and he smiled.

"Go ahead and order the stuff, Royce," he said. "I'll figure out some way to get you gas for your Bunsen burners."

He did, too. It took a little while, but he did it. He laid a small-diameter pipeline down Mad Dog Creek about ten miles to where the Hewlitt Oil Company had brought in some oil and gas wells. Not just for my burners, I might add. Mr. Hammond had it in mind to light the camp with gas, which he did, before the electricity came in. But my Bunsen burners might have speeded up the gaslighting project a little, I don't know.

NELSON FEATHERS

Sim Yates and I lived on the upper end of Rockhouse Creek which dumped into Mad Dog and went on down through the valley to Hammond. After Mr. Charles Hammond built the new school down there we all got a chance to go to it, and we used to meet under a big chestnut tree and walk down together.

33

One day as we walked along we got to talkin about what we were goin to be when we grew up. Sim Yates says he was goin to travel and see the world. They was so many wonderful things in it, like the new teacher, Mr. Royce, had said. It was a little hard to believe some of those things, but I guess Sim Yates believed em.

"You remember that big old tree Mr. Royce was tellin us about in California?" Sim says. "Old Grizzly, they call it. Boy I'd sure like to see that big old feller. Hit was two thousand years old already when Christ was borned. I wonder how many birds done nested in that tree since hit was a little sapling?"

"I don't know how many birds nested in hit," I said, "but I heered the preacher is sayin that Mr. Royce is fillin our heads full of evil lies. Like his tellin us that coal is made from a bunch of ferns and leaves and flowers and stuff that growed on the earth millions of years ago, and died and turned into coal. How kin ferns turn into coal, the preacher says—little piddly green plants like that, turnin into coal. It don't sound reasonable. And even if they done it, how did they get buried between those layers of rock? Nobody ever seed ferns growin underground, the preacher says, between layers of rock. He says Mr. Royce is tryin to make a liar out of the Bible. It says in the Bible that God done made everything that's in the heavens above and the earth beneath and the waters under the earth. He done it in six days. On the seventh day He rested from His labors. The job was done. He called the seventh day Sunday. If God made the ferns and the coal and everything else in six days, the preacher said, how could Mr. Royce be tellin the truth about them millions of years and stuff?"

"I don't know," Sim says. "But I'd ruther listen to Mr. Royce than that old preacher yellin all the time about what miserable sinners everbody is, and how we better repent or we'll burn in hell. I don't know if Mr. Royce is tellin the truth or not, but I'll tell you one thing, as soon as I can do hit, I'm gonna travel out to California and have me a look at that big old tree." Sim stops talkin and looks at me. "How about you, Nelse? What are you goin to do when you grow up?"

"Im goin to be a great violin player," I said. "My daddy promised to git me a violin as soon as he can, so I can git started."

"You got a good idea there," Sim said. "You can make a lot of money playin at square dances."

"I don't intend to play at no square dances," I said. "Mr. Royce has some records of a violin player named Mr. Kreisler, and he played them for me after school one time, and I decided right then. I decided to study up and learn to play as close to the way Mr. Kreisler done it as I could."

While we had been talkin, Angie Yates, Sim's big sister, had come up and was listenin to us.

"You boys want to know somethin?" Angie said. "Both of you will go to work in the mines, just like everybody else, and make money to pay your bills."

We looked at Angie and began to laugh.

"Yeah, sis," Sim says to her. "I reckon you're right. I reckon that's about what we'll really be doin, when you come right down to it."

ALICE MENEFEE

I don't believe anybody could have had a happier life than I had in Knight County, when I was a little girl. We lived in a cabin miles from anybody and my daddy raised pigs and we had a big garden. My daddy shot squirrel and possum and my mother cooked them up into a delicious stew. We didn't have an inside toilet, of course, and my daddy didn't like the idea of a privy close to his house, so he dug a deep trench in the woods about two hundred feet away and rigged a seat out of two stumps and a cross-pole. It wasn't very relaxing, particularly in the winter, but I can say this: there was never a fly or a smell from it. Daddy left a shovel there and after we were through we covered up what we'd done with a blanket of earth. We were poor but my mother had a saying: "Cleanliness is next to Godliness." She stuck to it too. Our cabin floor was made of logs that daddy had hewed flat on top, and then worked over and over until it was smooth as a big piece of glass, and pegged them tight together. The logs of our cabin were cut in a special way so they could be driven in place solidly as if they'd been spiked—but could be taken down and moved if we felt like moving our cabin. Hundreds of cabins and other buildings were built like this in Kentucky in the old days and many of them are still standing today. I'll never forget the smell of our cabin. It smelled of old rich wood. It was a wonderful smell, piney and sweet and with a few little stinks too, that were like salt and pepper on a good piece of meat.

I know a lot of families where the parents get old even before they reach forty, and they snap at each other and don't wash or shave and let things go to pieces. It seems that every word they speak to each other or to their kids is a harsh word, or a whine, or a snarl. The people in those families, from the little kids up to the old folks, seem to live on hate. They eat it and drink it and it is the only thing that keeps them going. I heard somebody say that hate is like moonshine. I can believe it. Some of the awfulest things that happen in these hills come out of the moonshine stills like old Bad John Bentley and his boys used to have up the holler from us.

One thing I'm glad about. My daddy never bought a drop from Bad John or anybody. He had his faults, but liquor wasn't one of them. He couldn't seem to keep hold of money. It just drifted through his fingers, when he did get hold of a little bit, like water through a sieve.

In the fall my brothers and sisters and I went chestnut hunting. There was a big orchard of them on the mountain behind our house. The burrs were green—like fat prickly apples and they hung in clusters of four or five on the ends of the branches. The leaves were long and almond shaped with little points on the sides. My brother climbed the tree and shook the limbs, or we knocked the burrs down with rocks. I liked it better when we used rocks. You fired away with all your might and you could see the rock shoot up and just barely graze the clump, and then fly off and land in the brush, and you'd go out and find it and throw it again because there aren't many loose rocks lying around in a chestnut orchard. And then you'd let one go that you just knew was going to connect the second it left your fingers, and there'd be a soft little smack in the middle of the cluster and the burrs would fly out in all directions and fall in the grass and bushes with heavy thuds, like stones.

We opened the green burrs on a flat rock by pounding them gently with another small rock, being careful not to mash the nuts inside. You could tell by looking at the burr itself what the nuts would be like. If the burr was a little pindly thing the nuts would be shriveled up and not developed. If there was a brown spot on the outside of a green burr you would always find a fat white grub inside, eating one of the nuts. But if the burr was big and heavy you knew it would hold three or four chestnuts, nested neat and tight like toes in a shoe. The best time to get them was when the skins turned from milky white through yellow to pale brown. The nuts weren't dead ripe—they were crisp, like the heart of a piece of celery, but sweeter. You could peel off the pale brown skin, with a little downy fuzz on it toward the top, and you'd find a crisp white meat shaped like a teardrop that tasted wonderful.

My brother said the reason that a chestnut tasted so good was because of all the trouble we went to to knock them down and open the burrs and peel off the skins, and I guess he was partly right. But I had another reason. The fields in the afternoons were brown and rolling in the bloody September sunset and the maples were like bonfires burning in the black pines and the insides of the chestnut were like little jewel boxes lined with gray plush. When you took out a ripe nut and held it up in the golden light of the setting sun, it glowed like a precious thing. I always imagined I was a fairy princess when we were out chestnut hunting. One of the saddest things that happened to me in my life was when the blight came and killed all the chestnut trees, not just in Kentucky, but all over the United States.

I went to school in Hammond and Mr. Royce, who was the teacher that Mr. Hammond had brought in from New York State, encouraged me to go on and get more education. He said I had a fine mind and it would be a shame if I didn't develop it as best I could.

"I'd love to go on to school," I said to Mr. Royce. "But I can't. My daddy don't ever have hardly any money atall. He feeds us and we have a nice warm house, but we don't have any money and we probably never will."

"Well Alice," Mr. Royce said. "If you did have some money, would you want to go ahead and study?"

"Would I?" I said. "Just try me and see!"

I didn't learn for a long time after I went down

to the Bluegrass to college who it was who supplied the money. But when I did find out, I can say this: I paid Mr. Charles Hammond back every cent of it, just as fast as I could, even though I don't suppose he'd have missed it if I hadn't.

BOOK TWO

1920–1933

BAD JOHN BENTLEY

I finally got tired of the revenoo agents sneakin up on me and bustin my stills and pourin my moonshine out on the ground and takin me to the Circuit Judge down in Booneville to be sentenced to go to Atlanta to the penitentiary. The thing that really made me mad was that some of these agents was local boys, sons of men that I'd been friendly with since I can remember, comin in with their badges and them big high-power Springfields that could kill a man by shootin plumb through the tree he was hidin behind. Them young bucks aint got no call to come messin into a neighbor's still, I said to my sons, particularly with times so hard around the mountains a man can't hardly make it lessen he has him a still, and I don't aim to let them put me out of business.

"Well what do you aim to do, daddy?" my boy Bob says. "They got more men and guns than we got."

"That's true," I said, "but I got a plan that even them big guns can't beat."

"What is it, daddy?" the boys asked.

So I told them, and they looked at me in surprise, because I guess they didn't expeck an old man like me could be so smart, and then they said, "Daddy, hit's a terrible thing to do to people."

"So is bustin up a still a man put all his saving into a terrible thing," I said. "You younguns gonna hep me or aint ye?"

"Oh we gonna hep you, daddy," they said. "When you want to start?"

"There aint no time like the present," I said.

We worked fully a month on the plan and when it was ready I put my still right in my house instead of out in some wild holler, and went to makin whiskey. Nobody bothered us for quite a spell and then somebody must of told, because one morning, just at dawn, my son Bob who was on duty as a lookout in his regular turn, come arunnin in.

"Daddy," he says. "The revenooers is acomin up the creek on horses."

"Who's leadin em?" I asked.

"It's young McCombs," Bob said.

"You mean old Ves McCombs' boy from Mad Dog Creek?"

"That's right," Bob said.

"Old Ves would roll over in his grave if he knowed what his son was doin," I said. "Old Ves and I used to lay drunk ever Saturday night under the hill after we got through raisin a ruckus in the dance hall down to Booneville. We was like brothers. The first man I ever killed, Ves was with me. He was the witness to hit. He testified the other feller drawed on me first, and I got off."

"I know, daddy," Bob says. "But we got to do somethin. Them fellers is all carryin rifles and they are comin up the holler toward the house. They be here in another ten minutes."

"All right," I said. "You know what to do. Go get your brothers and put them at their places. Then take your own place and wait until I give the signal."

"I already told them, daddy," Bob says. "They already at their places."

"Good," I said. "Everybody knows the signal?"

"We all know it," Bob says. "When you drop your left hand."

"That's right," I said.

I went out on the front porch and put my left hand up agin the post beside the steps and kind of leaned agin it. I didn't have no gun on me. Pretty soon Ves McCombs' boy comes ridin up through the trees with six of his revenoo agents and stops at my gate.

"Good morning, Mr. Bentley," young McCombs says. "I guess you know why we're here. Now if you cooperate, there won't be any trouble. All we want to do is take a look at your house. We hear you got a still in there."

"Who told you that?" I asked.

"I'm not at liberty to say," McCombs says. "But we are here in the name of the Federal Goverment and you will have to bow to that superior power."

"I don't have to bow to no power atall," I said. "And that includes the power of the goddam Federal Goverment. Now I'm tellin you somethin, young feller. You turn them horses aroun and ride out of here while you and them men you got are still able to ride."

McCombs huddled with his men and they whispered a little while and then he said, "I'm givin you one more chance, Mr. Bentley. Are you gonna let us come in peaceable, or do we come in by force?"

"All right," I said. "You give me one more chance. So I'll be fair. I'll give you one more chance. You gonna go away and leave us alone or are you gonna insist on comin in and botherin us? Because if you do, somebody is goin to get hurt."

"Don't waste no more time arguin with the old man," one of the agents yells. "Let's go git him!"

"Is that your last word, Mr. Bentley?" McCombs yells at me and I can see them all ease them big Springfield rifles up to easy position for quick shootin.

"Yes sir," I said. "That is my last word."

45

"Then you'll have to take the consequences," Mc-Combs says. "Come on boys—we're ridin in."

I didn't do a thing until all of their horses was inside my yard, all bunched together on account of the rail fence me and the boys had built right up to the house. When they was exactly where I wanted em I just took my left hand down from the post where I was leanin. My boys musta been a little nervous because my hand hadn't even hit my thigh when they pressed them buttons that set off the big bundles of dynamite we'd buried all along under the driveway. We figured we had to cover the whole driveway, regardless of where a man or a horse might be standin, so we put ten sticks to a bundle and we buried ten bundles. It was more than enough. It killed all the men and all but one of the horses and it blew me through the front door of the house back through the big room and agin the wall and broke my left arm. But I didn't realize it was broke for a minute or so. I heered this horse screamin out there and I grabbed up my rifle and run out and killed it. I hate to see a horse suffer. People are different. Most people got it comin. But a horse don't. A good horse never done anybody any harm and hit don't deserve to suffer if a person can prevent it.

RUFUS FUGATE

Old John Bentley was a friend of our family as long as I can remember. There are people that call him Bad John, and it's true he killed a lot of men in his time, but the way I look at it, if a man treats me right personally, I don't go around takin up for others that he might of harmed. When Bad John and his boys blew up young McCombs and his agents who was snoopin around to bust his still there was lots of people that said the old man was nothin but a murderer and he ought to be strung up from the nearest tree.

I didn't say nothin, but I didn't agree with that atall. If John had made rotgut whiskey it would have been a little different, but him and his boys made the best liquor you could get in the state of Kentucky as far as I know. They took a pride in their moonshine. They didn't rush it through with no sugartop, and they didn't put no lye in it to color. They used the best corn they could git and they took their time and then they let her age good. You could git drunk on John Bentley's whiskey as easy as rollin off a log. I never forgot one thing that happened to me. Young Anse Webb was agoin down to enlist in the army for four years and before he went he bought him a gallon of Bad John's best whiskey. He put hit in a stone jug with a redwood cork and he buried it in the garden back of his daddy's cabin and he only told one person where he buried it, and that person was me. Well I forgot all about it until one day Anse comes up to the mine where I was workin and says, "Rufe, I'm back from the army, and I want you to help me locate my stone jug I buried. I been diggin all over that garden and I caint locate her."

The way he was alookin at me I seed what he was thinkin.

"Anse," I says, "I didn't touch your whiskey, so hep me God. She's buried in that garden someplace or other."

"If you come and hep me find her," Anse says, "I'll split her with you."

"Just you wait a second," I says. "'I got to wash up, and I'll be with you."

Well we got us two spades and starts up the road to Anse's place. Whilst we was awalkin along, Anse tells me about how it was in the war against old Kaiser Bill in France. All about them muddy trenches and cooties and barbed wire and guys gettin their guts blowed out by the Germans. Anse said he must of bore a charmed life. He come through it all without a scratch. In fact, he never had so much fun in his life as one night down in Paris when he went to see them pretty little French girlies adancin without practically nothin on atall, ceptin a little glittery string of jewels around their hips.

"How you goin to stand it back in these hills?" I says to Anse, rememberin some song I'd heered, "after you seen Paree?"

"That stuff is all right for a little while," Anse says. "But there aint really no place like home."

Well, we got to Anse's place and we like to spaded up the whole garden lookin for that whiskey. And presently I seed Anse givin me the eye. "Nelse," Anse said finally, "you didn't get thirsty while I was gone, did you, buddy?"

"May God strike me dead," I says, "if I touched a drop of your whiskey."

All of a sudden, I figured out what was wrong.

"The hillside's been awashin all during them years you was gone," I said. "It must of put two feet of soil on top of the garden. We knowed where we thought you buried the jug. Hit was over there, about four feet from that birch tree on the fur end. Let's just go over there and dig a little deeper and I bet we find her."

So that's what we done, and sure enough, when we got down about two more feet there was a gratin sound and hit was that stone jug. The redwood cork was eat a little bit by the ground water but she warnt near eat through, and when Anse got the cork out and we took a couple of nips of old Bad John's whiskey, hit was like tastin honey and melted butter. We just took that old jug down by the creek and passed her back and forth until we felt like the Kings of Southeastern Kentucky and part of Virginia, too.

"Old Bad John sure can make whiskey," Anse says. "I got to run over and see him and his boys as soon as I get a chance."

"I guess you aint heered the news," I said.

"What news?" Anse says.

"Bad John and his boys blew up a bunch of revenoo agents with dynamite while you was over fighting the Kaiser," I said. "They killed seven men and seven horses—so the Federal Goverment sent a whole army of agents after em with high-power rifles and demanded they surrender. John and his boys knowed that they'd be hung for sure if they surrendered, so they decided to shoot her out. They didn't answer nary a word when the leader of that big army of goverment men yelled at them to give up and come peaceable. Old John and his boys just drawed a bead on them agents and started blastin away. That started the Battle of John Bentley's Farm, as the newspapers called it. It was the bloodiest fight in the history of Kentucky moonshinin, the way the papers told it. And for once I guess they was right. A whole slew of revenooers was killed outright and a sight more was so badly wounded they aint ever goin to be able to raid a still again."

"I'm glad to hear that," Anse Webb said. "What happened to Bad John and his boys?"

"They vowed none of them would be took alive," I said. "And they made good on that vow."

"Hit's a shame," Anse said. "There's enough misery

in these hills without the Federal Goverment trying to mess into it. If a man wants to make good whiskey he ought to be lef alone to do it."

"Amen," I said. "Hand me that jug again, will you, Anse?"

ELIZA CLAY

I was born and brought up a Baptist and I knew that everything in the Bible is true if we only know how to interpret it right, but I draw the line at certain things which other people put their faith in. I didn't believe in those Holiness preachers when they said that a person could "take up serpents" in his hands, because that was what it said in the Bible, and actually encouraged their congregation to try hit. I know of people that tried and they got bit and they died. But of course the Holiness preacher had the answer to that. He just claimed them poor people didn't have enough faith. To me that was just plumb crazy, taking up serpents.

Then one night me and a girl friend from Hammond went to a Holiness meetin in a cabin up in Rockhouse Creek where you had to be known to git in because they were goin to handle serpents that night and it was agin the law. I went just to see the excitement. I didn't believe a word of that stuff about handlin serpents. It was intended to be took as a parable, our Baptist minister said, and not to be took literal.

Well there was about two hundred people there that night, far too many to get into the cabin, so the

50

preacher came outside and stood in the light of a big
fire they'd built and done his snake handlin there.
His name was Brother Daniel Hawkes and he sure was
a big strong goodlookin feller. He must have stood
six feet and he had big shoulders and big muscles on
his arms and big strong hands. His sleeves was rolled
up high for the snake handlin and he had flashin
white teeth and red lips and his eyes burnt like the
coals of fire in the yard that was givin him the light.

There was a big basket on the ground. Brother
Hawkes looked around at all of us, smilin more like
the old Nick than like a man of God, and he told us
what the Good Book said about handlin serpents and
how if you had faith enough you could do it just as
safe as a little baby handlin its bottle, and I looked
around me and the people's eyes was glowin in the
firelight like we was all a bunch of animals instead
of people. Brother Hawkes begins yellin to the sinners
to repent, and he yells to Satan to retreat and let go
his grip on us sinners, and pretty soon the crowd is
moanin and talkin in tongues and swayin back and
forth. Then they begins to git up and confess their
sins. My girl frien, even, she done it. She started yellin
to sweet Jesus to take her and wash her in the blood
of the lamb until she is cleansed of all her black sins
and is white as snow. She tells her sins. She even names
the boys she has sinned with and I never dreamed of
such a thing because I had never been with a boy
myself.

I see Brother Hawkes starin at me and then he suddenly stops yellin and hit gets so quiet I could hear my
heart beatin in my head and the fire makin a soft little
fryin sound.

"Brothers and sisters," Hawkes whispers. "Now is
there anybody present here who has faith enough in the
Lord to take up one of my serpents?"

51

There is a long moment, and nobody even breathes, and nobody speaks.

"Nobody in this vast crowd has enough faith," Brother Hawkes whispers. "Is that right? Not a single one of you has the faith to do hit?"

I saw my girl friend lick her lips and I went cold all over and got ready to grab her and hold her back, but she didn't say anything. And then Brother Hawkes says, "If nobody else in this gatherin has enough faith, I do. I have told you the word of God, and now I will demonstrate that those who have faith can handle serpents and the Lord God Almighty and his Only Son Jesus Christ will protect them from those drippin fangs!"

He lifts the cover off the basket and reaches down and I thought my heart would stop. His hand is out of sight in the basket for an instant and then it comes out, slow and steady, and writhin in his grip is a great big Timber Rattler, as big around as a man's arm, and the rattles are whirrin and the snake is starin at Brother Hawkes with its eyes that look like big bright diamonds in the firelight, and then it strikes at his face, and I can see the fangs, curved like a couple of yellow needles, and I shut my eyes and somebody screams in the audience.

I have to open my eyes immediately because I can't miss seein what the bite looks like on Brother Hawkes' cheek, but there's no bite, and he's smilin at us, and the snake is still there, writhin in his grip.

"You see, brothers and sisters," Hawkes whispers, never takin his eyes off the serpent. "You see—God is protectin me! The snake struck but it did not touch me! This is the power of faith! Praise be to the Lord and His Son Jesus Christ!"

Then, very carefully, Brother Hawkes put the rattler back in the basket and shut the lid.

"Ah am baptizin in the creek now, brothers and sisters," he said in a big voice that sounded almost like he was singin a hymn. "You have seen the Power of The Lord. Who will be the first to receive His blessin in the water?"

Mostly at revivals the preacher is lucky if he gets even one person to come to Christ, but Brother Hawkes had about fifty. It took him almost the whole rest of the night to finish the baptizin. I hung back until near the end, because I loved the sight of Brother Hawkes holdin the Lambs of God in his big hands and shovin them deep out of sight in the creek and then liften them out, washed like newfallen snow, in the Blood of Our Dear Lord Jesus.

When it came my time, Brother Hawkes took me by the hand and as he was leadin me down to the water he says, "You're Eliza Clay, aint you, sister?"

"That I am," I said.

"I'm real proud to have you with us tonight, sister," Brother Hawkes says. "I took special note of you when I was about to take up the serpent."

I didn't say anything. I was quiverin, deep down inside, because I had a feelin of what was comin.

"After the baptizin," he says, real low. "I want you to wait for me down on the path. Under that big rock by the bend in the creek. The Lord has spoke to me this night and He has decreed it."

I didn't say a word and then he took me down in the creek and held me under and I thought he was goin to hold me under until I drowned but I didn't care. I didn't care what he done to me. When I come up I seed The Lord in a great big silvery cloud up above the pine trees in the moonlight. The Lord was lookin down on me and smilin.

I told my girl friend to go on ahead home, that I wanted to be alone to pray, and she looked at me funny but she left; so I waited under the rock by the bend in the creek like Brother Hawkes had told me to do. When he come to get me, and he was all alone, he said, "We are in the shadow of a great rock in a barren land." I didn't know what that meant but I knew it was the Lord's word. When Brother Hawkes started to undress me I didn't resist. I begun to hep him. And when he got on top of me I closed my eyes and thought: *This must have been how the Virgin Mary felt when the Holy Ghost done it to her.*

WARD THOMAS

I had worked for the Fletcher Coal Company as a surveyor for about five years when a tree that my brother-in-law, Ben Martin, and I were chopping took a bad turn and broke my right hip. It was a long time healing and I was off work almost four months, and when I finally got up I had a lot of pain and a limp. Still, I was able to get around, and I went out with my crew working a boundary near the Hammond line. I was surprised, a day or two after I started, to see Mr. Will Fletcher himself coming through the woods to where I was taking stadia readings.

"Hello there, Ward," Mr. Fletcher said. "How is it going?"

"All right, Mr. Fletcher," I said. "We should be cleaned up here by the end of the week."

"How's your hip feeling?"

"Not too bad," I said. "I still got pain but I can make out."

"They tell me you limp a little."

"Yes sir," I said. "That right hip doesn't seem to want to work the way it did before I was hurt."

"Well look, Ward," Mr. Fletcher said. "I've been keeping an eye one you for quite a while. I know you are a fine surveyor and a hard worker. But now that you've got that game leg I'd like to put you in a spot where you wouldn't have to walk so much. Have you ever thought of running for Public Office?"

"Oh no, sir," I said. "I figured that was out of my line."

"Well maybe not," Mr. Fletcher said. "You've had all this experience in surveying and looking into deeds and boundaries and leases. That's exactly the sort of experience that would make a crackajack County Tax Commissioner. How would you like to be County Tax Commissioner, Ward?"

I was amazed and scared.

"Gee, Mr. Fletcher," I said. "I don't know if I could handle a big job like that—even if I could get elected."

He smiled. "You don't have to worry about a thing, Ward. We like you. We'll back you in the campaign and after you are elected we'll give you any help you need. In fact, I'll help you myself. There won't be a thing to worry about."

"Well all right," I said. "If you say so, Mr. Fletcher, I'll give it a try."

Mr. Fletcher was right. With the Fletcher Coal Company behind me in the campaign I won the office of Tax Commissioner of Knight County by 919 votes, which was a landslide. After I got the job Mr. Fletcher called me into his office at the mine and explained how to go about it. It was simple. Take his own company, for example. Once a year I would come to him and he would give me a list of the company's holdings, and their estimated values. That was all there was to it. I would take that list back to the county seat and enter the figures Mr. Fletcher had given me in the official records.

"But I'm the Commissioner," I said. "It's my job to set these values, isn't it?"

"Of course, Ward," Mr. Fletcher said. "You go right ahead and set them, if you want to. Just remember that everything you do is subject to review by the Board of Tax Supervisors. I believe you know the chairman."

"Yes sir," I said. "It's Mr. David Randall."

"That's right, Ward," Mr. Fletcher said, smiling at me in a friendly way. "He's our company attorney."

I didn't say anything, but I understood.

"Well then, Ward," Mr. Fletcher said. "If you have any questions about anything, from time to time, don't fail to come in and let me help you."

"All right," I said. "I'll do that."

I went back to my office and did the job, but I didn't feel right. We had a standing in the community. My daddy was well known. He used to do a little preaching in his younger days, and everybody got to calling him Uncle Eb for some reason. Daddy was real proud of me when I got this high-paying job as Tax Commissioner. I had been elected by the influence of Will Fletcher. He put me in office so I would hold his taxes down. I suppose I realized that all along. I just didn't want to face up to it. But now I rassled with it in my mind and I finally decided I'd be better off broke than living high off the hog at the expense of my own people, and I went into Mr. Fletcher's office one morning and told him exactly that.

"Well, well, Ward," Mr. Fletcher said. "I certainly agree with every word you have said. I had no idea this was bothering you. I wish you'd have come right in and told me before you let it prey on your mind."

He stopped and lit a cigar. He puffed it a couple of times and blew out a big cloud of smoke. "Ward," he said, "let me ask you a question. What would happen to your friends in this county if the coal companies went out of business?"

"Well," I said, "I reckon it would go pretty hard on a lot of folks. A lot of men would be thrown out of work."

"Exactly," Mr. Fletcher said. "And that's why you are wrong in feeling guilty, Ward. You aren't hurting your friends. You are doing them a favor when you hold down taxes on coal operators. If taxes rise too far—and it doesn't take much, with all our other expenses in labor and equipment and interest and the rest of it—a lot of us would have to close our mines. But with the kind of fair taxes we have now—thanks to you, Ward—that won't happen. You should feel proud. You are one of the best friends the folks of Knight County will ever have!"

I'd never thought about it that way. I wasn't sure he was right, but I wasn't sure he was wrong, either. And to tell you the truth, Will Fletcher was too much for me. I wanted to agree with him, and he gave me a reasonable argument, and I just nodded. So he got up and smiled at me and we shook hands and I left. I guess lots of people have done a thing like this at one time or another in their lives. You aren't really satisfied, but you go along with it anyhow, rather than make a fuss.

LUCY MARTIN

I got my first teaching job when I was sixteen years old in a one-room schoolhouse at the head of Mad

Dog Creek. I got it through my daddy's brother-in-law, Mr. Ward Thomas, who is County Tax Commissioner of Knight County. We used to call him just plain Ward. But after he got so important in county politics everybody called him Mister. He spoke to me about the job.

"I know you're very young, Lucy," Mr. Ward Thomas said to me. "But I think you have good stuff in you or I wouldn't have asked the School Board to hire you." He patted my shoulder. "Do me proud, now, Lucy, you hear?"

"I sure will, sir," I said. "I aint had much training but I'll do my very best."

It was pretty rough, at first. I had six grades all in the one room and some of the boys in the sixth grade were older than I was, and of course like any young boys they were full of high spirits and big ideas. I was a little girl, but I'd been doing the chores right along with my brothers and sisters, and I was strong, and while I might not have been a Normal School graduate, I had a mind of my own.

I remember the second day, after school, Bob Evartz, whose daddy had been killed by Mr. Hammond in a pistol fight, and a friend of his, Jimmy Webster, waited for me on the back path that I took as a shortcut over the mountain to my daddy's house. It was a path nobody used much, and the laurel bushes had almost choked it shut. I was about half a mile from the school when Bob Evartz and Jimmy Webster rose up suddenly out of the laurel on the side of the path.

"Hello teacher," Bob Evartz said, grinning at me. "It's a surprise seein you way out here all by yourself."

I felt my stomach go tight as steel.

"Well hello Bob," I said, trying to keep my voice natural. "I'm on my way home. I'm taking this shortcut."

"Well don't be in a hurry, teacher," Bob Evartz said,

"We got lots of time. Jimmy and me figured you might be willin to teach us a few little games such as we couldn't learn in school."

Jimmy Webster hadn't said a word. He was a scary kid. He had a narrow gray face and no lips and a long nose and eyes that looked dead except they glittered. He looked like his daddy had been a wolf and his mother had been a snake.

"How about that, teacher?" Bob Evartz said. "You want to play some nice games with me and Jimmy?"

I guess a city girl would have screamed or fainted or started to run, but I'd been born and raised in the hollow, and I'd seen what happens to animals when they turn and run. It sets off something. The other animals drag them down and tear them. If I tried to run that same thing might happen to me. Bob Evartz and Jimmy Webster would do things to me that would scare them so bad after it was over that they'd only have one thing left to do. They'd have to kill me. If I was dead I couldn't tell on them.

I looked at Bob Evartz. "Bob," I said, "I'm not the kind of a girl who fools around with two boys. You ought to know that." I lowered my eyelids a little. "I'll admit I wouldn't mind playing around with a big good-looking boy like you, but—" I glanced at Jimmy Webster and left it hanging.

I held my breath. I knew my life probably hung on what came next. Bob Evartz's eyes got wide. His lips opened a little and they were wet and he was breathing through his mouth. "You—you aint lyin to me, Miss Martin?"

My knees were shaking under my dress.

"Why would I lie to you—sugar?" I said.

Bob turned on Jimmy Webster. "You heered what the teacher said, boy," he said.

Jimmy Webster's gray wolf-boy face didn't change a particle. He looked at me with those dead glittery eyes and then he did what I was hoping and praying he'd do. He stared at Bob Evartz and said, "I aint leavin."

Bob Evartz took a breath.

"Then I reckon I'm gonna have to make you leave," Bob said.

Jimmy Webster had his knife out so quick I didn't see it happen, but Bob Evartz was just as quick. He was on top of Jimmy before he could get the blade open and they were down in the laurel, grabbing and kicking and snarling like two dogs. I didn't even look to see a single thing. I just took off on a dead run and I never stopped until I ran into my own yard and fell on the ground, dead beat. I couldn't speak for two or three minutes. I was too weak and too out of breath. My daddy and my brother Lincoln were squatting beside me, all worried and scared. They thought I'd been chased by a bear. Then I got enough breath to tell them what happened. My daddy's eyes got funny. He rose up from where he was squatting.

"Well Link," he said to my brother, "I guess we got us a job to do."

"Don't kill them, daddy," I said. "They're just a couple of young fool kids."

"If they are big enough to try a thing like this," daddy said, "they aint kids no more. Go in the house and git the rifles, Link. We goin huntin."

Link gets up and goes in for the rifles. But it gives me a chance to talk to daddy. I said if they killed those boys I'd surely lose my job teaching the school, or if I didn't I'd probably not be rehired, and also that Jimmy Webster's father was one of the feuding Websters and he'd be sure to come around in the night and shoot some of us through the window, and even if he didn't, we'd be scared he would and we wouldn't draw another easy breath the rest of our lives.

"Well that's true, Lucy," my daddy said. "But there

aint anything else Link and me can do under the circumstances."

"Daddy," I said. "One of the big troubles with this country is everybody worrying all the time about their sacred honor. They hired me to teach that school and with the help of God I'm going to teach it. All by myself, and without you or Link messing into it."

"No you aint, Lucy," daddy said. "If we let them miserable young skunks git away with what they just done, you gonna be throwed down and tore up the very next time you get out by yourself in the woods."

I looked at my daddy real steady. "Oh no I aint," I said. "Because you are going to let me take your forty-four pistol with me to school. Bob Evartz and Jimmy Webster won't dare bother me with the other kids around. And I swear to you, daddy, if they come near me out in the woods, I'll kill them both without even saying a word to them."

Link was out with the rifles, listening, and he was against letting me try it. He said somebody might as well shoot Jimmy Webster now, because somebody was going to have to shoot him sooner or later, and as far as Bob Evartz was concerned, he was no good, just like his no-good daddy.

Well, I talked to them for nearly an hour before I persuaded them to let me take the .44 and handle things myself. My daddy finally gave in. But he said for me to tell those boys that if they touched a hair of my head after this they might as well go right out in the woods and start digging a pair of graves because they'd be needing them.

Neither Bob Evartz nor Jimmy Webster came to school the next day when I arrived with my daddy's .44. They didn't come for over a week, and then we sent out the truant officer to get them. By that time my daddy had made a trip up in the hollows and spoke to both Jimmy Webster and to Bob Evartz and their people. When those boys came back to school they didn't make any trouble. I guess they knew how it was. If I failed with my .44, Link and daddy sure wouldn't.

I have to say this for my brother Link. He was right about Jimmy Webster. That boy was born to die a violent death, and he did. But Link was wrong about Bob Evartz. About a week after Bob came back to school, when it was getting cold and I had to keep the potbellied stove going, he came up to me and said, "Miss Martin, I seed you got a problem with that stove. I'd be proud to take care of it for you."

I looked at him but he didn't meet my eyes.

"Bob," I said. "Look at me."

"I can't, Miss Martin," he said. "I'm shamed."

"Yes you can," I said. "Go ahead."

He looked up. His eyes wandered for a second, then steadied on mine.

"That's better," I said. "Now let me tell you something. Taking care of the stove you'll have to come early to school and stay late. I don't mind you coming early. But if you stay late, you and I will be alone in the schoolhouse. Now I'm asking you something, Bob. Do you really want to look after the stove, or are you trying to get another chance at me?"

Bob Evartz's eyes didn't waver. "Miss Martin," he said, "I have to tell you the truth. You are the prettiest girl I ever seed in my life and there aint anything in the world I'd like better than to have you. But that aint why I axed to fix the stove. I axed because you give me another chance when I didn't expect one, and I aint never goin to forget it."

"All right, Bob," I said. "I'll accept that. When do you want to start with the stove?"

"I'll start right now," Bob Evartz said. "You won't have to give that stove another thought, Miss Martin, as long as I'm a student in this school."

I didn't, either. But if you think I didn't keep my

.44 handy when I was alone in the schoolhouse with Bob Evartz you're crazy. I wanted to help him but I sure didn't want to get myself raped and killed if I'd made a mistake in my judgment.

WILLIARD FLETCHER

You always have to expect a little trouble with these local yokels, even the stupid ones, until you get them broken in properly. I put one of my surveyors, Ward Thomas, in office as County Tax Commissioner, and I wasn't surprised when he got pangs of conscience over the low assessments on my coal holdings. But when I gave him the story about his doing the people of Knight County a favor by keeping our taxes low, he went for it without any fuss. I don't know if he really believed it. Put it this way. It sounded plausible, and Ward wanted to believe it, because he'd never had things so good, so he believed it. Better men than Ward Thomas have handled their conscience in that manner.

Well I've been aware of the big influx of people to Knight County with the opening up of the coal fields from 1912 on and I know that our schools and roads and other public facilities in the county have not kept pace, and so I expected that Ward Thomas would be in about it. He'd have to. The pressure on him would force him to. So when he showed up I gave him a big grin and offered him a cigar, which he refused because he was nervous, and made him sit down in my leather chair I keep for important visitors.

63

"Well Ward," I said. "I'm sure glad to see you. I've been hearing some fine things about the way you've been handling your job. Some very fine things indeed."

Ward fidgeted. "Well I hate to say this, Mr. Fletcher," he said. "But this year I'm afraid I'm going to have to raise your taxes. We simply haven't got near enough money to pay for all the things the county needs."

"What things are those, Ward?" I asked, very sympathetic, but surprised. "I hadn't heard of them."

"Well schools, Mr. Fletcher," he said. "And roads, And sheriff expenses. There's an awful lot of violence going on since people moved into the camps and things got crowded."

I had been hoping he would mention sheriff money. I had fully intended to expand the sheriff's office myself, but it would look a lot better to Ward if I seemed to be giving in to pressure from him.

"Violence," I said. "Well now I'm very sorry to hear about that. I'd hate to think that we don't have proper enforcement of law and order for the fine folks in this county."

Ward seemed to take a kind of a deep breath. I guess he'd expected me to bat him down on everything.

"You really feel that way?" he said.

"I certainly do," I said. "In fact I'm not even going to ask the good people of Knight County to pay taxes for law and order, things which are theirs by right. I am going to send a check to the Sheriff's office myself, in the amount of five thousand dollars, and I am going to ask Sheriff McCabe to put on three more men right away."

"Well gee, Mr. Fletcher," Ward says, "that sure is nice of you."

"It's the least I can do," I said, and then I struck quick, before he could get set. "But as far as those

64

roads and schools and things are concerned, I think the people who use them all the time should pay for them. Have you reassessed the properties up in the hollows, Ward?"

"No sir," he said. "I used to live up in the hollers, Mr. Fletcher, and those folks are barely getting by, in many cases, without raising their taxes at all."

"Why that doesn't sound right to me, Ward," I said. "For years now there has been good work in the mines. What have those people been doing with all their money?"

"I don't know," Ward said. "I sure don't know."

"Well I do," I said. "It's management. Just a simple matter of management. Those people don't manage their money properly. Now if they have to pay their fair share of taxes it will give them a sense of community responsibility which they sorely need. By raising their taxes, Ward, you will be doing them a favor by forcing them to manage their money better."

But this time I saw I'd overplayed my hand. Ward didn't look convinced. He sat there looking down at his hands.

"Let me explain it to you another way," I put in quickly. "A family up in the hollow has only one little cabin to pay taxes on, right?"

"That's right," Ward said.

"Well it's different with a big employer like myself," I said. "I've got my tipples, my rolling stock, my commissary, a hundred houses for the miners, not to mention my carrying charges on my borrowings, my insurance, and the big payroll I have to meet every week. If you raise taxes on one man with one little house you don't hurt him much. But if you raise taxes on all these things I just named, you hurt me a lot. In fact you might just hurt me so much I'd have to close down. Now I ask you, Ward, man to man. Is it fair to ask the person who is providing all the work and all the services and all the payroll for this whole area to pay all the taxes too?"

"Well I guess not," Ward said. "When you put it that way."

I rose, smiling, and patted him on the shoulder. "You're a good man, Ward," I said. "Oh, by the way, I've been meaning to ask you something for some time but haven't got around to it. Now is as good a time as any. Are you pushed pretty hard for time down in the tax office?"

"Well no," Ward Thomas said. "Except around tax time we haven't very much to do at all."

"I'm glad to hear that," I said. "Because if you have time, I'd like you to handle a little surveying job for me every now and then. I want a man I can really trust."

Ward smiled. "Why sure, Mr. Fletcher," he said. "I'll be glad to. Any time."

"Fine," I said. "It's a deal. I'll just write you a little check and seal the bargain."

"Gee that won't be necessary," Ward said. "You already done so much for me. I'll be glad to survey for nothing."

But I was already writing the check. I handed it to him and he took it and put it in his pocket without looking at it. He thanked me and left. I sat there and waited. I knew that Ward would look at the check—which was written in the amount of $1000—as soon as he got outside my office. And when five minutes passed and Ward Thomas didn't come back with that check I knew I had him right where I wanted him—in my hip pocket.

ANDERSON WEBB

I knowed Ward Thomas from the time we was kids together and you wouldn't be able to find a nicer feller anywhere. Smart as a whip, too. Ward went on through High School down in Booneville and then got him a job workin for old Jacob Wright, the County Surveyor, and learned a fine trade. After he'd been with the old man Wright for about five years he went out on his own, workin for the Fletcher Coal Company, which is the big holdin next to Mr. Hammond's property, and he was doin fine when he broke his hip. Things looked bad for Ward for a while after that. He got very depressed and I went over and set with him regular and cheered him up with a seegar and the local gossip. I remember Ward sayin to me once, "Anse, you're a hell of a good fellow to come over here like this. If I ever get a chance I'm going to do you a good turn."

"Aw hell, Ward," I said. "I aint done nothin but come over here and bend your ear out of shape."

"You've done plenty," Ward said. "And I don't intend to forget it."

I was surprised to see Ward the other day, comin up the holler, all dressed up like a city feller. Course I knowed he was now the County Tax Commissioner and he had to dress like that or the other bigshots down in Booneville would look down on him.

"Well well," I said, at the door. "Come on in, Ward. It's sure good to see you. Come in and set a spell and I'll get Angie to rassle us up a bite to eat."

67

"I can't stay that long, Anse," Ward says. "I'm out on official business today."

"Well no business can be that official," I says. "Hey Angie, honey," I yelled to my wife. "Ward Thomas is here. You got those miner's strawberries on the stove?"

"I sure do, honey," my dear wife replied, and stepped out on the porch. "Hello there, Ward," she said. "It's mighty nice to see you. And congratulations on your fine big job. It couldn't come to a better man than you."

"Well hello, Angie," Ward said, but he sounded funny and he seemed to be lookin at the wall a few inches from Angie's face, and not right at her. "It's mighty nice to see you, too."

"Come in," Angie said, "and I'll warm up the miner's strawberries as Anse calls them. You know they's just old beans—but I got a fine brown gravy to go with them."

"Thanks a lot," Ward says. "But I really haven't got the time right now." He took a swaller and his voice was loud and it sounded almost as if he was mad at somethin when he spoke. "I hate to be the bearer of bad news, but I figured the least I could do was come out here in person instead of writin it in a letter. The fact is, we have to reassess the taxes on all rural properties. You both know how fast the county has growed. We need schools for the kids and roads and all sorts of stuff."

Angie and I looked at him.

"It aint my fault the county is growin," Ward said.

"Course it aint," Angie said. "You just doin your duty, Ward. We understand that."

Somehow or other that seemed to hit Ward harder than anything else that had been said. He got real red in the face and I swear for a second I thought he was goin to bust out cryin. But he didn't. He just kind of shook his head in a funny way, and made his lips

68

tight as if somethin inside was hurtin him, and then he turned around without sayin a word and started down the path.

"Good-bye, Ward," Angie said. "Hurry back."

Ward never said a word. And he didn't look back. When he got down to the bend in the creek, he begun to run.

FRANK McCABE

It is my private opinion that Knight County is misnamed. It should be called Fletcher County. The reason I say that is because Mr. Will Fletcher and his brothers Austin and Boyd run this county like their own kingdom. Mr. Will has his coal company, which is the biggest in the county. Austin is Vice President and principal stockholder in the Booneville and Ohio Railroad. And Boyd is in timber. Boyd bought out the Yulee Lumber Company back in 1910, and it wasn't very big when he got hold of it, but now in the boom years of the War against the Kaiser, that sure changed in a hurry. The three Fletcher brothers are on the Board of Directors of the Booneville First National Bank. Mr. Guthrie is President—but really just a pratt boy for the Fletchers. They can tap that bank for any amount of money they might need, at any time, no questions asked. But I have to say this. When the Fletchers do anything they do it big and they do it right. They aint ever lost a nickel for that bank and I doubt if they ever will.

Will Fletcher got Ward Thomas elected Tax Commissioner. That automatically took care of their tax problem. If all the Fletcher holdins was assessed fairly, they'd pay half a million dollars a year in taxes, or thereabouts. Will ships a hundred gondola cars of coal a day out of his mine over on the Rockhouse Branch of Mad Dog Creek. Austin's railroad does his haulin for him. Boyd's timber makes the ties and roundhouses and stations and the rest of it for Austin's railroad—clear down into Ohio.

Of course that's just a drop in the bucket for Boyd's timber outfit. They've been cuttin Knight County like a great big lawn mower. They don't leave nothin standin. They just slash her all down and run through her and grab the best and let the rest lay. This is mighty wasteful of timber, but it's like Boyd says: "Time is money in this business." He sure practices what he preaches. He cut over 5,000 acres up in the north end of the county. There wasn't much left but a lot of loggin roads and a big pile of stumps and shavins. The sun dried all that little stuff like tinder. One summer some hunter must have started a fire and gone off and left it. The whole 5,000 acres burned in one big ragin fire. The smoke was so thick the sun looked like an old red harvest moon. The fire didn't stop with the cutover scrub. It went on and took 15,000 acres of prime virgin timber. Boyd Fletcher was so mad about it he couldn't see straight. But there wasn't much he could do. Not even a Fletcher can stop a forest fire of that size, once she really starts to roll.

But I wouldn't want anybody to think I'm agin the Fletchers. I'm certainly not. In fact I'm their right-hand man, you might say. When I got through ram-roddin the track gang for Mr. Austin Fletcher while he was buildin his railroad, I was goin to return to the South where I was born, but Mr. Fletcher talked me out of it.

"You've done a fine job for me, Frank," he said. "I like the way you handle men."

"Well thank you, Mr. Fletcher," I said.

"How would you like to be Sheriff of Knight County?" Mr. Fletcher said then.

I grinned. "Well, I used to run a chain gang down in Georgia when I was a young man," I said.

A slow smile come over Mr. Fletcher's face. "You did?" he said. "Well I never knew that. Frank—I think you're the man we're looking for."

DICK HUFF

I was sitting in the office of our little newspaper, *The Booneville Vigilante,* when Sheriff Frank McCabe walked in. He was a bald-headed man, gone to fat, with a gold tooth in front. I'd heard about him a lot, how he'd been a railroad labor boss before he got to be sheriff, and how he'd had to shoot men, from time to time, in self defense. He didn't look like the type. He looked jolly and he was smiling.

"Hello Mr. and Mrs. Huff," he said to me and Ginny. "Nice mornin we're havin."

"Yes it is," I said. "What can I do for you, Sheriff?"

"Oh nothin much," he said. "I hate to bring it up, really, I can see you're busy."

"Go ahead," I said. "There's nothing that can't wait."

"Well do you recall that story in your newspaper a while back about the County Tax Commissioner, Mr. Ward Thomas?"

"Yes," I said.

"I believe you mentioned that Mr. Will Fletcher gave Mr. Thomas some checks in fairly big figures."

"Yes," I said. "That's true, isn't it?"

71

"That aint really the point, Mr. Huff," the Sheriff said. "If Mr. Fletcher wants to pay Ward Thomas for surveying his property, there's no reason to print it in the newspapers."

"No," I said. "You're right, except for one thing. I checked up and Mr. Thomas hasn't done any surveying for Mr. Fletcher since he worked for him, many years ago."

The Sheriff stopped smiling.

"Mr. Fletcher has done more for this town than all the other citizens combined," the Sheriff said. "Anything that hurts Mr. Fletcher hurts the town. I'm sure you wouldn't want to hurt the town, Mr. Huff."

"I certainly wouldn't," I said. "That's why I'd like to see Mr. Fletcher pay at least a small fraction of his fair taxes in this town. I looked at the assessments at the courthouse and I found—"

"You look at too much, Mr. Huff," Sheriff McCabe cut me off. "You look at a lot of things that are none of your business!"

"Anybody is free to look at the tax books," I said, but I could feel my knees shaking. "They are open to the public."

Sheriff McCabe stepped back toward the door. He seemed about to go out without saying any more. Then he stopped and spoke again.

"You're a nice young feller, Mr. Huff," he said. "And you've got a nice little wife. Maybe I ought to give you a little advice. This county is a right dangerous place at times. I mean, accidents happen. A house burns down. Some poor feller gets shot in the deer season. Like that. Makes a feller stop and think."

"Mr. McCabe," I said, and my voice shook in spite of all I could do to hold it steady. "I think you better get out of my office."

McCabe stared straight at me. Then he turned and walked out.

Ginny said, "Dick, for God's sake, hold your temper! That man has a terrible reputation around here. You can't tell what he might do if he gets mad at you."

"Nobody comes into my office and threatens me," I said, "and gets away with it."

Ginny looked at me.

"What about that story you wrote for this week's paper?" Ginny said.

"What story?" I said, but I knew well enough.

"Well, the story on Boyd Fletcher and the way he's scalping the county to get his timber."

I hesitated just a heartbeat. Then I said, "We'll run it. It's a true story and we'll run it and be damned to them."

DR. BOONE CALLAHAN

My philosophy of life is fairly simple: have as much fun as you possibly can every day and every night. The human body is at best a frail and faulty machine which is always getting out of kilter and giving liberal doses of light, intermediate and severe pain. If, in the interims when it is working well, it can give you a little pleasure, grab it. You may never pass this way again.

I have a few people I really like in Knight County and a few sons of bitches I really can't stand, but by and large I take everybody as they come and I hope they take me the same. One of my good friends is old Rufe Fugate. Rufe should have been a bullfighter, he loves to show off so much. Rufe will go in a mine shaft where the roof is barely hanging up there by its fingernails—and cut coal—just to prove he's the boy who can do it. Some day old Rufe is going to be smashed flatter than a beetle. But I admire the guy—even though I'll never admit it. It's part of my job to lecture people about obeying the rules of safety, even though most of them don't pay me the slightest heed.

Anse Webb, for instance. Anse is getting silicosis from breathing the rock dust they use in the mines to lay the coal dust and prevent those big explosions. I tell him to wear a mask when he's working in silicon dust and Anse always promises faithfully. "You bet, Doc! I shore will!" And I look at him. "Why goddam you, Anse," I say. "You are the lyinest patient I got. You know in your heart you aint goin to wear no mask, and that's the truth, aint it?"

Anse will give a little grin. He likes to hear me talk like that. It makes him feel at home. If I talked like one of those city doctors I wouldn't last a month out in the hollers. Some old moonshiner would mistake me for a revenooer and pot me with his 32-20 from a laurel patch.

The best thing to do in Kentucky, or anywhere, is live and let live. You take these Holiness ministers. Almost every one of them I ever run across will tell you that God appeared in person in front of him and told him to go preach the gospel. Now of course there are a few liars among these wild-eyed Holiness boys, but mostly they believe they are telling the truth. If a superstitious man gets some high-powered moonshine in his belly and listens to some old mountain auntie spin her tales of haints and madstones and such nonsense—and then an owl hoots or the lightning cracks as the man is on his way home through a dark forest— he can sure read some mighty strange things into it. He sees a funny-shaped patch of moonlight. Or a strange little cloud. Or some remarkable coincidence or dream occurs. It's the Almighty—summoning our man to service! And of course, as time goes by, and the man tells his wonderful story over and over, he naturally enlarges on it and points it up here and there and fills in little details he might have forgot—and the first thing you know he can tell you how many hairs the Almighty had in His beard at the time of the confrontation. Once they go that far, there is no stopping them. They go and hold "prayins" over sick people, lay on their hands, and tell them they are cured.

I have no doubt that city doctors would be horrified by that sort of thing. I myself am not. In fact I have seen a goodly number of people completely cured by Holiness preachers in a single prayin. Of course I suspect that their ailment was mostly imaginary—but anybody who tells you an imaginary ailment isn't serious is a damned fool. And I must add that I have seen Holiness preachers pray over TB patients who turned around and died in less than a week, but even in those cases I must report that the prayin had at least a temporary effect. People living up in a lonely hollow in a dismal cabin have little enough to occupy their minds. A good Holiness prayin is exciting. It brightens up the day. The preacher holds up his hand, palm out, to ward off Satan, and he puts the other hand firmly on the patient's shoulder, and then he really turns loose on the Old Nick. This is good for any patient. The devil has been tormenting him something awful —and here's a friend to give the devil the devil as it were. The patient usually joins in. He begins shouting as best he can, often "lapsing into tongues," as the saying goes. It is exhausting and the patient frequently weeps or even has a mild fit. But I have been present at many a prayin and I can report that almost without exception the patient felt better, the whole family felt better, smiling and cheerful, at the end. There is something really medically beneficial, I'm convinced, about telling the devil to go to hell.

To prove what an easygoing fellow I am, I admit I even like do-gooders, and everybody knows that a do-gooder is one of the hardest to stomach of all. Mostly he is a person who likes to appear on the scene during the high excitement, when the blood is flowing and the victims are screaming—wearing, if possible, some snappy uniform with a snappy cap and a nice-looking badge of some kind—and Lend a Hand in The Crisis. You have seen people like this. You find them handing out hot coffee at disasters, or driving an ambulance Monday nights, 7 to 11. This kind of a do-gooder loves misery. He can smell misery for miles, like a buzzard can spot a dead thing that is lying on the ground from high in the sky. Like the buzzard, the do-gooder circles down to the feast. It gives him a thrill—a kind of sadistic orgasm—and after he hands out his coffee or loads his accident victim he retires from the scene, sated, and waits for another tidbit of misery to come along. I regard him as a carrion bird—but even so, I do not hate him. Carrion birds are necessary. They clean up messes that you couldn't pay anybody to touch with a ten-foot pole—and smack their beaks for more.

I am a do-gooder myself. The very worst kind—a dishonest do-gooder. Let me give you an example from late in my life, when Kentucky turned into a Welfare State in the late 1950's and early 60's. I was out in the hollows making my rounds as County Health Officer and I dropped in on a fifty-year-old man I had certified as blind so he could get on the county welfare rolls. He wasn't completely blind when he came to my office but his eyes were all inflamed and he claimed he couldn't even see the big E on top of my eye chart. Well, I found this man sitting on the front porch of his shanty reading a newspaper without glasses, and I sneaked up behind him and said, "Morning, Ed. How about reading me a couple little news items out of that paper of yours?"

Poor Ed like to died.

"Oh for God's sake, Doc," he cried out. "Don't tell on me. I'm too old to go to work in the mines and I'm too young to draw a pension and this welfare check is all we've got to live on!"

I knew this was true, of course, which was probably the reason I'd persuaded myself the old boy was really blind when he came to my office. But now I was curious to know how his eyes could have been so terribly inflamed when he came to see me a short time ago—and were now obviously 20-20. So I asked him. He told me he had a very bad eye disease which came on him in vicious sudden attacks. His eyes were perfect one day, he said, and the next, Oh God, they were giving him fiery agony and he couldn't see his hand in front of his face. He was better now, he said. But the terrible eye disease might strike at any moment. Well, that made me good and mad.

"Ed," I said, "I don't mind helping you gyp the government. Everybody else is, so you and I might as well do it too. But I don't like to be lied to. Now you tell me what ailed your eyes when you came into my office the other day, or so help me I'll turn you in and you'll never draw another nickel of welfare the rest of your life!"

That scared him half to death. "Oh God, Doc," he yelled. "Don't do that. I'll tell you! I chewed up a plug of terbaccer and rubbed the juice in my eyes just afore I come into your office!"

"Well now that's better," I said. "Get on back to your paper, now. Don't let me disturb an old blind man at his reading. But let me give you a warning. If you ever come to town without rubbing tobacco juice in your eyes—at least enough so they water good

77

—I'll tear that welfare check right out of your thieving hand as quick as look at you."

Tears of gratitude appeared in the old boy's eyes.

"Oh God, Doc," he said. "I'll take your advice. I wouldn't come within ten miles of town without my eyes red and waterin and my younguns leadin me. May God strike me dead if I do!"

"God won't strike you dead," I said. "But old Doc Callahan sure as hell will!"

I shook hands with my grateful patient and continued on my rounds. We're all do-gooders around here now. We know it's a losing game, but things have gotten so fouled up we can't figure any cure. You've heard the old saying about it doesn't do any good to put a mustard plaster on a cancer. I don't think it's so funny. Myself, I'd slap one on in a minute if it would ease the patient's mind. Way I figure, life's made up of minutes. Good ones and bad ones. My idea is to give everybody as many good ones as I can, and the hell with the high and mighty reasons.

DICK HUFF

Ginny woke me up by gently pressing my arm under the covers, and when I sat up and began to mumble, not being awake yet and not knowing what was going on, she pinched my arm tight and I froze.

I sat there holding my breath and feeling Ginny trembling against me. I could hear the brush of my heart in my ears and the rustle of the leaves on the maple outside the house. Then it seemed as if some-body touched my stomach with a red-hot wire . . .

"Hear that?" Ginny whispered with her lips so close to my ear I could feel her breath, and yet so soft I could scarcely hear.

I gripped her arm. And then, moving very carefully, I edged my left foot out from under the sheet. The sheet made a rustle that sounded very loud in the still-ness. And then, suddenly, somebody struck a match out in the hall. I saw it through the partly open door. And then the hall was one big sucking mass of orange fire as the match lit in the kerosene they'd dumped there and a man's voice said something, quick and low, and Ginny was screaming beside me and we were run-ning for the window in our night clothes and feeling the heat of the burning house pressing on our backs.

It was twelve feet to the ground. I held on to Ginny's hands and let her drop. Then I hung from the window-sill and dropped and my right bare foot struck one of the rocks in the border of the flower bed and I felt the bone in my ankle snap like a dry stick, and then I was floundering away, holding Ginny's hand, through the flamelit yard, and behind me our house was becoming a blossoming torch.

Doc Callahan set my ankle that night in his office after my house burned to the ground. Ginny was with me. She was crying. Ginny doesn't often cry. And it shook me almost as bad as the fire and the pain in my ankle.

"We'll just have to leave," Ginny said to me. "We can't fight this kind of thing."

I admit I felt like it. If we'd been sleeping soundly we very well might have been overcome by smoke and burned alive in our own house. I was sure the Fletchers were behind it and that McCabe had either ordered it or touched the match himself. But of course I couldn't

79

prove a thing, and there was no way of getting proof. It would be a big joke if I went and asked McCabe to investigate his own crime.

I don't know how my uncle Morgan heard about the fire as quick as he did. Morgan lives out on Pity Me Creek, which is some miles up in the hills, but old Morgan shows up at Doc Callahan's office just as I'm getting ready to go over with Ginny and try to get a room in the Boone Hotel. I'm a member of a famous—or maybe a better word is infamous—family in Knight County. We are known as "The Feudin Huffs." If you look into it you will find that some of the Huffs have been just as wild as old Devil Anse Hatfield or Bad John Bentley in their prime. Personally I have always done my feuding in newsprint, but uncle Morgan is a different kettle of fish. Morgan is a big rangy dark-faced man with deepset eyes and wide craggy cheekbones and heavy dark hair. There is darkness, in fact, in his soul. Morgan killed a man on the streets of Booneville one time with his bare hands. He gouged out one of the man's eyes with his thumb and then beat his head to jelly on the courthouse steps. He did it in front of witnesses and they sent him to the Penitentiary for life, but he got out in three years for good behavior, which was about average in a case like that in Kentucky in those days.

Morgan's black eyes glittered when I told him about the fire, and how we'd heard a man strike a match in the hall and throw it on the kerosene. He looked at my ankle, which Doc Callahan had put in a cast.

"You got any ideers who done hit, Dickie?" old Morgan said.

I told him about McCabe's visit, and what he'd said. Then I told him about my story in the paper about Boyd Fletcher.

"I haven't got any proof," I said. "So I guess there's nothing that can be done."

80

Morgan didn't say anything to that.

"You younguns got a place to stay?" he asked me.

"We thought we'd stay in the hotel until we can get another house," I said. "I guess we'll rent this time. If anything happens"—I managed a feeble smile—"it'll be the landlord's problem, not mine."

Ginny said, "No we won't rent a house, Dick. We'll sell the paper and get out of this miserable town. That's what they want us to do. And we better do it before something worse happens."

Morgan looked at Ginny.

"Don't be in no hurry, honey," he said. "You and Dickie get you a good sleep now. Maybe things'll blow over." He spoke real soft, and it should have tipped me off, because Old Morgan, when he has murder on his mind, begins to talk like he has a mouthful of molasses honey. I was in pain and confused, or I'd have picked it up. Old Morgan gave Ginny's shoulder a little pat and walked out.

The next day around noon, eleven heavily armed men walked into the office of Sheriff Frank McCabe while he and his chief deputy, Bull Hargis, were eating ham sandwiches. The leader of the men was my uncle Morgan Huff. The rest were also Huffs, or in-laws of Huffs.

"Howdy, Sheriff," Morgan said. "Go right ahead and eat. Don't let me and the boys disturb you none."

McCabe stood up. "I'll have to ask you men to disarm," he said. "You are in the office of a duly elected officer of the law—"

Morgan lifted his 32-20 and shoved it against Mc-Cabe's belly. "That little Dickie Huff that runs this little newspaper," Morgan said. "He aint nothin but a writin feller—but he's a Huff. Now I heered how you said this county is a dangerous place. Lots of accidents happenin. Fires and like that. I agree, Sheriff. Hit's dangerous around here. So I want to be special sure that nothin happens to Dickie or his wife. No accident. Cause let me tell you somethin. If a accident should happen to Dick or Ginny Huff you and that big old fat boy you got settin over there munchin on that sand-widge are goin to be killed. I aint sayin which one of us Huffs will do hit. I aint sayin you won't git some of usen in the shootin. But I am sayin we got enough boys to git the job done. So you go right ahead, now, Sheriff, and do whatever you got a mind to."

There's a saying that the pen is mightier than the sword. I don't know about a pen. But I can tell you about a 32-20 rifle in the hands of an old feuder like Morgan Huff. Sheriff McCabe didn't make a peep. And neither did Bull Hargis. And having said what he'd come to say, Uncle Morgan turned around and he and the rest of the Huffs marched out of the Sheriff's office.

CHARLES HAMMOND

On my way home to Boston in the spring of 1927 I stopped off in New York and had lunch with Mr. Ralph Uhl, who is my financial adviser. Ralph runs an investment-counseling service in Wall Street. He is a very successful man even though he has ice water in his veins instead of blood. One thing I have to say for him. He doesn't mind calling a spade a shovel. He often tells me things I do not want to hear and makes me angry because he fails to become enthusiastic over some pet scheme of mine. But later, when I cool off, I usually find that old Ice Water Ralph was right.

I was telling him how little education the coal miners

and their children were getting in Eastern Kentucky and how concerned I was for them, and he listened politely for a while, and then he said, "Charlie, I know how dearly you love to play God with all those little miners of yours, but I now have to tell you something. I have been making a study of the coal industry since I took on your account, and it is getting in a very dangerous condition. In the first place it is grossly over-expanded. In the second place there will soon be very serious competition from gas, oil and electricity. And in the third place your biggest customers are the railroads and they are busily converting from steam engines to diesels."

"What are you trying to tell me?" I said. "To sell my coal holdings?"

"Exactly," Ralph said. "And at once. Before the Kentucky fields begin to slip."

"You sound very sure of yourself," I said.

"Let me ask you something, Charlie," Ralph said. "Do you pay me to tell you bedtime stories or protect your capital?"

"But I can't sell out," I said. "Those people out there are looking to me for help. God knows nobody else I know is giving them any."

"What kind of help?" Ralph asked.

"Decent wages. Decent houses. Education. You name it."

"All right," Ralph said. "If the bottom falls out of the coal industry, what are you going to do—sit out there and pay those little friends of yours for sitting and admiring you?"

"Don't be silly," I said.

"If you want to provide them with education," Ralph said, "why don't you sell out at a big profit right now—and set up a substantial permanent fund in their behalf."

I hesitated.

"You're really sure there's trouble ahead?"

"Let me tell you a little story," Ralph said. "Last week I was down in Philadelphia and I took time to run over to Eddystone, where Baldwin Locomotive has a big works. I had some business with a couple of their top people and in the course of the conversation they told me they don't expect to build any more steam engines at all for domestic use. None at all. Do you know what per cent of the coal you fellows mine goes to the railroads?"

"Quite a bit, I suppose."

"One ton out of every four," Ralph said. "And I found out another thing. There's a tremendous market for oil tank cars now—and it is growing all the time. And not only that. Big pipelines to handle oil and gas are being constructed from the Texas fields to the East. Oil and gas are simpler for a lot of people to use than coal."

I sat there thinking. I hated to sell out, but what Ralph said was very ominous. If the bottom did drop out of the market, as he predicted, I couldn't do much for my miners. Maybe he was right. Maybe my best course was to sell, and set up an education fund. Ralph seemed to read my mind.

"I know how you love to play God," he said. "But it's a tricky game. You must know that you can't wave a magic wand over a man and turn him into a winner. A man prospers or fails on his own efforts, his own brains, his own guts. Very often you don't do him a favor by trying to carry him over the rough spots on your back. You don't make him strong that way. You turn him into a dependent weakling."

It was a fine rationalization, and one the Republicans have been using since we first organized the party, and will use until the end of time, I suppose. There is a lot of truth in it, too.

"What would you call a substantial education fund?" I asked Ralph.

He considered it. Then he said, "Ten thousand a year would certainly be substantial by any standards."

"All right," I said. "I'll think this over and make up my mind."

"Better do it right away," Ralph said. "You may not have much time."

DICK HUFF

I'm kind of a bug on soil conservation. It was a toss-up with me as to whether I would be a newspaperman or a County Agent. The blanket of topsoil that covers the earth is our most precious possession. If it is damaged, we suffer. If it is destroyed, we die. I'll never forget poor old Noah Adams and his apple orchard. Noah and his wife slaved for years building up that place. Then the coal company came in and ruined it in a matter of days. Erosion is the same way. One fierce rain can wipe out the soil it took centuries to build.

When this young farm agent came into my office and wanted me to accompany him up into the hollows to give him some publicity on his new soil conservation program, I said I'd be glad to. It was his intention to visit as many farms as he could, one after the other, and pass on the latest ideas to the farmers.

At the first farm this young agent began giving his spiel to a grizzled old man who had just finished

hoeing a patch of corn. All wrong—as the agent pointed
out in loud but friendly tones. The way to plant
corn was "on the contour"—horizontally across the
side of a hill—not up and down the hill as this old coot
had done. When rains came, the farm agent explained,
a contour furrow acted like a dam. It held the precious
water and let it soak in. Thus the water was saved for
dry weather and was not lost immediately as run-off.
And even more important, as the young man explained, such contour-planting prevented gullies from
forming. He had some pictures with him which he
showed to the old man. They were "before and after"
pictures. They showed a field that had been plowed
straight up and down before a heavy rain struck it.
It looked just fine. Then the rain came and they took
a picture after it was over. Those up-and-down furrows
had been reamed out by the rushing water into deep
ruts, almost like little creeks. And you could see the
gritty subsoil lying exposed.

When the young man finished, the old farmer said,
"Mister, I been doin hit this way ever since I was a
little feller. I don't aim to make no changes at this
late date."

"But sir," the young farm agent says, real earnest.
"Look at your land! It's full of gullies already, and a
lot of your topsoil is gone! In a year or so this land
will be ruined and you will have to clear another field
if you hope to get anything to grow."

"Let me ax you a question, young feller," the old
farmer said, and I could see he was hot under the
collar. "How many farms have you ruined?"

"I never ruined any," the agent said.

"That's what I thought," the old farmer said. "I
done ruined half a dozen afore you was even borned.
I know what I'm talkın about."

The young farm agent thought the old farmer was
making a joke, and he laughed politely. But he found

out different in a mighty quick hurry. No Kentucky farmer—in fact no Kentucky man of any kind—likes to be laughed at, and this old gent's jaws snapped shut like the jaws of an old turtle and he glares at his would-be savior and yells, "Young feller, I'm agoin to git my rifle—and if you and this other dude aint offen my place afore I come back you'll be laughin out of the other side of your mouth!"

Well, I don't know if he really got his rifle or not, because when he started for his cabin, this young farm agent and I turned around and started down the hollow. We were quite some distance away, well out of sight, by the time the old man could have returned to his up-and-down corn patch.

CHARLES HAMMOND

My father never quite recovered from the memory that he had urged me to turn over my worthless coal holdings in Knight County to the friendly Booneville bank. I have never mentioned it, and I never will, but when I come home for a visit, such as I did in May of 1927, my father was a little nervous until things settled down. My mother, on the other hand, was delighted to see me. She likes to examine me, when I return from Kentucky for a visit, for signs of degeneration brought on by my associations with those horrible subhumans my mother believes inhabit the Kentucky hills.

I wouldn't want you to get the wrong idea. Mother is under a severe handicap. She was born on Beacon Hill—on Louisburg Square, on Beacon Hill—which to anyone who knows Boston means that mother saw the light of day not only in the sacred Inner Circle, but precisely at its center. Louisburg Square, in case you didn't know, is a small rather dingy place where children sing carols at Christmas. I am aware, of course, that children do this all over America, but mother and a good many Bostonians know where the Holy Spotlight is during this festive occasion. She is too well bred to come out and pin it down. I can say this much. The Holy Spotlight is not on Scranton, Pennsylvania, or Morgantown, West Virginia, if you get the point . . .

My uncle John Hammond, rest his soul, was of a different opinion in regard to Louisburg Square, and, in fact, Boston itself. After the unfortunate snubbing of his bride he never returned to the city at all, referring to it in the familiar manner of people who do not like a certain geographical location as the "orifice through which the world, etc."

I do not hold any of this against my family. They had their faults and so do I, but I do like to tease them gently, because they take everything so terribly seriously. Barbarisms in English are my mother's particular concern. She insisted, when I was quite young, that I pronounce the word "fortune" to rhyme with "neptune." She also drilled me to pronounce "picture" to rhyme with "picked your." Saying "fortchun" and "pitchur" were, as mother explained, the way the vulgar folks said it.

I always did as mother said, but I delighted in teasing her when a chance offered itself, and of course Kentucky usage was made to order. This time, at dinner, I asked mother solemnly to "please pass the taters." Poor mother was delightedly horrified. She lectured me for ten minutes. She called my attention to the habits of the British in their faraway possessions. The British never let down the bars for an instant, mother said. They dressed for dinner even if they were alone with some half-naked native servant. Mother dragged in a short story by Somerset Maugham, called "The Outstation," to prove her point. The hero of this story had his newspapers sent from England all the way to the Far East, by boat. This required many weeks. The papers came in a big bundle—a month's worth at a time—but did the hero grab hungrily for the latest one? No indeed. He arranged them in sequence and had his servant deliver them at breakfast, one each morning, just as if they were coming in fresh off the street in London. In this manner, mother said, the hero of the story "maintained his identity in an alien world." Mother was full of phrases like that, due, no doubt, to her early training in Louisburg Square.

I looked at her dutifully.

"I think that's a splendid idea," I said. "I'll tell you what we'll do. Save up a month's supply of the *Boston Evening Transcript*—"

"Please don't be impertinent, Charles!" my father cut in. "Your mother is only thinking of your best interests."

Poor father. He never understood the little game mother and I played. She would have been desolate if I had not given her a chance to deliver a corrective lecture or two.

"I'm sorry, sir," I said to my father. "I am sure you are right."

He peered at me suspiciously, but seeing my face solemn and filial, he offered a cryptic comment to the conversation. "Things," father said with a wise air, "are going rather well."

I did not know if he meant things were going well for himself, for me, or for the world in general, so I said yes they appeared to be going all right.

"The man in the White House is not a spectacular man," father said. "But he has his feet on the ground."

I had never been an admirer of Mr. Coolidge, and I could not resist a slightly malicious retort. "I've heard he takes a nap every afternoon," I said. "He has to take his feet off the ground to do that." And I chuckled at my own rather feeble witticism. Father did not chuckle.

"Mr. Coolidge understands America," he said. "He understands the American way. He has the greatness of character to stand aside and let this great nation work out its own destiny. I do not think he should be criticized for doing it."

At that moment I had a flash of insight. I saw Mr. Coolidge lying on the couch in the White House, allowing the nation to work out its own destiny, and at the same time, in a sort of double vision, I saw the nation doing it. I saw Mr. Boyd Fletcher tearing thousands of acres of fine trees to mincemeat, and Will Fletcher sicking that vicious sheriff McCabe on hapless enemies, and Knight County itself robbed of its resources and its hopes by this American Way my father was talking about, and I was sickened. Not only by little Mr. Coolidge and the Fletchers but by myself. I knew what I was going to do, and I didn't like myself for it. But at least, if I was going to run out, I could be generous about the running.

"Father," I said, "if you will excuse me, I think I'll go and pack. "I've decided to return to Kentucky tomorrow."

Father's eyebrows shot up. "But I thought you'd planned to tay another week."

"I'm going to set up an education fund for the area," I said. "A really big generous one. And then I'm going to sell my coal holdings, lock, stock and barrel, as quickly as possible, and pull out."

Father stared at me in amazement. Then, slowly, he smiled. "My boy," he said, "I was wondering how long it would take you to tire of that terrible place and come back where you belong."

Father drummed with his fingers. "As to this education fund you speak of," he said, "I can't see that it will do any harm to give the yokels a few dollars if it will ease your conscience any. But don't get carried away."

Monday, May 30, 1927, was a humid day, unseasonably warm, and toward evening when I came out of the mine office I noticed that enormous thunderheads had piled up in the sky. They were pure white and beautiful and I stopped a moment to admire them. One particular cloud, over Booneville, must have been 40,000 feet high. There was a wind blowing aloft. It smeared the top of that big white cliff like an anvil. The high sky was intensely blue, almost black, in the bright sunshine. There was a dull copper light under the clouds and the air was very still. The leaves hung limp. You could hear people talking in low voices a long way off.

I ate supper alone, as I usually do. I am not a heavy eater. Then I read a little of Plato's *Dialogues*. I hadn't been reading long when a shadow fell on the room. I looked out. The yard was in deep shadow. I glanced at my watch, thinking that I had read longer than I had realized, and that night was coming. This was not the case. We still had hours of daylight.

I put the book down and went outside. The sky was completely overcast. The clouds hung low and they were dark gray. No rain fell, but there was a feeling of rain in the air. Somehow the darkness was welcome to me. This was the evening I had called a meeting of my Education Fund—my "conscience fund" as father had rightly diagnosed it. I was going to explain my plan to them—but I was not proud of

91

myself—and it seemed fitting to be doing it on a lowering dismal day. When the meeting was over I could escape to my house and be shut in by the rain.

I arrived a little after eight in the schoolhouse, where we were having the meeting. Dick and Ginny Huff were there. They were friendly. They did not know I planned to pull out. I felt like a Judas. Doc Callahan had not arrived, and I delayed the speech I had in mind so I wouldn't have to repeat it. It had begun to rain, a scattering of big heavy drops, when Doc drove in with a girl he had picked up in his car on the road from Booneville. He introduced her as Lucy Martin, and I immediately looked at her with interest.

"Are you the Miss Martin who teaches school?" I asked.

"Yes sir."

"Did you have a pupil named Bob Evartz?"

"Yes sir," Miss Martin said. "Do you know him?"

"He's in our school here at Hammond now," I said. "My superintendent, Mr. Royce, told me his story."

"Yes sir," Miss Martin said.

Looking at her now, standing in the white light of the gas mantles we had lit against the night and the storm, she hardly seemed big enough to lift a heavy Colt .44, much less carry it to school daily with the idea of using it in self defense. She was a slender dark girl with a thin face and big dark restless eyes. Her brown hair had been blown by the wind and a stray curl hung down not unattractively over one eye. She looked at me directly, and even though she used the formal "Yes sir" which is taught to Kentucky children by their elders when addressing an older person, there was not the slightest trace of subservience in her manner. In fact she seemed to be examining me. I had the feeling that I was being appraised, for better or worse. It was disconcerting.

92

"Miss Martin," I said. "I would like you to meet some friends of mine. We are having a meeting which involves the future of education in this area, and I would very much like to have you join us if you will."

"I would like to, Mr. Hammond," Lucy Martin said. "But I want to get home before this storm. It appears to be a big one, and daddy may need some help. We've got a pig in a pen down near the creek. If the creek rises we'll have to get him out of there."

I smiled a little. The idea of this tiny creature getting a huge pig up out of its pen was a little incongruous to me. She saw my smile, and she frowned.

"I'm sorry," I said quickly. "It's just—you seem so little—and a pig is so big. I apologize if I have offended you."

She looked at me, apparently decided I really meant it, and said, "I accept your apology, sir."

Which really took me a little aback. I had become used to the independent ways of my Kentucky neighbors, but I had rather expected Miss Martin to melt up under a little sweet talk, like a pinch of sugar in a glass of water. I looked at her. Our eyes met. I noticed a funny sudden empty feeling in my wrists.

"Will you stay and help us?" I said. "I have my Buick outside. If the storm gets bad and you feel you want to go home, I'll drive you. Is that fair?"

Miss Martin smiled now, finally, and it was the most attractive smile I guess I'd seen in quite a while, because the weakness in the wrists did not go away. "Why, yes, sir," she said. "That'll be just fine, if you don't mind doin it."

"It will be my pleasure," I said, and almost added a gallant remark about helping fair ladies in distress, but stopped myself. Hammond my boy, I thought, let's not get carried away here. You are are not going to get emotionally involved with this young hillbilly child,

93

on the eve of your departure from this place. You had just better stop getting chills when you look at this tiny little Miss Martin.

Then I introduced Miss Martin to the Huffs and we started the meeting. I don't remember exactly what was said because the sound of the approaching rain came through the doorway then, in a sullen distant roar. It was a frightening sound, not like an ordinary rain. It sounded as if a huge dam had broken and a wall of water was rushing toward us, tearing the trees down as it boiled and foamed through the dark. We all went to the screened door; the wooden door was open because of the heat, and looked out onto the school porch where a few glittery drops of rain whirled in the glare of the mantles.

Lucy Martin suddenly said, "Mr. Hammond—this is going to be a real bad one. Will you please take me home right now, before it gets here?"

"I will indeed," I said. "Come on."

We left the school in the Buick and crossed the plank bridge over Mad Dog Creek and were on the woods road up in the hollow when the rain struck. It was a sudden blinding deluge that seemed to come straight down, with no wind, and the car's wipers could not clear it off the windshield fast enough for me to see in the blurred headlights and the darkness. Water was rushing down the road under our wheels like a stream. I stopped the car.

"How far is it to your house?" I asked Lucy.

"About a mile more."

"We'll have to drive it," I said. "We'd never make it on foot."

"But you can't see the road, can you?"

"I'll have to open the side window," I said.

"You'll be soaked in a minute."

"We'll both be soaked before this evening is over," I said.

I opened the window and the sound of the rain surged in, so loud we had to raise our voices to be heard. I stuck out my head and was instantly soaked. But in the headlights I could see the yellow sheet of splashing water which was the road. I squinted my eyes, put the car in low, and began to drive. The road was rough but it was all hardpan. There was no trouble with mud. It took quite a long time to reach Lucy's cabin. By that time we could hear Mad Dog Creek roaring over the steady thunder of the rain. It was the heaviest rain I had ever experienced. Still I was not worried. These cloudbursts never last long. It would no doubt be over in a few minutes and the big thunderheads would move into Virginia and the moon would come shining down into the dripping forest.

Lucy and I got out of the car and stumbled through the downpour to her house where we could see the light of a kerosene lamp. We were soaking and gasping when we burst in. Nobody was there.

"They're down at the pigpen," Lucy gasped. "You stay here. I'll go see if I can help."

"Come on," I said. "Where's the pen?"

It was down a steep slope through some trees and we could see a lantern bobbing as Mr. Martin labored to get a huge rubbery-looking beast to come across a patch of swirling brown water from the pen to the slope. The pig was confused and frightened and did not want to come through the shallow water, and Mr. Martin was beating it with a stick and cursing while Mrs. Martin held the lantern. Then, suddenly, the pen which had housed the pig, a rickety structure at best, sagged tiredly into the main current of the creek, threw up a splatter of muddy water as it crumbled, and was drawn out of sight in the darkness. The pig turned

95

brainlessly in the wrong direction, squealing mightily, and floundered headlong into the creek to its death.

"Daddy!" Lucy screamed. "Come on! Come on! You'll git drownded!"

I thought, at the time, how a crisis strips off the veneer of civilization and book-learning, and you revert to basic things. The Martins must have now realized the futility and danger of their position, because they waded through the shallows with their lantern and all four of us began scrambling up the slippery bank toward the cabin. The slope, like the road, was now running like a shallow streambed. I was crawling beside Lucy, to her left and behind, when I heard her scream and saw her fling herself sideways in the dark, and then a big slimy powerfully twisting worm of a thing writhed against me and past me, going along the flooded contour of the hill, and in the lantern light I saw the big timber rattler was going to run directly into Lucy's body in the next heartbeat, and I reacted automatically, I guess. An instant later the big snake was ten feet down hill, rolling and twisting from the momentum of the fling I'd given him with my hands and arms—but on the right side of my face there was a white-hot searing core of agony so intense that I heard myself screaming like a child as I clawed at my face as if my fingers could somehow scratch out the venom of the rattler's strike.

I do not recall how they got me to the cabin. I think Mr. Martin packed me up there on his back, but by the time they got me there I was seeing fiery skeins floating through the darkness and with each one the flame breathed across my cheek and eyes and blinded me, and I screamed in agony and horror of death.

Mr. Martin cut my face, then, with a hunting knife, but the pain of the poison, so close to my eyes and brain, was so high and intense that I scarcely felt the cut. I remember somebody, somebody little, and it must have been Lucy, bending to my face, and lips sucking fiercely at my flesh—and that is all I remember. A red burning furnace swirled up in my brain and ate it like acid and the pain got so bad I passed out.

DICK HUFF

The cloudburst that began on the evening of May 30, 1927, was the heaviest rain ever recorded in the history of Eastern Kentucky. The morning light revealed a ghastly scene. High brown water hurled itself through the narrow ravine in which the Hammond Coal Camp was built. The stream had over-run its banks and ripped away everything in its path. The coffee-colored water carried every sort of debris, from broken pitiful little children's playthings to smashed houses and giant trees. The corn, which had been sprouting on the hill farms, was wiped out almost to a plant. The worn-out soil that had nourished the corn had been melted loose and washed away, leaving raw gullies, some of them big enough to swallow a barn, and millions of smaller gullies, and even the forest floor, normally immune to erosion because of the protecting bushes and leaves and grasses, was veined with deep crooked gashes, and gradually, as the flood waters subsided, the sodden tragedy lay revealed.

A hundred human beings lay dead in the mud, half buried where the rushing torrent had jammed them, and the silt had piled in upon them. Whole towns along the banks of Kentucky rivers were virtually wiped out: houses smashed, store-stocks ruined, horses, cattle, sheep, pigs drowned by hundreds. The people stared dazedly at the awesome destruction which had fallen so savagely upon them in a single night. They poked listlessly in the ruins, their faces bleak, or dug frantically, hoping against hope that the boy or girl in the mudbank would not be a brother or a sister.

The rain of May 30, 1927, laid waste Eastern Kentucky like a vindictive enemy—intent upon killing and maiming and even destroying the hopes of those still unborn. The land lay defenseless. The hoed and weeded corn patches melted down in the slashing runoff like wax candles before a fire. The uphill furrows turned into trenches and the trenches turned into roaring funnels of muddy water. I knew the terrible damage because I had studied soil formation when I was planning to go into the conservation movement. Topsoil is the precious skin of the world. It produces plants, plants produce animals, and the human race grows strong. That precious skin of topsoil is built up by infinitely slow geological processes over centuries. It takes nature five hundred years to build one half inch of topsoil.

In a single night in Eastern Kentucky the rain removed the rich accretion of centuries from the shuddering hills. It struck a mortal blow. Such a loss could not be repaired in ten years—in a hundred years. That precious soil was gone forever.

Ginny and I covered the area, reporting for our paper. Attempts at rescue and first aid were now being made by the Red Cross. Later, Mr. Herbert Hoover came to Kentucky to observe the damage and went away. I suppose he made some sort of report. Those fellows always do. But if he did, nothing came of it that I could see. A reporter from a New York newspaper arrived, toured Knight County, and wrote a story in which he referred to it as "Nightmare County." His phrase was apt. Our towns were deep in mud, our roads were washed out, our bridges gone, our crops ruined, our bottom lands a garbage dump of wreckage. We did not realize it then, but the flood of May 30, 1927, was a turning point in Kentucky history. It was the beginning of the end of the long honeymoon we'd had with coal. I know. I was there, and I saw the nightmare begin and I am glad I could not look ahead and see what the future held in store.

We were all naturally very concerned about Charles Hammond's snake bite. Nobody expected Charles to live. He hovered on the brink for nearly ten days in bed in his home in Hammond. Doc Callahan saw him constantly and Lucy Martin, whom he had been protecting when he snatched up the rattler, nursed him night and day, only leaving him briefly for a snatch of sleep. Finally, he turned the corner and started back. In early July he rose from the bed, weak but alive and safe. His face would never be quite the same. The poison had withered some of the nerves, giving to his mouth a slight paralyzed droop, and to his cheek a shrunken look. But his sight was not injured.

And neither, I might add, was his judgment.

We were all making bets, of course, by this time— but the odds in favor finally got so high that there were no takers. Lucy Martin was without doubt one of the Kentucky belles you read about in books—and she had the brains to go with it—and there could hardly be a more romantic prelude to a proposal: a savage storm, a flood, a deadly snake, then the constant bed-care which necessitated intimacy between the wealthy Bostonian and the fiery little hill girl. Nobody was surprised when the marriage was announced and almost everybody in the Hammond organization and their friends and relatives were on hand for the wedding, which took place in the little Baptist church up in the hollow. I would say the crowd ran to at least two thousand people. The woods, as the saying goes, were full of them.

Lucy's daddy gave her away. I was Charles's Best Man. Naturally I got to kiss the bride. Ginny was mad, and I guess I can't blame her. She said I didn't give Lucy the polite peck on the cheek that was expected of any decent person in a bridal kiss: I kissed her warmly on the lips, as Ginny well knew because she was there and saw it, and she was heartily ashamed of me.

"Honey," I told her. "I'm ashamed of myself. I guess I got carried away by that sip of Sim Yates's mountain dew he was passing around."

Ginny glared at me. "You got carried away, Huff," she told me. "But it wasn't the mountain dew. You knew you'd never get another chance to give Lucy Martin a sweet kiss—and you darned well got hog greedy about it."

"I will go right to the fireplace and get me a big handful of ashes and rub them in my hair," I offered.

But I saw Ginny was grinning at me. "I'll have to forgive you," she said. "She is a very pretty girl. And I must confess you weren't alone. The kissing line ran out of sight up the holler."

"She's not as pretty as you, dear," I said in a sincere voice, because, in truth, it was a toss-up. "And she's not half as smart."

"Down boy," Ginny said fondly. "You're wagging your tail so hard you might knock over the furniture."

LUCY HAMMOND

As soon as Charles was strong enough to travel he took me to Massachusetts to meet his folks. They had never seen me at all, of course, and they had not seen Charles since he had been bitten by the rattler. They tried not to show any shock, but they didn't succeed. I had gotten used to the shrunken place on his cheek, which looked uglier because of the scars where daddy had cut it with his knife so we could suck the poison. But of course his parents hadn't seen it, and I guess they were not used to injuries and violence the way we were in Kentucky. When his mother looked at the wound there was a little tightening around her eyes and the pupils got bigger. His father's eyes sort of bugged out. I could see his father was a pretty stuffy old feller, but I had come prepared to be as sweet and polite as I could, no matter what happened. I had a sneaking suspicion that Charles's family expected me to be a rawboned creature with tobacco-stained teeth, who perhaps carried a loaded pistol, since Charles said he'd told them how I'd carried the .44 when I had that trouble with young Bob Evartz. I was as quiet as I could be, and smiled a lot, and said how pretty and amazing everything was.

Well, it was. Particularly the sea. I had never seen the sea, except in pictures. Charles took me to the beach and the waves scared me. They rose up real high and came crashing down and sent sheets of soap suds rushing up the beach right to your feet. The sand was

101

littered with piles of brown rubbery stuff that smelled like fish and iodine, and Charles said it was seaweed. I found a starfish in a shallow pool. There were lots of round gray rocks lying around, about the size of potatoes. They were smooth from having been rolled in the surf for many years, Charles said. He said I must come here in the winter when the nor-easters came in. The waves today were little bittie ones, he said. When there was a winter storm they got fifty feet high and hit the sea wall and shook the earth and sent sheets of foam as high as the houses on the bluff. It was great then, Charles said. Nobody was around. The wind howled at night like a lost soul and when you walked the beach the only sound you could hear was the mewing of the gulls and the hoarse whisper of the wind past your ears and the rise and fall of the surf. I saw that Charles loved the sea.

Charles took me to a restaurant called The Adams House, which was built out over the water in Marblehead harbor. They kept the lobsters alive in big wooden tanks in the sea. When you wanted a lobster you pointed him out through the wire netting and they reached down with a dip net and got him for you. I didn't think I could bring myself to eat a lobster when I saw it come up, black and glistening with its spidery legs waving and its big claws wedged tight shut with little wooden plugs so they couldn't pinch the cook. But when it arrived, bright red from the broiler, with the melted butter in a little tiny glass and a nutcracker and a tiny fork I gave it a try and it was sweet as honey.

But I didn't like the raw oysters on the half shell. I managed to dip one in the horseradish-and-ketchup sauce and I got it in my mouth, but when I bit into it I felt my mouth watering and my stomach contracting and I gulped it down real quick and sat there praying I wouldn't vomit and embarrass Charles.

"Don't you like the oysters, honey?" he said.

102

I didn't trust myself to speak. I shook my head no, and tried to smile. Charles took the blue points over on his side of the table. He speared those great big slimy things off their half shells, plunked them into the sauce, popped them in his mouth and chewed them as if they were delicious. I could hardly bear to watch him. Charles said raw oysters were an acquired taste. I said I'd work on it and maybe in a couple of years I'd get to like them, but I knew I wouldn't, and so did Charles, I think.

"Honey," he said. "Now you know the way I felt the day I was up in the hollow and Anse Webb invited me in—and Angie had a hog's head she'd just cooked, and they cut a nice tender chunk right out below the eye and told me to go ahead . . ."

"You can't beat Angie's hog's head," I said.

"You can't beat the Adams House blue points," Charles said.

We both laughed.

While I was with Charles's folks I tried very hard with my English. Of course I'm a schoolteacher and I've had a better chance to learn to speak correctly than most, but you can't change a Kentucky accent overnight, or perhaps ever, and you can't eliminate mistakes in grammar you've been making since you were old enough to speak, by marrying a Harvard graduate. I could see Mrs. Hammond wince when I'd make some slip in my grammar or use some odd little expression she wasn't used to. But she never said a word. I liked her. I had an aunt quite a bit like her, who lived in Pikeville, in Pike County—which may be small by Boston standards but is mighty high and fine by ours, I can tell you. Before my aunt moved to Pikeville everybody used to call her Maggie. But that soon changed. Her given name was Margaret, my aunt told us, and she'd be pleased if we would use it. When she drank coffee she lifted her little finger and held it out,

103

and she started speaking of arms and legs as "limbs." My daddy like to died laughing when we'd come home after a visit at Aunt Margaret's. "Keerful there, young-uns," he'd say as we climbed out of the wagon. "Keerful you don't skin them there little limbs!" We all laughed and hollered. But aunt Margaret was as good-hearted as they come, and it didn't make any difference to us if she wanted to put out her little finger and piddle with it when she drank her coffee.

I could see that Mrs. Hammond was good-hearted too. She just hadn't had the proper advantages in her upbringing. If she had been born in Kentucky I'll just bet she'd be out potting possum with the old hog rifle, like my mother did at times, and mighty proud of her aim. She might even have done fine in a place like Boston if she hadn't married Mr. Hammond Senior.

I am not going to make up a story about how I liked Mr. Hammond after I got to know him, and how he was frosty outside but the salt of the earth, really. Father Hammond was not the salt of the earth. He's got bright eyes, a high color, and he knows the answers to all questions concerning art, politics, religion, history, current events and human nature. He talks in a loud gushy voice when he is excited, and he won't let anybody else in. If you don't agree with him he doesn't hesitate to straighten you out. A young airplane pilot called Charles Lindbergh had flown across the Atlantic Ocean not long before we went to Boston in a plane called *The Spirit of St. Louis*. I thought it was a brave and wonderful thing to do and I said so at dinner one evening.

Father Hammond looked at me with one of his smiles and said that I was young and when I grew older and more understanding of the motives of the world I would see that this young feller, whatever his name was (one of Mr. Hammond's favorite habits was not to remember the names of people he felt beneath him), was a common publicity seeker, that the trip was a cheap stunt, and that all the excitement about this pilot was a sad commentary on the mentality of the American people. If it was a sad commentary on the mentality of the American people it was clearly a sad commentary on my mentality, because I had just gone on record as saying I thought Mr. Lindbergh was a fine young man and had done a thrilling thing.

I suppose I shouldn't criticize pride in Mr. Hammond because a Martin from Kentucky has pride too, you better believe. A Martin from Kentucky has a temper as well. I smiled at Mr. Hammond and said, just as sweet as pie: "I'm sorry, Father Hammond, but I just can't agree with you. I think Mr. Charles Lindbergh is a real brave feller and he done a real brave thing." I made these mistakes in English purposely. "Furthermore," I said, "it seems to me that it is a sad commentary on any American who don't realize it."

You could have heard a pin drop. Mrs. Hammond turned pale. Nobody had ever spoken to Mr. Hammond that way in his life, I guess. I didn't care. I had been listening to his high and mighty nonsense for almost a week—not only to me, but to Mrs. Hammond and Charles—and I had had enough. Mr. Hammond's face got very red and he stared at me as if I was a toadstool he'd suddenly found sprouting up beside his plate, and then he said one little word, under his breath. I just barely caught it. The word he muttered was "scrub."

Charles and I left Boston for Kentucky the next morning. We had a little tiff in our bedroom that night. Charles didn't exactly bawl me out for talking back to his father, but he indicated that he expected me to "rise above" certain things. Well I gave it to Charlie, just like I gave it to his daddy. "I've been rising above that silly stuff ever since I came here," I said. "And I'm not about to rise above it any more! I love you and I think I could love your mother, but your daddy is a great big pain in the rear end, and somebody ought to have told him so when he was about five years old instead of waiting until now. And furthermore, if you don't like the way I am, Charles Hammond, you can just get you a new—"

Charles did the smartest thing any young husband can do at a time like that. He grabbed me and threw me on the bed, clamped his mouth over mine in a great big smothering kiss and shoved his knee between my legs. I am sure Father Hammond never tried that on Mother Hammond, but maybe he should have. It sure worked fine in my case.

WILLIARD FLETCHER

After the big flood of May 30, things were in a mess all over Kentucky. My own coal camp, fortunately, was far enough up the slopes of Rockhouse Creek to avoid the total destruction which came to many buildings in the low areas. I had a lot of damage, however, as did everybody. We had a couple of shanties collapse when the run-off water loosened the poles they were propped up with, and one child was hurt. A couple of mine shafts were flooded and required extensive pumping to clear out. By and large, however, we escaped fairly lightly.

This didn't mean we escaped the troubles and expenses that followed the flood in the area. The people were really in bad shape. Many of them were homeless and without the proper clothing and food, and too stupid and demoralized to do much about it. People think of me as a hard and heartless man, but I'm not quite as bad as I'm painted. I'm a businessman. In business you do what you have to do to make a profit. If you haven't got the guts to do these things you shouldn't be in business. I'll go even further. If you haven't got the guts to do these things you probably *won't* be in business for too long. Because there are lots of other people who do have the guts.

I would like to make myself clear, once and for all, on how I stand concerning the so-called Little Man or the Common Man. I am aware that the Little Man and the Common Man have been glorified by bleeding hearts and sentimentalists who have never seen the viciousness and the violence and the stupidity of the darling Little Common Man when he sets out to satisfy his sweaty little lusts, even as you and I. I know for a fact that many coal miners beat their wives—particularly on Saturday night, when they come home drunk. It is a favorite sport. "Guess I'll go home now and whup the old lady afore I lay her," is how the drunken miner puts it to his friends in the drinking party.

Everybody has his own philosophy of life, or should have, and I have mine. I do not for a moment think that Lincoln was anything more than a flowery political speaker. "We hold these truths to be self-evident," says Lincoln. "That all men are created equal . . ." Well any fool knows that's eyewash. I was born with a silver spoon in my mouth, but if I had been born in a coal-mining family I'd at least be a foreman now, I'll bet you—and the truth is I probably wouldn't be working in the mines at all. I'd be long gone. Nobody with any brains or imagination or guts would put up with the way I run my coal camp. I wouldn't, myself, if I was a miner. I'd pull out.

Now I have been watching the national business picture carefully and so have my brothers Boyd and Austin. We know that oil is coming fast. We know coal is overexpanded. There's going to be a shake-out in coal operators in Kentucky one of these days. We don't welcome it, God knows, but on the other hand we don't shrink from it. There have been shake-outs in every industry from time to time. The tough, well-run, soundly financed outfits survive. The slobs go to the wall. This is how it should be. Even Mr. Darwin agrees with me. Darwin says nature is run on the tough but realistic rule of Survival of The Fittest. If you think about it one way, this is really why the world gets better and stronger all the time, instead of weaker and more sentimental.

I have been criticized for my political maneuvers in Knight County. I do not give one hoot in hell about that criticism. The results are what count, and I have certainly gotten results. Ward Thomas holds my taxes down. Frank McCabe browbeats my hecklers, with notable exceptions like old Morgan Huff the other day. I wouldn't admit it in public, but I admire that murderous old man. I'd have him on my payroll if I could get him, but these mountaineers are a queer lot. They will kill you over some trivial little insult that a businessman like myself would take without even getting angry. But they will let you underpay them, maim them and kill them in your mine, throw them out of their houses when they are old or sick, and work them into an early grave without raising a murmur. They may even thank you. I know the secret. They are like children. They want to be smiled at and patted on the head and praised. I do that all the time, just like the politicians. It pays big. It's all these poor ignorant people need to keep them happy.

All we have to worry about is the union. If the union gets in here, we are cooked. Austin and Boyd and I have already talked it over and made up our mind. If the union tries to come in we are going to fight them with every trick in the bag, and we can't afford to pinch pennies in doing it. I've already started to look ahead. We'll need more than the Sheriff and the Tax Commissioner. We'll need the judge. Floyd Cooper is an honorable man. But every man has his price, and Floyd's, I discovered, was a nice fat juicy coal boundary up on Mad Dog Creek near the Hammond holdings. I don't know if Judge Cooper realized he was selling his soul to the devil when he took that gift, but he must have. He is not a stupid man.

JUDGE FLOYD COOPER

This country was just a backwoods when I started out as a young circuit judge. The work was harder then and a lot more dangerous. You rode from place to place holding court, and like as not the case involved a feud of some kind. I have to laugh when I look at these modern television shows where the gunmen all have lightning draws and shoot from the hip and kill their men like clockwork. Anybody who knows the slightest thing about shooting a pistol knows you can't hit the broad side of a barn if you shoot from the hip unless you are close enough to a man to shove your gun in his belly. The way to kill a man, if you really set out to do that, is with a rifle. Even with a rifle you have to take careful aim and squeeze off the shot as you would do shooting a deer or a rabbit. All this fast gun-slinging is pretty childish to a person who knew how it really was in Kentucky when the feuds were at their height.

I was just a boy but I can recall hearing the old folks tell about the gunfights on the courthouse lawn in places like Jackson over in Bloody Breathitt County, and also other places. They weren't lying. You can still find bullet holes in courthouses in both Kentucky and Virginia. There were times when the friends of a feudist came into the courtroom while court was in session and removed the defendant from the stand at gun-point. Once they shot the poor judge off his bench, then went ahead and mowed down the Commonwealth Attorney and three jurors. A timid circuit judge couldn't hope to last. A man got the job and held it as much on his bravery and stubbornness as on his knowledge of law. I recall one Judge, Mr. Colin Marcus, who was about as brave as you can get, I guess. He was just a little fellow, didn't weigh over a hundred and fifteen pounds, they said, but what he lacked in poundage he made up in sheer nerve. He took over a case involving a multiple murder—the latest outbreak of a very long and bitter feud. There had already been several judges on the case. The feudists had run them off with threats of death.

Judge Marcus was threatened as soon as he arrived in Booneville to try the case. He replied that he had come here to settle this matter and he intended to proceed, and if the defendant was found guilty it was the Judge's intention to hang him. Bets were actually made in the bar of the Boone House as to which exact day Judge Marcus would be shot. Some claimed he wouldn't even get a chance to mount the bench; he would be picked off on the street (a common practice) as he made his way over to the courthouse from the hotel. Others felt that the friends of the defendant would at least wait and see how the case came out. If by some wild chance their boy was acquitted, even though any number of people had seen him commit the crime in broad daylight, the Judge would have to

110

let him off. There wouldn't be any need to kill the little feller then.

Judge Marcus was seated on the bench in court when the attack came. A rifleman had stationed himself on the hillside above the town, where he could see down through the tall windows into the courtroom. He put a high-powered rifle bullet through the window and it hit the walnut panel beside the Judge's head—about three inches from his right ear. Judge Marcus adjourned court for the day. Everybody stood around on the street waiting to see him come out of the Boone Hotel, fully packed, and flee for his life.

Judge Marcus came out, but he was not packed to flee for his life. He was packing a .38 special in a holster on his hip, and he went down the street to Big Anse Webb's blacksmith shop and went in and he and Big Anse had a long pow-wow. Two days later Anse and his boy and three men carried a sheet-iron box which Anse had fabricated up the courthouse steps and into the courtroom and carefully installed it like a little open-fronted house over the chair at which Judge Marcus sat when he held court. Several interested parties examined the iron box with care. It was believed by those who should know that not even a bullet from the highest-powered rifle in the county could put a hole in that iron box. Judge Marcus conducted the rest of the trial sitting inside his iron box. And not empty handed. Each day before he opened court, Judge Marcus held a little ceremony. He loaded his .38 special revolver and a 30-30 Springfield rifle. He placed them on the table within easy reach. Then he announced that court was in session.

Judge Marcus finished the case. The man was convicted of murder. Judge Marcus sentenced him to be hanged, and hanged he was. I sometimes think, when I wake up in the night and can't get back to sleep, how it would be to be Judge Marcus. He died a poor

111

man. He was never elected to the State Legislature, an office he was said to wish to hold. I have never met him. I have served many terms in the Legislature, and I have called several Governors of Kentucky by their first names, and I am a wealthy man. I have a large coal holding up on Mad Dog Creek. But I sometimes think, when I lie awake at night, that I would trade it all for an iron box like Judge Marcus's in my record. There was a joke about little Judge Marcus that people used to tell. He didn't stand over five feet three, and he was, as I have said, of slight build. People said they couldn't understand how a puny little rabbit of a man like Judge Marcus could go around carrying that great big old lion's heart.

ELIZA CLAY

About a month after I laid with the preacher up at the snake-handlin meeting I begun to get sick to my stomach in the morning and I realized I was pregnant. It scared me but it didn't worry me too much. I knowed that Daniel Hawkes would marry me. The Lord had decreed that he would take me under that big rock and the Lord must have meant for me to get pregnant and so it was all right. I wanted Daniel. I wanted him to do what he did. I never realized how hot-natured I was until we done it that night. After that I kep thinkin about it and wonderin when Daniel would come and git me and we could slip off sommers and do hit again.

But he didn't come. I knowed he was busy preachin so I didn't try to get in touch with him. But when I found out I was pregnant, of course then I had to. I heard he was over in Leslie County holdin snake-handlin sessions and I rode the railroad as far as I could and then I walked and asked people until I found the holler he was goin to use that night. That night I figured to surprise him, so I just snuck in quiet and waited in the back until after it was over. He didn't handle no snakes that night. He explained to the people that his snakes was sick. Hit sounded kind of funny to me at the time; I didn't know snakes got sick, but I didn't pay it no mind. I was too excited thinkin of seein Daniel afterward and probly us layin together, and I was all quiverin and tremblin when I got a chance to talk to him alone after it was over.

"Hello Brother Hawkes," I said. "How are you?"

He give me a funny look, like he didn't know me, and I got a sudden sick awful feelin.

"It's me," I said. "Eliza Clay."

"Eliza Clay," he says. "Yes, Eliza. What can I do for you, sister?"

"You remember the night," I said, and my voice cracked. "Rockhouse Creek . . ."

"Rockhouse Creek," he says. "Oh—oh yes, now I remember. I baptized you, didn't I?"

"You—made me—told me—"

"What's the matter, sister?" Daniel Hawkes said.

"I'm pregnant," I said. "We got to get married. Right away."

Then I begun to cry. Daniel Hawkes put his arms around me and told me not to cry, that he'd marry me, and that it would be all right. I felt so wonderful. I felt as if I'd been raised from the dead. I kissed him and hugged him and told him how terrible much I loved him. And he said he loved me too, and kissed me

113

back. And when I asked him when we'd be married he said soon. Soon, I said. When is that? I have to know. I'm awful scared.

He thought a second.

"How about next Tuesday?" he said. "I'll finish my swing around the county then. I'll be by to get you."

"Oh, I love you," I told him. "Oh, God how I love you. I'll be waitin."

I was, too. I waited all day in my best clothes and all night and never closed my eyes until the sun come up Wednesday; and he never come. He never come Wednesday, neither, and not that week, and not ever. He done left the county, I guess. I heered he was preachin over in Virginny, but that was after I married Jimmy Webster and it didn't make no difference. I didn't love Jim. He had an awful snaky look around the eyes, and he was a terrible feller to drink, even then, but I was pregnant and I had to have a daddy for my baby. I just had to. Even Jim. So I married him.

One thing I got to say for Jimmy, he sure has to have it regular and he don't care what's the matter. I was six months pregnant when he took me and he done it to me six times that night, with the baby kickin inside me, and me grittin my teeth to keep from throwin up. Jim didn't know about that, or if he did, he didn't care. He was pretty drunk at the time.

ANNIE FUGATE

I had a little ruckus with Angie Webb the other day and I felt bad about it. Angie and I are best friends. Still I couldn't let it pass. Angie says: "You are makin a big mistake, foolin around with Bob Evartz. That boy is no good. I've had no use for him ever since he and that snaky Webster kid got after little Lucy Martin up in the woods."

"Look Angie," I says. "Bob Evartz aint got no daddy. He lives next door to us. You mean to tell me you would turn your back on a kid cause he made one mistake? You never would in this world and you know it! There aint a chicken-hearteder person in this whole holler when it comes to lookin after younguns than you, Angie Webb!"

"Chicken-hearted?" Angie screams. "One of these days I'm goin to show you how chicken-hearted I am. I'm goin down to Booneville and hunt up that miserable Ward Thomas and give him hell for raisin our taxes like he done!"

"That aint the same thing," I said. "We're talkin about young Bob Evartz. All I do is feed the boy and listen to his troubles. It aint the same thing atall as old Ward Thomas." I give her a sly dig then. "You better not fool with Ward Thomas," I says. "Or he'll sick the High Sheriff on you."

"High Sheriff," Angie yells. "I aint scared of no High Sheriff!"

"Uh-huh," I says.

Angie got so mad she jumps up and runs out. Angie is old Sim Yates's sister, and all the Yateses has got bad tempers. They'll blow off like a skyrocket and then they'll be sorry and come back and make up. Course in Sim's case, when he blows off there just might not be nobody left to apologize to. Sim is a mighty active feller in a scuffle. I expected Angie would be back. I waited a couple of days and she didn't come. I figures it's both our fault, but I couldn't stand it no more. I baked me the finest huckleberry pie I could make and I puts it on a plate with a napkin over it and I runs down the holler to Angie's house while it's still smokin hot. Angie and Anse are settin on the porch.

"Hello Mrs. Fugate," Angie says to me, like some high and mighty lady on Silk Stocking Row. I would of been mad but it struck me funny instead.

"Hello Mrs. Webb," I says. "How is you and Mr. Webb this fine evenin?"

"We are fine, Mrs. Fugate," Angie says.

"Well I'm mighty glad to hear that," I says. "Because I done baked me a smokin-hot huckleberry pie and I dusted her with cimmonon and nutmeg and powdered sugar so she'll just about melt in your mouth, and I brung her over to give you."

I whipped the napkin off of the pie and Angie gets a look at it.

"Should I put it in the kitchen for you, Mrs. Webb?" I asked then.

Angie gets up and comes down the steps. "Annie," she says, "can you forgive a old fool?"

"Why sure," I says, laughin out loud. "I'm a old fool myself."

Then I sets down the pie and we throws our arms around each other like a couple little school kids. Then me and Angie and Anse goes inside and cuts the pie and eats her right to the last crumb. It was one of the best huckleberry pies I ever made in my life.

LUCY HAMMOND

I'd always wanted to teach school kids my own way, but when I was hired by the county I couldn't. There was no time. I was trying to handle six grades, wipe

116

runny noses, sew on buttons for kids whose mothers had no thread, separate fights, lime the privies, patch the roof, and fight off the big boys who had ideas about teaching the teacher. I loved most of it. But I hankered to change it . . .

Take a boy. He's interested in guns and hunting more than almost anything. A girl wants to learn how to make herself pretty: sew, fix her hair, make the boys look at her. The Kentucky schools had always been run sternly. Nobody risked spoiling any child by sparing the rod. A good whuppin was considered an education in itself. And the textbooks were pitiful. Most of them had missing pages and scribbles on the pages, put there by bored and disgruntled students. If you tried to study those books you couldn't completely blame the students. They were dull as dishwater, and the problems all dealt with cities. Distances were spoken of in city blocks. People rode elevators up and down tall buildings. That was fine, except none of the kids had ever seen a city block or a tall building. I made up my own problems. I used tons of coal, buckets of water, bullets, squirrels, and pecks of beans. They all knew these things, and they took an interest in figuring out, for example, how long it would take Sim Yates to shoot twenty squirrels up in the Flatwoods, if Nelson Feathers ran for each bullet down the hill to his house, and each trip took three minutes and twelve seconds. I knew that most of my students would not go on to high school. Knowing that, I tried to do two things: teach them how to read simple English, and write simple English. If they could do that, and nothing else, they would be a little harder to "rob with a pencil."

When I married Charles and he showed such an interest in education, I got interested in it again myself. Al Royce, Charles's superintendent, was glad to have me come in and talk about it with him. Together we came up with some pretty fair ideas. The best one was to have guest speakers—people who wouldn't put the kids to sleep with long-winded platitudes—but would tell them things they could really use, and liked to hear. Doc Callahan came over and told the school about mountain First Aid, bringing in exciting cases he'd handled, and the children were sitting on the edges of their seats. Lee Harrod, the Commonwealth Attorney, came up to discuss Kentucky laws, but got off on the famous Marcum Feud and never did get to the laws. The students were much more interested in the feud—but I made Lee take my students down to Booneville one day and listen to a trial. I didn't bother to check up what the trial was about. It turned out that they had poor old Sim Yates, Sim's daddy, up for bootlegging, and I was very embarrassed. I apologized to Sim. But he said not to pay it no heed. His daddy didn't.

The last week in September, we got a telegram from Mr. Ralph Uhl, Charles's financial adviser, saying he was coming down to see us. The first thing I thought of was to get him to talk to our class. I mentioned it to him shortly after we met him at the station, but Charles said, "Oh, for goodness sakes, Lucy—Ralph doesn't have time for lecturing your students. He's down here to relax."

"On the contrary," Mr. Uhl said. "I'd be honored to talk to the class. I never mentioned this, Charles, but my home town, before I came to New York, was Wilkes Barre, Pennsylvania. It's a coal town, as you probably know, and I was a coal-town kid."

Well, you might as well know that Mr. Ralph Uhl won me over that very instant. He addressed the class and even though a lot of what he said was over their heads they were polite and it was a nice occasion. Sim Yates invited Mr. Uhl to come out for a squirrel shoot after Mr. Uhl found out that Sim was the best shot in the hollow and remarked about it. Ralph went. He didn't get any squirrels but he did come back with a very rosy account of the expedition, due, no doubt, to a few liberal drafts of Sim's daddy's finest shine.

The last evening Ralph was with us he told us the real reason he had come down all this way to see us. He was worried about the stock market. He had been watching it carefully for the past two or three years, he said, and it had gotten into a very unhealthy condition. He knew Charles had invested almost a million dollars in various stocks and he wanted him to switch those stocks into bonds right away.

Charles didn't agree. He said he'd read some financial bulletin which said that the stock market expansion was healthy and orderly and might be expected to go on for years, rising steadily.

Ralph shook his head sadly. "Charles," he said, "I hate to have to be the bearer of ugly information about my own compatriots, but the truth is this. Those people who write those enthusiastic bulletins are the guiltiest of all. What you don't realize—and what most Americans don't realize—is that these high prices are merely figures printed on paper. They don't represent real values: hardware, inventory, patents, real estate—capital strength. They are falsely inflated, and God help all of us if the people find out and start unloading."

"Ralph," Charles said, "you are a fine fellow but you've always been a real stick in the mud when it comes to taking a chance."

But Ralph wouldn't give up. He told Charles and me about the various clever schemes that had been hatched in Wall Street to bilk innocent investors. Holding companies were piled one on top of the other in a big glittering pyramid—and men like Insull sat up on the top with a golden straw and sucked the profits and the heart out of the whole pack of them. Ralph mentioned a trick he called "security affiliates" which banks were setting up and using as a method of illegally using their depositors' funds for investments. Then there were stock-market pools which quietly drove a stock artificially high—then unloaded it at a thundering profit. There was, in fact, Ralph Uhl told us, a lot of outright criminal stuff going on in American finances these days. Nobody stopped it. Coolidge was asleep on the White House couch. But even if the little man was awake, Ralph said, it wouldn't make much difference. Coolidge had roughly the same financial understanding as a jack rabbit. In a way it was probably just as well that he had adopted a policy of napping and letting the government run itself.

"Old Andy Mellon, now," Ralph said, "is a different story altogether. Andy Mellon is one of the shrewdest financiers this nation has ever had—and one of the smartest Secretaries of the Treasury."

"What does Mellon say?" Charles asked.

Ralph's eyes twinkled. "I was hoping you'd ask that," he said. "Mr. Mellon advises to buy bonds."

Charles kind of shook his head, the way a man will when he's argued as much as he can, and is giving up.

"All right, Ralph," he said. "You win. Sell my stocks and put the money in bonds. If I'm right, and the market keeps on going up, we can always switch back again, and all we'll lose is the rise."

"All of your stocks?" said Ralph, pressing his advantage.

"Yes, yes," Charles said. "All of them."

"I'll do it as soon as I get back to New York," Ralph said. "Day after tomorrow."

He did, too. The confirmation of sale and the confirmation of the purchase of U.S. Government bonds—close to a million dollars' worth—came through to us the first week in October, 1929.

ANDERSON WEBB

It was late in October and I had come back from the mine and was washed up and sittin listenin to station KDKA in Pittsburgh over my new Atwater Kent radio. The name of the dance band that was playin was Happy Felton. He was playin one of the purtiest pieces I ever heered. Hit was called "Little White Lies," which might seem like a foolish name, but the sound was sure awful sweet and kind of sad.

Angie was out in the kitchen cookin up the supper but she stopped and come out when the girl singer of Happy Felton's band started in on the chorus. The drums was whisperin and the saxophones was surgin soft and slow, there was a little flutter of drums, and everthing cut, and this girl's voice come in, like she was cryin, sort of . . . *The moon was all aglow* . . .

Boy it sent prickles through you. You felt young again, like a kid acourtin, and I looked at Angie and I knowed she felt the same way. We was both pretty tard by then, but a person can be dead tard and still shet his eyes and see it like it was when that big old moon was ashinin like a white bonfire through the trees and the woods was black and you could hear your heart abeatin and feel the breath of your little gal blowin hot and quick on your face . . .

I don't know what Angie was thinkin about, but I was thinkin about a little redheaded girl I was courtin once, over in Virginia. I'd took her in my

121

daddy's buggy up nearly to the top of Pine Mountain and we'd been there about an hour and we was both right to the point. It was in the month of June, and there was a warm south wind blowin up over the hills and medders and I could smell buckwheat flowers and a little smoke, mixed up together, and I know as long as I live when I smell that same smell I can shut my eyes and be back there on Pine Mountain in the dark —and about that time the moon showed on the edge of the hills to the east and it was so big and close you felt like you could of reached out and touched it . . .

Now, as I listened to this girl singer I felt my throat git tight, and there was a hot, blowed-up feelin behind my eyes, and I thought, *Jesus, if I could just go back there—just for one night—just for one hour . . .*

Then the music snapped off short and an announcer said he was breakin into the program to give us the latest news of the big crash in Wall Street. I hadn't heard about any crash. We knowed they was havin trouble, of course. A couple of weeks back the market had dropped and them big bankers had run in, we heard, with great gobs of money and got up some kind of a buyin pool and stopped the panic. We didn't pay much attention. We never had no stocks or bonds and never expected to have none.

"The stock market declined today," the announcer said, "in the most severe panic selling in history. Sixteen million shares were thrown on the market. Prices have been falling out of control. Reports are that the decline will continue. Several persons jumped to their death out of windows in the financial area of downtown New York. Veteran financial observers say we may be entering the greatest disaster of our time. We will bring further bulletins to you as they come in. And now, back to Happy Felton."

Happy was announcing his next number, and Angie

said to me, "Oh darn it, we missed the rest of that purty song about the Little White Lies."

"What day is today?" I asked Angie.

She looked at the Booneville paper.

"Tuesday, the twenty-ninth."

"I'm sure glad we don't own no stocks," I said. "Them poor fellers jumpin out the winder. They must of felt pretty bad."

"They's no use worryin about it," Angie says. "Hit aint got nothin to do with us, thank God."

"That's right," I said. "What you got cookin for supper?"

"I got some fine pork and beans," Angie said. "You just set back now, and relax, and listen to the band, and I'll call you when it's ready."

I sat back. Happy Felton was playin another purty piece which was took from a movie, they said. Hit was called "Broadway Melody." I must of dozed off then, because Angie had to shake me to wake me up so I could come and eat her pork and beans.

WILLIARD FLETCHER

When the crash came we took a realistic view right from the start. We knew there would be only one way to survive, and that was to retrench swiftly and ruthlessly. We cut the men's wages at once. There was grumbling, but we didn't pay any attention. We told the men if they weren't satisfied with the cuts they were free to look for work elsewhere. A few of them did. They were back in a week, trying to get us to rehire them. We said we were sorry. Orders were slow and we couldn't use them. We added that they had made their bed, and now they would have to lie in it, and they could pass that on if they cared to.

Other companies in the area were more soft-hearted than we were. They were slower to cut wages and they were more reluctant to evict sick or injured miners from company houses. We were not. We needed those houses for strong young workers. It was in every one of our leases that we could take possession of a house as soon as the man stopped work in the mines. We did it, even if we had to get Frank McCabe to go over with Bull Hargis, with the van, and move them out at gunpoint.

Other companies advanced scrip to a man to use in their company store if he was sick or injured and couldn't work. We advanced scrip, but only from one payday to another. If a man still owed us scrip on payday and couldn't settle, we wouldn't advance him more.

We started doing these things right away, as soon as the situation began to deteriorate, and as a result we were the strongest coal company in Knight County when the men finally began to get desperate in 1931, and the union organizers began to come in stronger than they had ever done. One thing my brothers and I had decided. We were going to keep the unions out, no matter what he had to do, and no matter what it cost. If the unions got in, we were finished.

CHARLES HAMMOND

One day not long after the stock-market crash I got a phone call from one of my coal brokers saying that a big customer was shifting his order to another firm.

"Which firm?" I asked.

"Fletcher Coal," the broker said. "Will Fletcher has knocked ten cents a ton off your price."

"Is the deal closed?" I asked.

"Not yet," the broker said. "The customer says he'll stay with you if you'll shave Fletcher's price."

I hesitated.

"All right," I said. "Twelve cents."

"Good," the broker said. "I'll get right back to the customer and close for you."

That was the start of the price war as far as I was concerned. It got worse as the months went on. Presently it got so bad that I was making no profit on the coal we mined. I was merely breaking even. But the war raged on. After a while I was selling coal at less than it cost me to mine it. This isn't as ridiculous as it sounds. A big coal mine depreciates very rapidly if left unworked. The roof shifts and buckles, water fills the shafts, and the mine may actually fall into total ruin. Many companies in the Kentucky and Virginia fields were working their mines and selling coal at a loss for this reason.

I had another reason, of course. I felt responsible for the men. Still, if I hadn't been married to Lucy,

I think I'd have pulled out anyhow, as the depression deepened. As time went on and I lost money steadily I began to hate the sight of the men coming to the pay window. I wished they'd die, or vanish. I knew I was going to stick with it, but not as a hero. I just didn't have the moral courage to pull out—and then face my wife and tell her. It simply boiled down to that: a lack of moral courage.

RALPH UHL

As the shock waves of the great stock-market crash in October and November of 1929 rippled across the nation, there were frantic attempts by the business community to stem the tide of recession. They recalled how Pierpont Morgan had nipped the Panic of 1907 in the bud by bold buying. They tried it. A powerful pool headed by Dick Whitney rushed in after the first break and bought U. S. Steel for 205—and touched off a brief rally. But it was over almost as soon as it began, and the panic-selling wave rose like a nightmare into the sky and broke over everybody . . .

President Hoover was in office, having taken over from Calvin Coolidge. Mr. Hoover meant well, but he was dealing with a situation which was new and strange to him. He tried to stop the slide and bring about recovery by calling top businessmen to Washington to give out public statements to the effect that there was nothing to worry about. The country was solvent. Business was built on solid rock. There would be no wage cutting. Shortly the tide would turn and prosperity would come back, brighter and warmer than before.

It did not work.

Mr. Hoover was silent then, for a time, placing his faith in the normal operation of the market. A market automatically corrected itself, if let alone. It always had. If it went down, and you were patient and had faith, it would come back up again. Mr. Hoover was patient, and presumably had faith, but the months passed and the market simply went farther down and showed no signs of coming up.

Mr. Hoover then looked across the Atlantic and decided that the cause of our trouble lay in Europe, where a financial panic was paralyzing business. He diagnosed Europe's trouble. It was war debts and reparations owed to the United States for 1918. Hoover promptly declared a moratorium on these debts and reparations, and predicted a world-wide upturn as the result.

It didn't come.

Finally Mr. Hoover realized, with a great shock, that for once the automatic working of the market was going to fail him. It would need some artificial help. This must have been a bitter thing for Mr. Hoover to accept. American businessmen had been preaching *Laissez Faire* ever since they read Adam Smith. If you just kept your hands off, and let business alone, all would go well. When it didn't, and businesses were failing right and left, Mr. Hoover set up the Reconstruction Finance Corporation to lend federal funds to banks or businesses which were in trouble. This was fine for the banks and businesses. But the RFC sternly prohibited the loan of a thin dime to any individual—and there were, by now, millions of individuals who were wondering where their next meal was coming from.

And so, as 1929 passed into 1930 and 1930 passed

into 1931, the lonely despair of joblessness, hunger and ruin spread like a blight throughout the United States. And the despair was the deepest in the hollows and creekbeds of Kentucky. I know this because Charles Hammond told me. He told me the coal operators were engaged in a suicidal price war. They were like senseless animals tearing at each other's vitals. If he had not taken my advice when he did, Charles Hammond said, and sold his stocks before the crash, he would be in desperate trouble himself, right now.

RUFE FUGATE

Annie says I am the dumbest white man in the state of Kentucky, and I hate to admit it, but she's right. Mr. Hammond has been keepin us at work in his mine even though the coal business has gone to hell. I guess he aint makin much money, if any, and just does it because he is good-hearted and has so much money in the bank.

But that young foreman on my shift is a horse of a different color. He's been after me ever since I worked for him with one little naggin instruction after another. I'm a feller that puts out a good day's work. I always have and I always will. Nobody could ever accuse me of gold-brickin. But one thing I can't stand is to have a feller leanin over my shoulder all the time, breathin down my neck, tellin me to do this, do that, watch out for loose rock, don't forget my safety shoes, and little nit-pickin crud like that.

Well this foreman was just like a damn old woman,

and he wouldn't let me alone and finally I told him. "Look brother," I says, "I was cuttin coal when you was suckin your mamma's tit. Just you get the hell out and let me load the coal. If the roof falls on me it aint no skin off you."

The young feller jumps up like a fighten cock and starts givin me a bawlin out. Tells me I'll do it his way, he's the foreman by God, and if I don't he fire my ass right outen that mine.

Well there's where I pulled my dumb trick.

"You aint man enough to fire nobody," I says, and gives him a shove.

Well, he come at me with a shovel and he didn't give me no choice. I took that shovel away from him and hit him over the head with it and knocked him cold. And then I didn't wait to have nobody fire me. I walked out of that mine and quit. Everbody knows me around the county. They know I cut as much coal as two guys when I'm goin good, and I managed to get me a job over at the Fletcher mine. But it wasn't like workin for Mr. Hammond—even though I was shut of that miserable foreman. It was lousy. But I'd made my bed and now I had to lie in it.

UNCLE EB THOMAS

I know what's causin all this misery. It aint Mr. Fletcher or the Wall Street crash. We turned our back on God. Now God is turnin His back on us. The Bible says that when the people gets too wicked, times will be hard. Well we sure been wicked, and so I tell my neighbors we just brung it all on ourselves.

129

"Oh come on, Uncle Eb," they said. "You got a boy makin big money down to Booneville. You kin afford to go around actin high and mighty and preachin at people about their sins. We aint got no boy that's Tax Commissioner of the county to lay back on. So go away and let us alone."

"Listen," I said. "I never took a nickel from my boy Ward, and I don't never intend to. I'm not talkin about him. I'm talkin about God. We got God hoppin mad. He aint even begun to whup us. You'll see!"

Them people turned their backs and walked off. They don't want to admit that we're all black sinners. They don't want to admit that God has every right to pile miseries on us the way he's adoin. God made this earth, and we're ruttin in it like a bunch of hogs in a pen, and no wonder he's mad!

CLABE TURNER

I been livin with my young brother Jim and his family since the hard times begun, helping Jim out with the bills. Even between us we can't make it. The other night was payday night. We had three dollars and seventeen cents between us after the company made all their deductions for rent, coal, doctor, insurance and overdraft. And that was in scrip—not cash. Jim told me to go to the company store and buy some groceries with the money, and that's what I done. Jim has a little daughter, name of Connie, that's cuter than a button. Jim and his wife kids me about Connie. They say if Connie was to put a ring in my nose and tell

130

me to get down on my hands and knees and ride her into Booneville on my back I'd sure enough do it. I didn't give them no argument. That little Connie has a couple of dimples and her eyewinkers is about a inch long and when she looks at me and says, "Please, Uncle Clabe . . ." I just turn to jelly. I never had no kids of my own. I guess that's why I love Connie so much.

Well when I was in the store I got to thinkin about Connie as I walked around lookin at the stuff. They had coffee, fruit, fresh meat, cans of peaches and sardines in olive oil and boxes of dates.

I'll just get a box of dates, I thought. Connie will go wild when she sees them dates.

Then I walked a little farther and I saw a big old spread of hamburger layin on the ice, all red and fresh.

I'll get that hamburger, I thought, and felt my mouth begin to water. We'll cook it up real rich, with lots of salt and pepper, and soak bread in the juice, and we'll eat it slow to make it last.

Then the man that runs the store steps over to me and asks me what I'll have.

I looked at him careless like and I says, "Oh give me a couple of loaves of bread and a can of beans."

"Is that all?" he asked me.

"Yes sir," I said. "I guess that's all we'll be needin tonight."

I didn't look at them dates when I walked out. I knowed I couldn't bring Connie home no dates when the family hadn't had nothin but lard drippins and potatoes for weeks. I know old Fletcher's got the mine full of spies. I know I'll be fired if I'm caught talkin to a UMW man. But so what? What have I got to lose? I'd be just as well off—maybe better—out in the hollers huntin squirrel as buckin this company store and all them items that gets took off my pay at the office before I get anything for myself.

MARIE WINGATE

My baby girl Evie has been ailin for quite a spell and we didn't know what it was that was plagin her. The other night in the middle of the night somethin woke me up and it was Evie, chokin in the bed with the other kids. It was pitch dark and I jumped up and run over and lifted her and spanked her good on the back but she didn't stop chokin so I run out in the kitchen with her in my arms and struck a match to see what it was.

A worm was crawlin out of her left nostril.

I screamed, and almost dropped her, but I didn't. I forced her mouth open and stuck my finger down her throat and she puked. She puked up worms, a whole big gob of them, that was stuck in the back of her throat. That was what had been chokin her.

After that she laid there in my arms and cried a little bit, and then she went back to sleep and slept real good.

ARTHUR TREADWILL

The Federal Government finally got concerned about the plight of the coal miners as the depression went on, and a sum of money was allotted to the Friends Service Committee of the Quakers to go to the mountain areas and feed hot lunches to undernourished children. My job was supervising such a program in Knight County in a small one-room school. The other day I was observing a teacher conducting her classes and a little girl wasn't paying attention. She was bent over her desk and seemed to be looking at something. But when the teacher walked over to her there was nothing.

"Honey," the teacher said. "What's wrong? Are you sick?"

"No ma'am," the child said. "I'm hungry."

"Well then you better go on home," the teacher said, "and get something to eat."

"That won't do me no good," the child said.

"Why not?" the teacher asked.

The child didn't answer. She bent her head and looked sullenly down at her desk again. One of the other children supplied the answer. She said they ate in relays in that girl's home, because food was so short, and today wasn't her day. I know this food shortage is a fact. Not long ago a group of women pushed into one of the school lunchrooms and took the food from the children and ate it. They were like animals. They were starving. A gang of men went in a delegation to see Judge Cooper, in Booneville. They were from an isolated coal camp that had been shut for a long time and they had been out of food for four days. The men said if they were not given food at once they would break into a store and take it at gun-point. Judge Cooper arranged to have bags of potatoes given to the men that very day, which no doubt averted bloodshed.

I have to write a report on what I see for the Committee. So I try to find out as much as I can from the people when I visit a community. I toured the Fletcher Coal Camp with a man I happened to run into walking down the street of the camp. He said his name was

Rufe Fugate and he lived in one of the company houses but he wasn't working but three days a week, and this was one of his days off. He surprised me. Most men you talk to don't seem to like the work in the mines. Rufe Fugate did. In fact he said he'd rather be a coal miner than anything. The only thing he objected to was being laid off or on short hours, the way he was now.

I found out a lot about the mines from Fugate. When we passed the various buildings I asked him what they were for and he told me. I learned about the tipple, the scale, the head house, and the names of things inside the mine. Where a man cuts coal is called his "working place." He enters the mine through the "drift mouth" and travels in an empty car pulled by a little low electric locomotive, or by a mule, and that is called "the mantrip."

Fugate seemed pleased to be able to tell me these things. He explained that a coal miner holds up the tunnel by stout poles five or six inches thick, known as "jack props" and further increases his safety by laying heavy timbers across the roof from one jack prop to another. These are called "collar poles." After a shot of dynamite, Fugate said, there is a big pile of broken coal lying at the working place ready to be loaded. Mixed with it is slate and sandstone which is known as "gob" and powdered coal known as "bug dust." Fugate said a man could breathe bug dust all his life and feel no ill effects. It was the rock dust which they used in the mines to lay the coal dust and prevent explosions that was dangerous to breathe. It brought on miner's "asme." I gathered that he meant miner's asthma, which of course is silicosis—a deadly disease. Once contracted, there is no cure for silicosis. It is common among miners all over the area.

As we made our way through the camp, Fugate

pointed out the various facilities. He pointed to the restaurant and I asked who operated it.

"The Fletcher Company," he said.

There was a bank and I asked about it. Fletcher operated it too. Of course I knew they operated the company store, but I was surprised to learn that they also operated an insurance agency, a funeral home, a light plant, a medical clinic, and, in fact, everything in sight.

Finally I started laughing. "It looks to me as if the Fletcher Company owns everything in this camp except the people."

Fugate stared at me. He did not laugh.

"I'm sorry," I said.

"That's all right, mister," Fugate said. "You're from outside. You just got here. I guess you aint had time to find out how things really are."

ELIZA WEBSTER

I wish I knowed then what I know now. I wouldn't marry Jim Webster nor any man, even though the preacher had me knocked up. I wouldn't let anybody touch me that way, never. Sex is the meanest trick God plays on us human beins, and I know that is an awful big statement but it is a true one. If anyone should be able to say, I'm the person. I just never knowed what it was like not to be pregnant after Jim and I got married. He was at me ever night for a long spell, but when the depression come and he was out of work we used to lay and do it half the day, drawin it out and holdin off, or maybe four or five times, with the kids playin around on the floor but too young to know what we was about. I liked it myself, at first. I admit it. I was just as eager to git in bed as Jim was. But when the kids begun to get older and they was underfoot all the time, things changed. I never seemed to get rested. And no matter how hard I worked at the washin and the sweepin and the cleanin I never seemed to get caught up. The kids got dirty too fast. I'd be fixin a batch of clean clothes and they'd be dirtyin another batch at the same time. And of course in the winter they all got colds and their noses run and they wiped it with their fingers and wiped their fingers on their clothes.

It would have been different if I'd had some help from Jim, or even a decent way to wash. I washed in the creek when the weather was warm enough, but in winter the creek froze and I finally got so I just couldn't go and bust a hole in the ice and git the water and lug it up to the house and build a fire to heat it and wash the clothes and hang them out. I just couldn't make myself do hit, even though I was brought up in a clean house and I hate dirt. So finally our place started smellin and lookin like a hog pen.

The County Health Officer, Doc Callahan, would come by ever so often and ketch me sittin in front of the fire with the kids dirty and the floor messed up and the kitchen full of dirty dishes and garbage, and he'd say, "Eliza, honey—you got to do better than this. This is one of the worst houses in the whole county. You a Clay, honey. Now promise me you'll clean up and take care of your kids."

"Sure, Doc," I'd say. "I will. I promise."

Both of us knowed I wouldn't. I was half sick most of the time, and I didn't have any teeth to chew my food so I could digest it right. I lost my teeth on account of all the babies comin so fast. That's what Doc said. The babies used up all my calcium, or somethin. Anyhow, my teeth went bad. They got big cavities in em and ached like fury and then they'd beel at the roots and pus would come out, and then the rotted stump would get loose and fall out. I was sure glad when that happened because the misery stopped, at least on that one tooth. By the time I was twenty-five I looked like a woman fifty years old. I knowed I was a mess, and I had a crook in my nose where Jim hit me one night when he come home drunk. He broke it and it growed back crooked. But by that time I didn't care how I looked. I wished I looked so bad that even Jim wouldn't get after me, and he didn't, when he was sober. But when he was drunk I looked like a woman and he wanted a woman and it was dark and he just took me. He'd come home from Booneville, reelin and slobberin, and throw me on the bed and force my legs apart and do it to me right in front of the kids. They'd begin shriekin. They thought he was tryin to kill me before they found out what he was really doin. Then the oldest, Ruth Ann, would take them out in the next room and shut the door.

I tried to talk to Jim when he was sober, but it didn't do no good. He just got mean. "Shet your mouth, old woman," he'd say to me. "You aint got no teeth, so I can't knock em out. I done fixed your nose for you. But I aint broke your jaw yet. You keep arter me, I'm sure as hell gonna do that."

I knowed he meant it so I shet up. I would of left him but I didn't have no way to look after the kids, and even though I was a poor mother, I didn't intend to let them freeze or starve. I knowed if I left them with Jim they'd likely die.

Then one night the whole thing come to an end. It was Ruth Ann's birthday. She was twelve years old. I wanted it nice for her, on that day, and I had some money—two dollars and eighty-four cents I'd made off some berries I picked and sold in Hammond Camp— and I said I was goin down and buy somethin for Ruth Ann for her birthday. A nice hankie with lace on it, maybe. And Jim said I was right, a little kid deserved a nice birthday, and he'd go down and git the hankie for me. I didn't really believe him. I guess I knowed all along he wouldn't do it, but I was so tired of arguin and fussin and he got so loud and mean when I crossed him that I just handed over the money.

After he left we made a plate of fudge out of some sugar and cocoa I'd been savin and brought out some little iced cakes that Mrs. Fugate had made for the birthday party, and all the kids pitched in and we fixed the cabin up nicer than it had been in months.

We got all ready and was waitin for Jim to bring the present, but suppertime come and went and he didn't come. About eight o'clock I said we might as well sit down and have the party. We ate the fudge and the little cakes and we all sung Happy Birthday to You to Ruth Ann, and we was really happy and laughin, havin forgot Jim, when the door opened and there he stood, rockin back and forth, glarin at us, drunk as a Lord.

"Well," he yells. "I see you couldn wait for the old man! You had to go ahead and eat up all the stuff!"

I seed he was in a beatin mood so I didn't say anything back. I kind of shooed the kids into the other room and tried to smooth Jim down, but he wasn't havin none of it.

"I tell you what I'm goin to do to you, old lady," he says. "You old beat-up bitch, I'm gonna screw you to death!"

He grabbed me and I tried to get away and he throwed me agin the wall and I seen stars when my head hit the boards. Then he grabs the front of my dress—the only decent one I owned, that I'd put on for

138

the party—and rips it from the neck clean down through the skirt so it's hangin on me like a bath robe. Then he stands there lookin at me and laughin. He got all blurred then. I started cryin and I just couldn't stop. I couldn't stop even when he throwed me on the bed and yelled for me to stop my blubberin, it was spoilin his fun. And when I couldn't stop he hit me and kep hittin me for a while and then he throwed me on the floor and went after me like a wild animal.

I laid there for a long time when it was over. I was too sick and in too much pain to move. Jim was layin on the bed without no clothes on, passed out, and I got up and looked at him with his mouth open and spittle runnin out of the corner of his mouth and needin a shave and I could smell the stink of the liquor he'd drunk with the money I'd saved to buy Ruth Ann's present, and I could hear him snorin, like a pig snores in the mud of its pen. In the other room, then, I heard one of my kids cryin, real soft, and it was the most lonely hopeless little sound I ever heered in my life, and suddenly I knowed what I was gonna do.

I went in the kitchen and found the butcher knife. I was suddenly cold, like I was freezen. My teeth chattered, even though it was hot in the room. I tested the knife with my finger. It was good and sharp. I tiptoed back into the room where Jim was sleepin on the bed. I knelt down. Then I cut, quick and hard, and the whole bed was a big waller of blood and Jim was screamin and clawin at hisself and I jumped up and run into the other room where the kids was and shut the door and threw myself agin it, in case Jim tried to kill me.

I didn't need to worry. Jim got off of the bed and run across to the front door. I guess he was tryin to run to the doctor, but he never made it off the porch. He was losin blood like a fire hose, and when he got through the door he fell on his face and passed out.

139

That was how I found him later when I went out with the candle. He was layin face down in the candlelight and the blood had spread out in a big dark glittery pool from under his thighs. I knelt beside him and looked at his eyes, which were turned to the side. They stared straight into the candle without winkin. I put the candle flame close to his nose and mouth and the flame never wavered.

I took the candle away.

Well, I thought, *you won't have no more trouble with Jim Webster, Eliza, and that's a real blessin, even if they hang you.*

WILLIARD FLETCHER

As time went on I saw that the union organizers were turning up in Knight County again, more of them than ever before, and smarter and tougher than ever before. And I saw that this time it wouldn't be just a matter of letting McCabe beat one of them up and run him over the county line. This time the men were in a different mood. They realized they didn't have much of anything to lose. Men like that are very dangerous, and to handle them you have to take the strongest possible measures. Thanks to my retrenchment I was in about the best financial shape of any operator in the county, except Charles Hammond, maybe. I'd heard that somebody had tipped him off to the crash and he'd unloaded on top of the market. I don't know if it was true but I do know the silly sonofabitch was still paying his men the same wages he'd paid them before the depression began, so he must be loaded, and he must be crazy. I never could figure him out. I always thought he was a big phony, with his fancy camp and his high wages and all this fooforah about education. But now, I heard, he was getting friendly with the union, and that was something else. I could afford to stand aside and let him play God on his own property, but when he starts helping the union he starts getting on my property, so to speak, and we can't have it. In fact, we won't have it.

I called together the other coal operators in the county and we set up the Knight County Coal Operators' Association. I explained to the mine operators at the meeting that we were now in for a fight to the finish and we might as well face it. It was going to be dog eat dog, kill or be killed, and if we were finicky about what we did now, we'd lose. I pointed to my own operations since the crash. I reminded them that there'd been some criticism, early in the game, that I was being heartless and cruel. Well, I said, if anybody wanted to check my books against the books of people who'd tried to hold up their wages and coddle their miners with scrip and keep them in the company houses when they couldn't produce, and like that, I would lay my books on the table right now. I saw some men in the audience look down. Some of them had done just that, and they had learned, through bitter experience, that I was right.

"When you go to war," I said, "half measures are worse than no measures. They cost money, and they don't win anything. You have to go all the way. If you haven't got the stomach for it, you lose."

I paused, to let that sink in. The men were looking at me, very sober and serious. I saw they had my point.

"Now then," I said. "If anybody in this room is

141

squeamish about the methods we may have to use, I want him to be honest with himself and with us, and get up and leave."

I paused again. I saw a couple of men were squeamish, but nobody got up and left. I hadn't expected them to. I didn't make it intolerable to them by spelling out the methods, because I knew that once the war started and the miners did these things to us, all the operators would harden up in good shape and back whatever we had to do to the miners.

"Our problem is the unions," I said. "The United Mine Workers particularly. You all know John L. Lewis. I hate the big overgrown sonofabitch, and I know every man in this room hates him, but we can't afford to underestimate him. He is a tough man, and a brave man—and a smart man. That makes him dangerous. To lick him and the UMW will cost money, a very great deal of money. But look at the alternative. If we don't spend the money and Lewis and his cruddy union gets in, we are all finished. Lewis will insist on higher wages and shorter hours and a bunch of expensive safety rules and compensations and so forth. We can't pay it. We are barely making out as it is. If they hang those other costs on us, every man in this room will be completely ruined."

An operator raised his hand and I recognized him. "What do you want us to do, Will?" he said.

"I was just getting to that," I said. "I'm not talking about some little piddling hundred dollar contribution here. I'm talking about full-scale war. I'm talking about hiring an army of tough men and deputizing them and putting official badges and uniforms on them and arming them with pistols and rifles and submachine guns and keeping them on the payroll as a permanent operating expense—until we smash this man Lewis and his union once and for all. If we are not

142

prepared to do this, we might as well start looking for a buyer for our mines right now."

There was a little mirthless laughter at this point, as the operators contemplated the ridiculous notion that anybody would buy a mine now.

"How much do you figure it'll cost, Mr. Fletcher?" another operator asked.

I paused and let the tension build up a little. It was very quiet.

"A hundred thousand dollars," I said.

There was a kind of mass indrawing of breath, which was clearly audible in the room.

"Yeah, I know," I said. "That's a lot of money. But it's that or lose the shirt off our backs. We can take our choice."

I was silent. Finally an operator stood up. He said, "I make a motion that we take Mr. Will Fletcher's advice and organize this police force and fight for our property that we've all built up around here. Even if the cost goes to a hundred thousand. All those in favor will now stand up."

There was a slight hesitation. Then one man stood up. Within ten seconds the entire group was on its feet. I smiled. I had made the point I had come to make. There was only one miscalculation on my part. It didn't cost $100,000 to fight Lewis and the UMW. Before we were through it cost a cool $1,000,000.

BOYD FLETCHER

It never rains but it pours. I had a big fire loss in my property over on the edge of Pike County some years

143

ago. Burned down roughly 15,000 acres of prime timber. So I figured I'd had my quota of fire.

But I hadn't.

Some knucklehead threw a butt out of his car on Route 119 while there was a stiff wind blowing, and before the thing burnt itself out, it was almost into Booneville. Otter Creek stopped it. But a lot of cabins along the creek went, and they went fast, because the fire was really jumping by the time it got that far. Most of the people got away, except one cabinful of kids. Some woman killed her man with a butcher knife, the way I heard it, and they had her down in the Booneville jail. The neighbors were supposed to be looking after her kids but the fire spread so fast I guess everybody just left whatever they were doing and ran for their lives. None of the kids in that one house made it. But one way to look at it, I guess: what did the poor little devils have to look forward to anyhow? Maybe they're better off dead.

Thing that worries me, frankly, is my losses. Even at these rock-bottom depression prices I must have lost close to a hundred thousand dollars in timber off that tract.

ELIZA WEBSTER

They had me in jail down in Booneville for quite a while after I cut Jimmy and he died. They said I was insane. Or my lawyer did, so he could git me off. He said I was drove out of my mind by the things Jim done to me and I didn't rightly know what I was about when I cut him that way. I kep tellin my lawyer I wasn't insane when I done it. I might of been insane when I married Jim in the first place, or when I stuck to him and kep havin babies, but I wasn't insane when I killed him. That was about the only sane thing I done the whole miserable time, as far as I can see. Course I wasn't even tryin to kill him. I was just tryin to fix it so he wouldn't make no more little kids. The bleedin is what killed him.

The trial was a big one. A lot of people was there. They all wanted to hear what I done to Jim. I'd be darned if I'd tell em. I just said my mind went black, and stuck to it. No matter what the other lawyer said I just kep sayin my mind had went black.

Course hit hadn't. I could see ever single detail of what I done like it was passin right in front of me. I'd cut real quick and the knife was real sharp and I got it off clean afore Jim knowed what hit him.

My lawyer give a real touchin speech to the jury. I almost cried to hear him tellin what a terrible life I'd had. I hadn't realized it was so bad myself until I heered him atellin it.

"This poor woman aint responsible," my lawyer said. "I hate to have to say it in her presence but this poor woman is mentally deranged."

He said it so often I begun to believe it myself. I was really crazy. I must be. Everybody thought I was, so it must be so.

Then a terrible think took place. It happened in court durin the trial.

I started to smell smoke. I looked out the winders and the whole valley was blue with it. And shortly a man come runnin in and went up and whispered to the Judge and the Judge got an awful look on his face. Then the Judge made an announcement that court was adjourned and he called me right into his chambers and told me what happened. Judge Cooper

145

is a wonderful man. Nobody can tell me different. I seen how hard it was for him to tell me, and I says to him to go ahead, whatever it is it can't be much worse than I've had already. But when he told it to me, it was so bad I couldn't believe it. I thought it was probably the fact I was crazy and was dreamin it.

We couldn't go up in the holler right away. Things was too hot. The whole place was burnt up. Even the next mornin, when they let me out of my cell and Judge Cooper drove me up there, the ground was so hot it liked to burn your feet when you walked on it. When we got to my house it wasn't there no more. There wasn't no sign of it. The whole place had changed. Everything was charred black and the smoke was still comin out of stumps and logs that laid on the ground. It was so strong I got to coughin, just from breathin in.

They can't all have been burnt up, I thought. The big ones must of got out. There must be some of them around here in the woods somewheres.

I told Judge Cooper I'd better look in the woods for my kids, and he kind of bit his lower lip and says, "Eliza, the bodies are in the funeral home down in Booneville. They was picked up this morning by Mr. Elkins, the funeral director."

"But not all of them," I said. "Some of them must have seen the fire comin and got away."

"I'm sorry, Eliza," Judge Cooper said.

But I didn't believe it. I jumped out of the car and ran out in the woods. As I run I yelled for my kids by their names. I run all over the holler for a long time, yellin, callin their names, lookin everywhere. But not a soul answered.

Finally I was wore out. I couldn't run another step or call another name. I set down on a stone that was cool. I knowed the truth then. My kids was all dead, all burnt up in that forest fire. It wasn't no use tryin to run around and call no more. I set there. I finally got rested but I didn't get up. I didn't have no urge to get up and go nowhere. I don't know how long I set there on that rock, but it must have been an awful long time, because finally it got dark.

JUDGE FLOYD COOPER

I had to call in the Kentucky National Guard last Sunday during the funeral of Jim Sizemore. Booneville was flooded with circulars calling on the miners to make a mass protest by a demonstration in front of the church. Sizemore was known to me. He had married one of our nicest girls up in Mad Dog Hollow, Alice Menefee. They had three fine little kids. Sizemore was shot and killed by a mine guard hired by the Knight County Coal Operators' Association. He used a Thompson machine gun and he tore up Sizemore's body pretty badly. I hadn't seen the policeman before, but Will Fletcher said he had only been doing his duty. Sizemore had been going to dynamite his tipple, Will said. No dynamite was found, but Will assured me that the miners had made off with it after the shooting.

I talked to the guard who had done the killing, and he jibed with Will's statement. His name, he said, was Dominic Strelli, and he had been working in Chicago before he came here.

"Who did you work for in Chicago, Strelli?" I asked him.

"Oh different guys, Judge," he said.

"What sort of work?"

He smiled. "Judge," he said, "what difference does it make? You and I are both on the same payroll, aint we?"

I gave him to understand, there and then, that he was wrong. I was not on anybody's payroll. He nodded his head and said, "Yes, Judge. Sure, Judge. I'm sorry, Judge."

I finally had to let him out on Will Fletcher's bail money. I passed young Lee Harrod in the hall of the courthouse the other day, when I was leaving my chambers. I never thought I'd see the day when I couldn't look a young lawyer in the eye. It really shocked me when I spoke to Lee without meeting his eyes. I guess that was the first time I really realized that something had happened to me. That night I sat up trying to figure out what to do. I couldn't. So I drank about half a pint of bourbon and after it took effect and I got drowsy I went to bed and went right to sleep.

JIM TURNER

I don't know about the others, but I am now at the end of my rope. I can stand it when they cut my wages. I know the price of coal is fallin all the time and that the operators have to make a profit to stay in business. But when they start riggin the scales and robbin me of the tonnage I really dig, I can't stand it. Somethin inside me just can't stand it. I know exactly how big a coal car is because I have measured it. It is eleven feet long by six feet wide by eighteen inches deep. I know exactly how much coal that car will hold. Three and a half tons. That's 7,000 pounds of coal in every car I load full.

Now I have been loadin my cars over full, just to make sure, and now I am sure. The Fletchers have tinkered with the scales. They have set them back. I get credit for only 3,500 to 4,000 pounds a car. In other words they are gyppin me out of half a car of coal every time I load one.

The other day I just couldn't stand it no more. I spoke to the foreman about it, and he said he'd take it up with the boss. I waited awhile and he never said anything so I asked him again.

"Jim," he says, "I've always liked you. You are a hard worker. One of the best men I got. So I'm goin to stick my neck out and give you a tip. Just lay low and do as you are told. If you don't you'll be fired. They can get lots of men who won't make any fuss about their scale."

"But it aint right," I said. "If they got to do it to us, why can't they just tell us the truth? Why do they have to sneak around and jigger the scale?"

"I don't know, Jim," the foreman said. "But that's how it is. You'll just have to put up with it."

"The hell I will!" I yelled. "I'm goin in and tell old Will Fletcher right now, what kind of an S.O.B. he is!"

Well I was wrong about that. I never even got close to Mr. Will Fletcher. They've got uniformed company police standin guard everywhere these days. A couple of them stopped me in front of the main office and asked me my business and when I told them, they told me to leave. I refused. One of them looked at the other and sort of smiled. Then, all of a sudden, they went for me. One of them hit me on the side of the face with a billy club. I thought for a while my jaw was broke, but it wasn't. It was just two of my teeth that was cracked off on the upper jaw, below the gum line, that was causin the pain. My face was sure a sight though, after them company cops worked me over. I didn't want to worry my wife or my kids. I told them that I'd been in an accident in the mine. But I had to tell my brother Clabe the truth, and he was wild. He wanted to get a rifle and go kill those guards, but I talked him out of it. There wasn't no use. If Clabe shot those guards they'd come after us, and my wife and little Connie might get hurt. That slowed Clabe down, when I mentioned Connie gettin hurt. But of course he quit. He couldn't stand to go and work for a man that had had his brother beat up, even though God knows we needed every penny we could rake together. There are just some things a person can't do, even if he starves.

BOB EVARTZ

I was very lucky, and I knew it, to get on the payroll of the Knight County Coal Operators' Association as a full-time deputy. I got a fine-lookin uniform and a badge and a big broadbrimmed hat with little woven cords around the brim like the Staties, which made the girls look at me when I passed. I was allowed to carry a pistol. In fact it was an order to carry one at all times, and I bought me a big beautiful .44 with nickel plate and an ivory handle. I have never had it so good. I was paid more money than a miner could make, and people kind of looked down when I came along the street—or they smiled at me and tried to get in good with me, and says, "Hi Bob. What's new?" I answered them with

150

a grin at first, but we had a lecture on that later, and I stopped. It wasn't a good plan to be friendly with the miners, Sheriff McCabe said. We'd be inclined to be easy on em if we got to smilin at em. Just give em a curt little nod, McCabe says.

Boy, I hated that, at least at first. But I got used to it, like anything else, and finally I got so's I got a kick out of seein them react to that little nod. It scared em. They thought I was mad at em. Or they might feel guilty about somethin, some union trouble they was hatchin and they might think I was on to em.

As time went on it got easier to be rough with the miners. They were rough with us, if they got a chance. I'd find stuff written on the fence when I'd be walkin home to my room in Booneville. *Bob Evartz is a yellow bastard. Bob Evartz eats shit. Watch it, Evartz, we going to kill you . . .*
You see enough stuff like that written on a fence and you begin to stop givin a damn for these miners. After all, they join the union, don't they? And what's the union but a bunch of lousy Reds and Communists that are tryin to destroy the United States? That's what they swear to do, when they join up, them Red bastards. It's right in the oath they take to get in the stinkin Communist party. And if a miner wants to throw in with a lot of cruddy bastards that are tryin to overthrow this country he deserves every punch in the mouth and kick in the crotch we can give him.

I worried awhile about the warning that they were goin to kill me. We've had a couple of company police shot from ambush, but not killed. Nobody shot at me, and I got over bein scared, and instead I got mad at them for writin that stuff on the fence and givin me sleepless nights. I decided that as soon as I got a chance I'd kick hell out of one of those smart sons of bitches, even though it wasn't the one who wrote that warnin. I'd begun to hate them all, just like they was hatin us.

151

It was a showdown fight, like Mr. Will Fletcher said, and all was fair in a showdown fight. The thing to do was win, Mr. Fletcher said. After a person won, it didn't matter how he done it: that was soon forgot.

Course I didn't exactly let my love-life suffer. I had a little waitress lined up at the Boone House, a little bittie girl no bigger than a button, but just cuter than hell. I used to take her drivin in my car out in the country, and we'd stop in some lonely place and fool around and hug and kiss. She'd get me about half nuts and then it was no, no, no. If we was married, she said, it would be different. Hell I didn't want to marry nobody. I've seen too much grief come out of that stuff. But this little gal was pretty as a little live doll and I guess one of these days I'm gonna weaken, like all the other suckers. I might as well be married to her, the money I'm spendin for bracelets and nicknacks she's got a hankerin after. If I'm gonna pay the bills I might as well get in on the fun.

I had to give myself a talkin to from time to time. I knew that miners' families was havin it tough, and I'd get to thinkin about it and feel bad. One man was seen eatin potato peelins and lard out of his lunch pail in a mine, I heard. That made me feel bad. I remembered how it had been with me up in the holler when I was a kid. But I put it out of my mind. There wasn't a damned thing Bob Evartz could do about the fact that a bunch of Red Communists were tryin to wreck the coal companies, who were the best friends the country ever had, except try to help the companies fight them Communists off. If that meant that some poor devil had to eat potato peelins, it was just too bad, but Bob Evartz wasn't goin to go over there and cry on his shoulder. Sheriff McCabe had given me a personal pat on the back not too long ago when we scared off a bunch of miners who were tryin to turn over a company coal truck. I got one of them good with my billy club, right across the head—after he tried to kill me with his pick.

"You're a good man, Evartz," McCabe said. "Stay with it boy. You'll make out just fine around here."

"I'll stay with it all right," I said. "No sonofabitch is gonna try to gut me with a pick and get away with it."

"That's the stuff, Bob," McCabe said.

I was doin fine and I intended to keep it that way. The company had a standard lease they made all the miners sign if they lived in a company house. The Fletcher lease was no different from all the leases the other companies used. They was all the same. If a man got sick or hurt and couldn't work in the mines any more he had to vacate his house right away. Not in a week or a month. That very day, if the company wanted him out of there. I suppose it was a tough rule, but the way Mr. Will Fletcher explained it, the company really didn't have any choice. A man that's sick or hurt can't cut coal. If you don't get him out of the company house he's stayin in you'll pretty soon find yourself with a camp full of cripples. And you can't mine coal with a camp full of cripples, now, can you? That was the way Mr. Fletcher put it to us. and we had to give him the answer he was lookin for. You certainly can't mine coal with a camp full of cripples.

"So get em out," Fletcher said. "It's legal. It's right there in the lease they signed, and you can damned well show it to them if they give you an argument."

I took a look at one of the leases and he was right. It was there in black and white. If a man didn't want to sign it he didn't have to—just like Mr. Fletcher said.

One day we went out, me and Bull Hargis and two other company policemen, to do a little evictin in the Fletcher Camp on Rockhouse Creek. I'd been doin it for a couple of months now, off and on, and I was hardened up to it. The thing to do, as Hargis said, was to be so tough and mean and quick about it that they never got a chance to know what hit em. Beat em to the punch. Knock em down and throw em out before they had a chance to think what was happenin. Hargis was right. I once tried to tell a family that I hated to do this to them, and if it was up to me I wouldn't do it, and so forth and so on. Well, we were half a day jabberin before I finally got them out.

But I got a shock when we came up on the porch and the woman we were goin to evict was Mrs. Annie Fugate, Rufe's wife, that I'd known over on Mad Dog Creek when I was growin up. I didn't expect to see her here. I thought Rufe was workin for Mr. Hammond. Rufe had had a fight with his foreman and quit, but I didn't know it; and then he was too proud to go back there, and he got a job with Fletcher before the layoffs began. Anyhow, I didn't know any of that and I was sure surprised to see Mrs. Fugate.

Mrs. Fugate saw me, and her lips quivered and she said, "Bob—it's you—" And then she grabbed a hold of me and began to cry. Well I tell you I didn't know what to do. It scared me to see Mrs. Fugate cry. Mrs. Fugate had been an awful close thing to bein my own ma after my daddy was shot, and I'd seen her stand up to things that would buckle lots of men, without turnin a hair. You know how little kids get a feelin about a grownup—like they are Gods and nothin can touch them. That was how I used to feel about Aunt Annie Fugate, which was what I always called her. So I guess it was natural for me to call it to her now. "Aunt Annie," I said, and she kind of went rigid in my arms and then opened her eyes and looked straight into mine, and I swear it was funny but I was a little kid again, all of a sudden, and she kind of blurred in front of me and I squinched my eyes real tight shut a couple of times.

"Bob," Aunt Annie Fugate said. "Come in and speak to Rufe, will you, son?"

I wiped my eyes real quick and tried to get hold of myself. I knowed Hargis and them other men was watchin me. "What's wrong with him?" I said.

Mrs. Fugate didn't say anything. Then I heard the cursin comin from inside. It was Rufe. He was mad as hell, and his voice was good and loud, so he couldn't be hurt too bad. I felt a relief come over me.

"All right," I said. "I guess it won't do no harm to speak to him."

I stepped past Hargis and the other police and walked into the house. Rufe was sittin up in a chair facin the door. The room was kind of dark and it took a second before I could see well enough to see his face clearly. He was cursin steadily and his eyes were bandaged over solid with a white bandage.

"Hello Rufe," I said. "It's Bob Evartz."

He stopped cursin. "Bob who?" he yelled.

"Bob Evartz," I said. "Remember me? I used to live up the holler a piece."

"Oh hell yes," Rufe yelled. "Sure, Bob. Glad you come. I heered you was with them goddam company cops down to Booneville."

There was a silence. Hargis and the other police had come in and were standin in the room, and so was Mrs. Fugate. I licked my lips. I could feel my heart poundin.

"What's wrong with your eyes, Rufe?" was all I could think of to say.

He didn't reply for a second. And then he laughed. It was an awful sound.

"There aint nothin wrong with my eyes, Bob," Rufe Fugate says. "Ceptin one thing. I aint got them no more. They was blowed out about a week ago, up in the mine. I lit my fuse and she didn't go. I waited almost an hour, and then I was sure she had gone out,

155

and I went back and when I bent down to take a look, she went. It was a crazy fool thing to do but I done it. So now I aint got no eyes. The company doctor took em out, they was so bad tore up."

I looked around at Hargis and the others. They were standin there lookin at the floor.

"Bull," I said.

He looks up at me.

I jerked my head toward the door. His black eyebrows ridged up in a furry line over his black eyes and he stared at me—and then he shook his head.

And then Rufe says, real quick, "Annie—Annie—you there?"

"Yes I'm here," Annie Fugate says, and she's over there in an instant with her hand holdin Rufe's.

"Are they cops?" Rufe says. "Are they cops, Annie?"

And then, suddenly, I don't know why, but there I was, standin in front of Rufe and Annie facin Hargis and the others, and I had my .44 pistol with the ivory handle out, and the hammer back, and I was makin a little motion with it toward the door, and I heard my voice sayin, "There aint no cops here, Uncle Rufe. Just young Bob Evartz is all—come to pay you a visit."

And I looked into Bull Hargis's eyes and I wished he would draw, or any of them would draw—but they didn't. They just backed out, not sayin a word. I heard a car start and drive away. Then I put my gun back in the holster and turned around to Rufe. Annie was still holdin his hand. I was finished forever with the Knight County Coal Operators' Association and I figured I was a big damn fool, but you want to know somethin: there aint enough money in the world to buy the kind of a look I saw in Aunt Annie Fugate's eyes when I turned toward her and caught her lookin at me.

CHARLES HAMMOND

As I was coming from my house to the office in Hammond Coal Camp this morning I saw Angie Webb standing on a corner. She must have been waiting for me, because when I neared her she spoke. "Mr. Hammond, could I see you a minute?"

"Of course, Angie," I said.

"You know Rufe Fugate—the man who got his eyes blowed out."

"Certainly."

"Well Mr. Fletcher sent his men to evict Rufe and Annie yesterday—and young Bob Evartz was one of them. Bob used to live up the holler. He's been on the Knight County police force for a month or so."

I nodded, wondering what she was getting at.

"When the time come," Angie said, "Bob Evartz couldn't stomick throwin out a blind man—particularly one that had been his friend. So he drawed his gun and run the other police out of there. Old Bull Hargis was one of em."

"I know Hargis," I said. "I hope Evartz realizes what he's done."

"Oh he does," Angie said. "He aint about to take no chances. He moved his stuff out of the Boone Hotel right after he left the Fugates with us. That's what I wanted to see you about, Mr. Hammond. Rufe and Annie aint got no place to go and I was wonderin if it would be all right if we took em in permanent?"

"Of course it's all right," I said. "It's your house."

"No it aint, Mr. Hammond. It's yours. We just rentin it."

157

"Take them in," I said. "And if there's anything I can do for Rufe, let me know."

"Golly Mr. Hammond," Angie said. "I sure do thank you, and I know Rufe and Annie will too. I just hope it don't git you in no trouble."

"Trouble?" I said. "How could it get me in trouble?"

"Well, a lot of folks in this camp has wanted to do what I'm doin'," Angie said. "But they was scared to ask you. They figured you been so nice to us they didn't want to be hogs. But of course if I take in Rufe and Annie there'll be people around botherin you, and I know it."

I hadn't thought of that. But I realized what she said was true, and for a second I wished I hadn't been so hasty. Still—what other answer could I have given? I walked on toward my office, wishing I had had the courage to pull out of Kentucky before the price war on coal started. Well, I hadn't. I'd played God, and kept on playing it, and now I was stuck with it. My only trouble is, I'm not God. The only real solution I can see for this mess is to close the mine and get out—which might solve a lot of my problems, but it certainly wouldn't do much to help Rufe and Annie Fugate and the hundreds of other families which my God-playing had encouraged to look to me for whatever help they might get.

BULL HARGIS

I passed the word on Bob Evartz. I told my men to pick him up, the first chance they got, on any charge they liked. Loitering was always a good one. If a man stopped to tie his shoe he could be picked up for loitering, the way we were operatin in Knight County these days. The only law in the county was Company Law. Our Law.

But Bob Evartz was no fool. He hightailed it to his room and skipped out with his stuff, and we lost track of him for about a week. Then we heard through our spies—Mr. Fletcher had about twenty Pinkerton detectives posin as miners around the county—that Evartz was livin in the Hammond Coal Camp. This news made Mr. Fletcher good and sore. Hammond has been lettin all kinds of people come and double up with people in his camp. Some are labor organizers. I've been itchin to go in there and burn the place down, but Mr. Fletcher says no—not yet—maybe if somethin happens that's a real provocation, but we can't move cold turkey, even though we have the law in our pocket. Be patient, Mr. Fletcher said. Our time will come.

So the best I could do on Evartz was to tell my men to watch little Helen McCombs, the waitress at the Boone Hotel that he's been playin around with. Evartz spent most of his salary on that little gal and I figured he wouldn't be able to walk away and leave all that investment for somebody else to muscle in on.

I was right.

About two weeks after that smart sonofabitch drawed on me in old Fugate's cabin, he tried to sneak into Booneville and date his little honey, and my boys nailed him. They brought him over to the jail with the cuffs on him where McCabe and I were killin time with a couple of cigars and a pinochle board.

"Well hello there Bob," I said when I saw him. "Glad to see you. Where you been keepin yourself?"

"These men picked me up without no reason," Evartz said.

159

"Now that's where you're wrong, Bob," I said. "They had a reason. I told them to do it."

I looked at the boys.

"Nice work," I said. "You just leave this boy with us. We want to do a little questionin."

The boys left and McCabe and I went to work on Evartz. We asked him about the Hammond Camp, how many miners that we'd evicted had been took in. Evartz said he didn't know. We asked him how many labor organizers were there. He said he didn't know. We asked him if the miners had any plan to give us trouble, and he said he didn't know. All the time we were talkin I could feel the urge to beat him buildin up inside me. I remembered the look on his face when he drawed on me in that cabin. I knowed then, and I knowed it now, that he was itchin to kill me and if I had drawed he would have done it.

I says, "Bob, you don't know much, do you?"

"No," he said.

"Maybe this will smarten you up a little," I said, and hit him across the mouth with my billy club. The blow broke his teeth in front and knocked him down. Seein him on the floor like that and the blood and all kind of drove me off my nut for a minute, and Sheriff McCabe had to drag me away from kickin and poundin on him.

Then we both looked at him. He was layin face down and there was blood comin out of both his ears. He was layin mighty still.

"Jesus, Bull," Sheriff McCabe said. "I reckon you killed the sonofabitch."

"Na," I said. "You can't kill a hillbilly with a club. You got to use a gun."

McCabe bent down and felt around for a pulse beat. Then he turned Evartz over and looked at his eyes. Then he looked up and there was a little grin on his face.

160

"This poor feller just suffered a heart attack," McCabe says. "He's just about as dead as anybody can get."

And that's how we wrote it up in the book. Robert Evartz died of a heart attack in the Boone County Jail, with Sheriff Frank McCabe and Deputy Elwood Hargis as the witnesses. Elwood's the name my mother gave me. Nobody calls me that because they know I don't like it. They just call me Bull.

CHARLES HAMMOND

The news that Bob Evartz had been picked up and taken to the Booneville jail and had died there, in the presence of Hargis and McCabe, had a profound effect on the miners. The story of what young Bob had done at the Fugate cabin had gotten around, of course, and the miners felt strongly about it. They are like children —sentimental children. They will suffer terrible things but when their feelings are touched by something, you can't predict what will happen. There was talk of organizing an army out of the hollers and marching on Booneville with the idea of rooting out the hired police force, once and for all. Nobody believed for a moment that young Evartz had died of a heart attack. And when Fletcher had him buried (there were no relatives to do it) in a closed coffin, the miners were all certain the boy had been beaten to death. I agreed, but there was nothing I could do. I strongly opposed any violence. In the first place I knew that the police—hundreds of them—and armed with

Thompson guns, would make a bloody shambles of any mass of miners who appeared on the streets of Booneville. And in the second place I could not see anything to be gained, except revenge, which was sweet in the mouth but could leave a bitter aftertaste.

I took things into my own hands then. I called up the Governor and told him the situation. I told him we had what amounted to Company Law in Knight County, and that something terrible might happen if he did not break it up. He was very eager to help, he said, but the Sheriff was a duly-elected officer of the law, and the hired policemen were Security Guards, as it had been explained to him. Their purpose was to prevent disgruntled miners from burning or dynamiting company property. I couldn't argue with the fact that without the police there might have been such acts of sabotage. I tried to explain to the Governor how dangerous and complex the situation had become, with both sides gradually getting more and more implacable, as incidents piled up over the days and months. He said he was aware of it, that my situation in Knight County was in no way unique, and that he hoped and prayed for a peaceful solution to the whole problem. He had sent out the state militia a number of times to the hill counties already, the Governor said, and if we had an outbreak, which he certainly hoped we would not have, he would send them to Booneville.

Well I thanked the Governor and hung up. I could see his point. He was probably doing the best he could with the powers at his disposal, but it did not alter the fact that my call had brought nothing tangible in the way of hope for a solution.

And Angie Webb's prediction about people wanting to come into my camp had been correct. Taking in the Fugates touched off a wave of similar requests. Fletcher's crowd, and the other operators around the county, were evicting routinely now. As soon as a miner was dropped from the payroll, for any reason, he was moved out of the company house at once. They did it by force if they had to. They brought in a van and armed police and picked up the possessions of the hapless miner and drove it out and unloaded it off company property beside some county road. It was a familiar sight to see a miserable family huddled by their belongings, and now that I had opened the door to my camp, so to speak, requests to bring in homeless relatives and friends came to me in a flood. I had set a precedent. It was very hard to say no. As time went on our camp began to look like a refuge camp in a war. I began to see that the consequences of being a Good Samaritan were many, difficult and irksome. There were squabbles among the newcomers, complaints, petty thefts, and all the troubles you must expect when people are miserable and are crowded in tightly together. I was getting a little desperate. To tell the truth, I was beginning to hate the sight of bedraggled people and dirty mattresses tied to old cars and the grateful faces when I said yes, yes, they could double up with this family or that family, just be careful to keep the place clean and orderly . . .

BULL HARGIS

I couldn't mention this to a living soul, but the most fun I ever had in my life was when I was about twenty-six or -seven, and me and another feller was huntin deer up in Martin County. Martin's one of the wildest counties in the state. They didn't even have the law in parts of it, nor doctors, nor nothin. We was tired as hell and we hadn't shot a thing and we was disgusted. We had us a jug of shine along, so we started in on it, and before we was through we'd emptied it. Both of us was feelin high as hell and my buddy says, "Let's see if we can't find us some little old gal."

"Little old gal," I said. "Why hell man, these hollers is full of little old gals, but you go foolin around em and their daddy'll fill you so full of buckshot you'll die just from the extra weight."

"You got any money?" he asked me. "These here people is poor as hell, and if they seen a ten dollar bill they might just decide to give us a little jump and not tell their daddy."

"Stop talkin crazy," I said. "You go around here wavin ten dollar bills, and you gonna get us shot."

Well, drunk as he was, he knowed I was talkin sense, so we starts walkin out. Well I guess our luck was bound to turn. We hadn't seen a deer all day, nor nothin, and we comes out of the woods into this clearin and here's this little kid gatherin chestnuts. She couldn't of been more than fourteen, and she wasn't too pretty, but drunk as we was she looked mighty fine.

"Hello there, sister," my buddy says. "You gettin many chestnuts?"

"A right smart few, mister," she said.

"Aint you afeered to be all alone out in the woods like this?" my buddy said.

"Oh no," this girl says, "I come out here often. Nothin ever happens."

I seen this kid wasn't too bright. They's a lot like that around in the hollers, what with cousins marryin cousins and brothers foolin with sisters and like that. So I smiles at this little kid and I says, "Well, of course you got no worries. All you got to do is yell and your

164

daddy comes arunnin from your cabin down the creek a piece."

This kid looks at me, and busts out gigglin. "You must not be from around here, mister," she says. "I aint got no daddy. I'm Janie Pigman, and I'm livin with my old grannie down by the river. I'm gatherin these nuts for usen in the squirrel stew."

I looked at my buddy. He looked at me. Then, all of a sudden, we grabbed her . . .

When we was both through and she was lyin there moanin and cryin we both got sober, and we realized what we done, and we thought what might happen to us if this little kid told on us. So we talked her over quick, and then we throwed fingers, odds or evens. I took odds and I lost. I knowed I had to do it so I done it quick. I took careful aim at the back of that kid's head and pulled the trigger. Then me and my buddy hightailed it, and we never went back to Martin County again. We read in the papers about it, though. The paper said a girl had been killed in Martin County by a stray bullet that had been fired by some hunter. That was the end of it as far as we was concerned.

SIS SIZEMORE

My daddy was Clarence Sizemore, who was shot by that Strelli feller, that works for the County police, and my mother was Alice Menefee. Everybody knows us around here for hard-workin god-fearin people. But after daddy was gone things got awful hard. We was too proud to beg. But there were times when all of us

165

were hungry. Mother got cornmeal from a feed store down in Booneville and we had a garden and Brother shot varmints with his twenty-two whenever he could see one and hit it, but we was just livin from hand to mouth, and finally I couldn't stand it no longer.

"I'm goin down to Booneville, ma," I says. "Maybe I kin get a job and make us some money. Our clothes is patches on patches right now, and gettin worse."

"You can't do it, Sis," my mother says. "You're too young."

"I'm fifteen and I'm big for my age," I says.

"Yes," ma says, "I know that. I'd go down myself if I didn't have the baby."

"I'll be all right," I says. "It won't do no harm to try. If I can't get a job I'll come home."

Mother was worried to death. She give me a big lecture on boys and men and what they are after and how to protect myself, and I listened, but I already knew. When I was just a little shaver I come across Bill Ott's sister Francie up in the hayloft of the old barn the Otts used to own before their family kind of fell apart. I'd gone up there lookin for pigeon eggs and I climbed up the wooden ladder between the beams without expectin to find anything except a pigeon nest. I was barefoot and little and I guess I didn't make much noise, but when I got almost to the top, my hair stood on end. I heard this soft moanin sound. I crep up, quiet as a mouse, and peeked over the top of the haymow and there is Francie Ott layin on her back with her legs wrapped around the back of some boy, makin that moanin sound. I couldn't see who the boy was but I could see Francie's face, half buried in the hay. Her eyes was squinched shut as if she was in some kind of pain, but then I noticed that one of her hands was gently strokin the boy's head, so I figured she wasn't in pain, or she'd be fightin and screechin, so I just backs down the ladder, real quiet, and tiptoes

166

out of the barn. But I did hang aroun in the bushes to see who the boy was, because I was curious, and it was Dave Beckley, whose father owns the Beckley Drygoods Store in Booneville, one of biggest and most expensive stores in the whole area. I thought that Dave might marry Francie Ott, seeing he was sweet on her, but he didn't. I never heard any more about it, except one thing; mother mentioned one day that old man Ott must of finally got up the gumption to get a job, because young Francie was sportin a real pretty pink silk dress. I knowed old man Ott never hit a tap in his life and never would. So the dress was a mystery to me for a spell, until I found out what things was all about.

When I went to Booneville to look for work I had a hard time. I tried all the stores and even the private homes, lookin for anything, maid work, washin, anything atall. But times were hard, even for folks in Booneville; women was doin their own maidin and washin. I was about ready to give up when I remembered about Dave Beckley and Francie Ott. Dave was now workin in his father's store. He was the Buyer, or somethin, and he wore a snazzy blue suit and white shirt and red tie, and his black shoes was polished to a high gloss. I'd seen him when I was in there askin old lady Taulbee for a job. Old lady Taulbee was a sour old person and she just looked at me and sniffed as if I wasn't very bright to be askin such a question in the middle of the depression when every job was filled by people that had had them, like she'd had, since Lincoln was assassinated.

Now I thought about Dave Beckley, and I won't try to be a liar about it. I'd seen Dave look at me in the store as I walked out. I knowed what that look meant. And I knowed good and well what I'd be gettin into if I went to Dave and asked for a job. I thought about it for about half an hour. Then I went and washed my face in the ladies room of the Boone Hotel, combed my hair, put on some lipstick and straightened up as pretty as I could. Then I walked up the street and went in the Beckley Drygoods Store and was goin right through to the office where I knowed Dave would probably be when old lady Taulbee called out to me and asked what I wanted now.

"I want to see Mr. Beckley," I says.

"Now look young lady," Mrs. Taulbee says, "I already told you there's no job open in this store. If that's what's on your mind, you just turn right around and march right out of here."

Well I guess I might have done it. Mrs. Taulbee is a big red-faced woman with a little mustache and she had me half scared before I even started. But just then Mr. Dave Beckley steps out of his office and asks what the trouble is. Mrs. Taulbee says I'd been in here botherin her about a job, and there was none, and now she figured I was back to pester him—and she was just tryin to pertect him from me.

Dave Beckley looks at me. I look straight back. Then he says, "You're Dinah Sizemore, aren't you?"

"Yes sir," I said.

"I heard about your father," Dave Beckley said, "and I was very sorry about it."

"Thank you, sir," I said.

Dave Beckley looks at Mrs. Taulbee, and I knew he was feelin a little strange, but he brung it off. "This young lady is a special case," he said. "She's entitled to help if we can give her any."

Mrs. Taulbee's face got awful red, but she didn't say anything. Then Mr. Beckley told me to come into his office and we'd sit down and see if there was anything that could be done for me. And I did. He gave me a job in Lingerie, which he explained was pronounced Lonjer-A. I won't lie to anybody. I knew what Dave Beckley had in mind when he hired me, and it wasn't to sell Lonjer-A as much as somethin else. But I didn't

168

let it stop me. Even before I sat down to be interviewed for that job, I'd made up my mind to go through with it, no matter what.

BULL HARGIS

I got ways of gettin relief. I can buy it any time I want it over at Ma Gerardi's place. It costs five dollars, since Ma got them new girls in from Chicago through Dom Strelli's friends. Them girls is younger than the ones Ma used to scare up out of the hollers, and they are prettier. Some of the old bags that used to work at Ma's you had to be half shot before you could stomick em. It a man wants a little piece of pussy he can't be choosy, specially if he's got a gut on him like me. Still, those new broads are hard as nails and the paint on em is thick as dirt. And the truth is, I never liked to buy it. I liked to take it—like I done that time off of that little Janie Pigman in Martin County. I like to take it when they are young and little and kickin and screamin. For that I would pay the devil with red hot silver dollars with my bare hands.

So that's why I'm half crazy when Strelli and I make the rounds up between Booneville and Hammond Camp. Young Sis Sizemore got her a job workin for Dave Beckley. Everybody knows Beck is gettin it. That's why he hired the kid. And if it's there and Beck is gettin it I can't hardly stand to see it walkin along the road at night, on the way home. When I see that young kid and her bare legs and her hair hangin down her back up there in the headlights I get so goddam shook up I can't hardly breathe. One of these nights I don't know. If that Sizemore kid aint got no more sense than to keep walkin home at night, its just like shovin my face in it, and I aint gonna be able to hold off. I'm just gonna take me some of it, off the road a piece, in the bushes, just like I did in Martin County.

LUCY HAMMOND

I don't know where this is going to end. Our camp is full. There are even people living in tents. And now that Charles has more or less declared Open House, and the county police patrol are picking up anybody even suspected of being a labor organizer and railroading them over the county line, the key men in the United Mine Workers of America have come to our camp as a sort of sanctuary. It's private property. The Knight County men have no right to come into our camp and arrest people on these phony charges of loitering and disturbing the peace and they don't try it. I knew it must be a thorn in Will Fletcher's side, but I didn't really think he'd do anything about it. I was wrong. Last night a man called up on the phone while Charles and I were having dinner, and I took it.

He called me a filthy name as soon as I spoke, and I put my hand over the phone and called Charles.

Charles said hello.

Then the man talked. I couldn't hear what he said, but I could see Charles's face. It got absolutely grim. He didn't say a word. He just listened. When the man was through talking I guess he hung up, because Charles just put the receiver back on the hook.

170

"Who was it?" I said.

Charles looked at me and I was scared. Charles is usually very calm. But when he spoke, his voice shook. "They called me a Communist," he said. "They claimed I'm harboring dangerous criminals in this camp. They are ordering me to get rid of them. If I don't, they won't be responsible for what happens to this camp."

"Dangerous criminals?" I said.

"They mean the UMW men," he said.

"But they aren't criminals," I said. "They—"

"They are labor organizers," Charles said. "That's a dangerous criminal in Will Fletcher's opinion."

I looked at him.

"What are you going to do?" I said.

"I tried to get help from the Governor," Charles said. "I couldn't. There's no justice in this county now. It's goon law. I have two choices. I can pull out—close my camp and throw the people to the goon squad—or I can fight."

He smiled slightly. And then he lapsed, for the first time in my life I ever heard him do it, into Kentucky slang. "I aint about to throw them men to the goon squad," he said, and his face was pale and his eyes were very bright. "I think I'll just put me in a phone call to New York."

DUNN BROS. HARDWARE

About an hour ago Clabe Turner came in and went over to our gun counter. Mr. Dunn waited on him. Clabe asked if we had any .38 special ammunition, and

Mr. Dunn said yes, we certainly did, we'd just got in a big shipment last week. Clabe asked how many boxes were in the shipment. Mr. Dunn said two hundred boxes. Clabe said he would take them all. We all know Clabe around here, and how he's been out of work. We figured Clabe was joking, that he didn't have enough money to buy one box of .38 special shells.

We were wrong.

Clabe took the two hundred boxes and paid cash.

Mr. Dunn had me call Pikeville to ask Halley and Sons if they could let us have a supply of .38 special shells to tide us over until we could reorder, but Mr. Halley said he was sorry, a man had come in this very morning and bought him out. Forty boxes. I asked if he knew the man and he said yes, it was Clabe Turner.

When I told Mr. Dunn he kind of whistled and told me to call Ames Supply Company, in Harlan. I wasn't surprised when Mr. Ames said he didn't have any either. A man had come in yesterday and bought out his whole stock. He didn't know the man, but when I described Clabe Turner he said yes, that was the feller all right, and he asked me what was goin on. I said I didn't know, but it must be somethin, and hung up. Mr. Dunn said I better put in a long-distance phone call and reorder, seein as how we couldn't get any help in the local area.

NEWTON TURNER

We live way to hell and gone up Pity Me Creek and nobody hardly ever comes to see us. So we sure was surprised to see old uncle Clabe comin up the path the other night.

"Well by dammit," my daddy yelled. "If it aint old Clabe. Where you been keepin yourself, boy?"

Clabe said he'd been out of work for quite awhile, but now he was workin for Charles Hammond.

"What you doin?" my daddy yelled. He always yells on account of he's deaf as a post. "That poor man aint still cuttin coal is he?"

"Not no more," Clabe says.

Then Clabe tells us about young Bob Evartz gettin killed—and also about hundreds of families gettin throwed out of the company camps onto the highway.

"Mr. Hammond's a fine feller," Clabe says. "He don't want no fightin nor bloodshed. But he says we can't just stand there and let them beat on us forever. So he's got this plan for buildin up a big powerful force of men. Like the government has an army, he says, to back up its rules and regulations. A big stick, kind of."

"No fightin," daddy yells. "How in hell kin Mr. Hammond spect there won't be no fightin? Them sons of bitches been givin it to us for years, and you know it!"

Clabe kind of gives a little smile.

"I knows it," he said. "And you knows it. But there aint no use in upsettin Mr. Hammond. He's our friend. He done bought a thousand thirty-eight specials from someplace in New York and he's give us men the job of handin them out where they'll do the most good. To the standin army, you might say."

Boy, old daddy jumps up like he's been jagged with a pin. "You lookin at one of the standin army right now!" he yells. "Where's my thirty-eight special? Let's go down and blow the balls off them sons of bitches!"

Uncle Clabe grins a little and tells daddy not so fast. All in good time. Once everything is organized, and the

power is on tap, Mr. Hammond is goin to help the
United Mine Workers organize Knight County. That
will jack up the miners' pay and give them all kinds
of benefits. Then when coal makes a comeback, if it
does, everybody will be protected.

"The hell with pertected!" daddy yells. "I aint interested in no goddam unions. I just want to get a crack
at them operators. Where's that thirty-eight?"

"I got her down in my car," Clabe said. "These con-
founded creek beds is gettin so rough a feller don't
dare drive em no more. Bust a axle. I had to walk the
last half a mile."

"Well let's go down to the car and git her!" daddy
yells.

I touched Clabe's arm. "How about me?" I said.
"You got a thirty-eight special for me?"

"Hell, Newt," Uncle Clabe says. "You just a baby.
You don't want to get mixed up in no shootin."

"I'm nineteen," I yells, "and by God I intend to git
mixed up in this shootin if I got to use my twenty-two!"

Uncle Clabe looks kind of pleased.

"Well damn, Newt," he says. "If you feel that way
we just got to git you a thirty-eight, and there aint no
two ways about it."

NOAH ADAMS

Young Newt Turner come by the cabin the other
day totin a new .38 special in a new holster, and I was
out in the garden hoein beans and I seen it and asked
him where he got it. He come over to the fence and

spoke in a low voice. "Mr. Adams," he said, "there's big things stirrin. Mr. Hammond done finally got his back up over this killin of young Bob Evartz or somethin. Anyhow, he's fixin to get the union recognized all over Knight County, and he's handin out these here little persuaders to some of the men."

I felt a funny kind of thrill. I done give up thinkin about the minin company that tore out my apple trees and forced me off my land. Hit had just about killed me, hatin em, and I stopped it years back. Or I thought I had.

"What's goin to happen?" I asked young Newt Turner. "Is they gonna be a big fight?"

"I don't reckon so," Newt says. "Mr. Hammond is agin it. He just wants us to have bargainin power, as he puts it."

"I'm a real old feller," I says, "but I sure as hell would like to get in on that bargainin power. You reckon you kin git me one of them thirty-eights?"

"Gee I wish I could, Mr. Adams," young Newt says. "But all the guns Mr. Hammond bought is done give out. The whole thousand of em."

"A thousand?" I says. "Did you say a thousand, son?"

"That's right, Mr. Adams," Newt says.

"There's a mighty lot of bargainin power in a thousand thirty-eight specials," I said.

Newt grins. "You're damn betcha, Mr. Adams," he says. "Well I got to be goin. Nice to of seen you. So long."

"So long, son," I said, and I watched him go off along the creek. But when I went back to my hoein I realized I'd been wrong when I thought I'd forgot the sound them axes made when the coal company men started choppin down my fruit trees. I hadn't forgot that sound. As I stood there watchin young Newt walkin away I could hear them axes just like it was yesterday.

175

MORGAN HUFF

When Clabe Turner come to my place and offered me a job workin for Mr. Hammond I wasn't busy. I was just makin a little shine and shootin a few varmints. Nothin that couldn't wait. Clabe told me about this idea Mr. Hammond had—a kind of standin army, so to speak—and he needed some people to guard the camp.

"Mr. Hammond says to git the best men I kin find," Clabe says, "and hand em out thirty-eight specials." Clabe grins at me. "I heered you knowed how to shoot one of them guns, so I come over to see if you was interested."

"Who else you goin to hire?" I says. "I'll shoot agin any man livin—but I'm a mite particular who I got heppin me. It could git kind of important."

"Well Morgan," Clabe said. "I knowed you'd probly feel that way, so I kind of figured to leave the rest of the pickin up to you. We'll need about ten men in all."

"When will you need them?" I says.

"Quick as we can," Clabe said.

"Okay," I says. "I'll be over around sundown tonight. I'll have a couple of real good fellers with me. The rest we kin round up in the mornin."

SILENT SAM MAGOFFIN

I can't read, write or speak. When I was just a little shaver my brother and I was foolin with a twenty-two and it went off and the bullet went through my throat and neck and come out under my ear. I run in to my daddy and he looked at it and about died. He figured I was a goner. No use hardly takin me to the doctor, it'll be over in a minute or two. Ma runs in and grabs me and starts kissin and prayin, and they laid me on the bed, all over blood from the throat wound, and I don't die. Somehow or another the bullet missed them big blood vessels and just tore up the vocal cords and the nerves leadin to them or somethin. Finally the doc come and examined me and says its a miracle but the kid is gonna be all right. They didn't know until later that my power of speech had been took away forever. Hit was lucky I was eight or nine and knowed how to understand when others spoke or I would have been in a hell of a fix.

So I've been this way all my life. People thinks I'm a halfwit because I don't talk. They wrong about that. A feller that can't speak has got to listen, and you learn a heap sight more alistenin than you do talkin. Also you caint waste so much time because nobody will gas with you. I got in the habit of goin out in the woods by myself with my gun shootin. I got to be a fine shot. I guess nobody knows how good I really am. A few does. Old Morgan Huff for one. Morgan likes to hunt hisself and him and I been out together and he seed me shoot.

177

He told me I was the best feller with a rifle in the county. I just grinned. That's all I can do without no vocal cords. My name is Sam Magoffin. So naturally everybody calls me Silent Sam. When old Morgan come to the house and explained to me what he wanted me to do about the Hammond camp I set until he was finished, and then I nodded my head up and down that I would do it.

So old Morgan hires me and puts me up in the woods on a rocky point overlookin the Booneville road. A man with a rifle, up at that point, could stop anybody he felt like stoppin, if he could hit. Morgan figured I could hit.

SIM YATES

I'm young Sim Yates. My daddy, old Sim, has been a lifelong crony of Morgan Huff. I can remember old Uncle Morgan, as we used to call him, comin to our house when I was just a little feller and them drinkin moonshine and playin cards and raisin hell. Nobody ever got killed around there but it was a wonder. My daddy was a hothead and so was Morgan. I guess the Devil was watchin out after his own. At least that was how my poor ma put hit. But ma was secretly proud of the old man, even though he was a heller and one night shot a hole in her prize picture of old Lazarus bein raised from the dead by Jesus. Jesus has this big light around His head, and he looks just holier than all hell, and old Lazarus looks like a damn old sick monkey, shriveled up like, and daddy is drinkin and he just notices the picture and the mood takes him and he says, "I'll just put old Lazarus back in the grave, by damn," and he takes a careful aim and plugs old Lazarus right between the eyes.

Ma just took on terrible. She predicted the old man was gonna be struck by lightnin the next time hit stormed, for defilin the friends of the Lord Jesus, and the old man half believed her. The next big thundercracker we had, he goes and hides in the cave where he hides his moonshine. Ma forgive him after that. But she used to tease him afterward, when company come, by askin little questions like, "Simpson honey, tell the Otts where you was durin that last big thunderstorm we had." Hit used to burn the old man, but he didn't let loose or nothin. He figured he had it comin.

One night when I was real little, Morgan Huff was over to see daddy, and he got to teasin me. They was a little tin whistle he had that I wanted, and he promised it to me. He'd hold it out, and I'd reach for it, and then he'd jerk hit away. Then everbody there would laugh. I wasn't no bigger than a rabbit, but I got my fill of that. And the last time he jerks it away and they laugh I grabs up daddy's huntin knife, which was layin on the table, and takes a lunge at Morgan's belly with her. I never knowed Morgan was so quick till I done that. He blocked the knife with his hand, and I cut a slash in his palm and the blood gushed out.

That could of been the end of all of us, I guess, if Morgan had took it up. Old Morgan give a big curse and leaped up, holdin his hand and then, all of a sudden, he laughs. When he laughs, everbody laughs, and it's a big joke instead of a big killin. "Make up with little Simmie, now, Morgan," my daddy said. "If you don't, son of a gun, he'll gitcha. By God he'll bushwhack you with his beebee gun."

Morgan sticks out his bloody hand to me and I dropped the knife and we shook. But I never in my life

179

done anything to Morgan Huff again. I just had a feelin hit wouldn't be healthy, even though I was a little kid. We been friends ever since. When he come to me and asked me if I'd take a job up in Mad Dog holler where the creek takes a hard dogleg, and told me the reason was that some dude might try to blow the hangin rock into the creek and flood the Hammond mine, I said I sure would. I was only seventeen then. I was real proud Morgan put that faith in me. I told him the only way somebody would dynamite that hangin rock was because they'd already shot me dead —and I didn't aim to let them do that. Morgan said he knowed that in advance or he wouldn't be here talkin to me.

CLABE TURNER

I got the miner's asme, like so many of us, and Mr. Hammond give me a cushy job settin in the storeroom handin out stuff to people that needed em. Since we got that threat to burn the camp down, Mr. Hammond stopped minin operations altogether, and put the men on to various other jobs which he figured were now more important. He really didn't look for a mass attack on our camp by the Knight County Police Force, but he said there were a few things we could do to fill up the time, and if the attack ever came, we'd have our life insurance in force, so to speak.

We had a lot of very heavy-duty preformed plow-steel rope—which is the strongest you can get—for use around the mines. There is a great big boulder on

Booneville road, on Hammond's property, about half a mile from the camp. Mr. Hammond had the men drill a couple of holes in that big boulder and set a couple of big steel eyebolts. He fastened two stands of inch-and-quarter steel rope to them big eyebolts with woven splices that are just as strong as the body of the rope. The ropes was long enough to stretch across the road. Both had thimbles spliced on the ends. If we wanted to block that road against anything, even a truck, all we had to do was run them heavy cables acrost it and bend em around the railroad track that run parallel right beside the highway and lock em there. Mr. Hammond bought a special pair of big locks, with long shanks on the hasp, like U-bolts, just for the purpose. Then the men made a game out of seein how fast they could run the cables over, slide em around the rail and lock em. They got so they could do it in between ten and eleven seconds. We didn't have a stopwatch so we couldn't figure it in fractions.

There is a big reinforced concrete pit, buried under the storehouse, where we keep the dynamite for blastin in the mine. Now that we aren't blowin down the coal any more, the supply don't go down none. There's about twenty-five boxes in there now, fifty sticks to a box. I guess one of the reasons I got the job in the storeroom is because I'd had some experience with dynamite in the mines. Blowin down coal and cappin and fuzin and touchin off dynamite was my job for a couple of years, and I guess Mr. Hammond wanted a powder man handlin high explosives in the storehouse.

I was settin in a touchy spot, and Mr. Hammond pointed it out to me. If things did get out of hand and the camp was invaded, the first place they'd head for would be the storehouse and the dynamite. They'd have plenty of powder men on their side, and they'd use our dynamite—or they might, if they thought about

181

it—to blow the tipple and the head house and the machinery to hell and gone. So Mr. Hammond suggested I keep a loaded pistol and a loaded rifle on my desk at all times. More of that life insurance.

CONNIE TURNER

I'm a senior in high school down in Booneville and I've got a part in the school play, which is a musical comedy. I play a beautiful rich American girl who takes a trip to Europe and a nobleman who is secretly after her money pretends to fall in love with me. I am overwhelmed by his handsome appearance and his lofty manners and ignore the loyal American boy who is really in love with me and who keeps following me around, but who I can't see because of the nobleman. There are many exciting adventures, including the big scene where I am held up by robbers and the nobleman that I was crazy about proves to be a coward and the loyal American boy rushes in and saves me and is the hero. It is a wonderful play and Earl Marshall plays the part of the nobleman and Darryl Eakins the loyal American boy. The only thing I don't like about it is that Earl Marshall is the handsomest boy in the world, and the brightest and is going to college if he can save up the money, and I am in love with him, I think, and instead of kissing him at the end of the big scene I have to kiss Darryl Eakins, who is nice, but not Earl Marshall by any manner of means.

Uncle Clabe likes to tease me about Earl Marshall. He knows how crazy I am about him. Uncle Clabe is my favorite uncle, and next to daddy he's my favorite man. I saved up my money and bought some dark blue yarn and knitted him a sweater for his last Christmas. He wears it a lot now that the fall is coming and the weather is cold and he has to sit in that storeroom in the Hammond camp. There's heat from a pot stove near his chair but the place is very drafty and he says my sweater keeps him good and warm.

When I was a little girl Uncle Clabe used to call me his Fairy Princess, on account of a story in a book mother read, and now that I've got big and am in my last year in high school he still calls me Princess. It makes me feel good when he does that, kind of special, even though I pretend I don't like it and think it's silly and babyish. I don't fool Uncle Clabe a bit. He just grins and says, "Now Princess, you just come down off your high horse, you hear?"

Last night we practiced until a little after nine o'clock and Miss Wheeler, who is directing the play wanted me and several of the others to stay and go over some point in the play she felt could be improved. So it was nearly ten when I started home. I was about halfway, on the Booneville Road, when a car's lights lit up the road behind me. I heard the car put on the brakes and slow down and I thought, Oh, boy, I'm going to let a lift. I kept walking so I wouldn't seem eager, and the car stopped beside me and I heard the door open. I turned then, surprised that anybody would get out, and there was a big man standing there. He made a grab for me and I tried to duck but I couldn't. He grabbed me and I screamed once. Then he hit me in the face with his fist and I saw stars and everything went black.

BULL HARGIS

Dom Strelli and I had a bottle of moonshine with us last night when we started our road patrol. It was only a pint and we passed it back and forth until we killed it and then I threw it out the side window. We made the run from Booneville down river to the Pike County Line, then took the shortcut up Rockhouse Creek and over through the Flatwoods and came back down onto the Hammond-Booneville road. It was a little before ten o'clock. The liquor I'd drunk was warm in my belly and the headlights looked yella in the dark. I thought to myself, Wouldn't it be nice if I had me a woman right now. Then, as we turned west on the Hammond Road, I saw Sis Sizemore walking up ahead in the headlight beams. I felt a tight stitch in my belly, down low, and I felt it swell inside my pants, and the light of the headlights got kind of orange instead of yella and I said to Dom, "That little bitch walked this road once too often. Slow down."

"What you gonna do, Bull?" Dom said.

"What you think?" I said.

And Dom kind of laughed.

"I'll slow down on one condition, Bull," he said. "Share and share alike."

"Why not," I said. "But I go first. It was my idea."

We was very close to the girl now and Dom slowed and stopped beside her and I jumped out. Just as I went to grab her she turned and I seen her face in the reflections from the headlights. It wasn't Sis Sizemore.

184

It was the little Turner kid. But at that point it didn't matter a goddam to me. I hit her with my fist and knocked her cold. "Douse the lights, Strelli," I said. "I'll take it right here in the ditch, while the takin's good . . ."

I must of hit her pretty hard, because I give it to her and so did Strelli, there in the ditch, and she's limp as a rag, out like a light. When we was through I pulled out my .38. I was sure she hadn't seen me to recognize me, but I wasn't about to take no chances. Then there's a big flash of fire from the laurel up the hillside and a bullet plows into my leg and knocks me sideways.

"Jesus Christ, Bull!" Strelli says, and dives into the car. I didn't wait to do another damned thing. I'm right in there behind him and we're hightailin it out of there. Strelli held it in second gear until we hit sixty, before he shifted. My leg was beginnin to hurt like hell. As we roared into the outskirts of Booneville I began to curse the lousy luck. If I hadn't had that goddam pint I probly wouldn't of done it, I thought. But I knowed that was a crock. I'd of done it, pint or no pint. The thing now was to put up a hell of a front. I've done worse things than this and got away with it, and by Jesus I probly will again.

"Drive to the jail," I told Strelli. "I got to get this bullet out of my leg before I do anything else."

SILENT SAM MAGOFFIN

I was on watch on my high point about three hundred yards above the Booneville road. It was a nice night. The stars was out and there was a little thin sickle of a moon. I listened to the night sounds. Off in the distance I heard a freight train makin a funny rushin sound like they make when they move fast and I knowed it was probly a coal train on that long straightaway goin down the valley into Pike County.

I noticed a car headlights comin up the road and I watched them, more for somethin to do than anything. Then I saw this girl walkin along the side of the road in the lights. She was too far away for me to know who she was. I saw the car stop when it got to her, and I thought I heard a scream, but I wasn't sure. It was about a mile away. Then the lights of the car went out.

There's somethin bad here, I thought.

I left my rifle, just takin my .38 and begun to run through the laurel. It was dark and steep and rough and it took me quite a while to get to the place where the car was. I was too late to stop them from what they done to the girl, but I was in time to save her from gettin shot. One of the men had his gun out and was startin to take aim on the girl in the ditch. I pulled my .38 and took aim and shot him. I was in a hurry or I would have killed him. I guess I hit him in the arm or someplace, because he didn't drop. The other guy says, "Jesus Christ, Bull!" I heard that very plain. I slipped on a patch of shale when I shot and lost my balance and almost dropped the gun. By the time I was set again, the car was gone. So I ran down and looked at the girl and when I saw who it was I felt real bad. It was little Connie Turner, Clabe's brother's kid, all over blood and just now beginnin to moan. I wished to God I could speak. When she come to I wanted to speak to her and comfort her. But I couldn't. And when she come to she begun to scream. She screamed like that for quite a spell, and then when she

186

realized I wasn't goin to hurt her, she stopped. I helped her up and put my arm around her and we begun to walk up the road toward the Coal camp . . .

CLABE TURNER

I was just fixin to lock the storeroom for the night and go home when the door opened and Silent Sam Magoffin stepped in holdin a girl. It was shadowy in the room and I didn't see who it was for a second. Then I saw who it was. I run over and Sam let go and Connie come into my arms and clung to me, whimperin like a little puppy, and I looked down and saw one side of her jaw was all out of shape and swelled up blue like, and there was dried blood on her mouth and nose and chin. I picked her up and carried her over to the cot I use to relax on when I'm not busy and put a blanket over her. Then I crouched down beside her and stroked her hair and talked to her real easy and quiet, tellin her it would be all right.

I didn't notice Sam leave.

I didn't notice he was even gone, I was just strokin Connie's hair and talkin to her, and then I looked up and I seed Morgan Huff standin there lookin down at us. I realized, when I looked at Morgan, that I was cryin. He was blurred in front of my eyes in the lights.

"Send for Doc Callahan," I said to Morgan. "Will you do that?"

"I already done it," Morgan said. "Doc will be on his way any minute now." He didn't raise his voice or nothin. He spoke real low. But even though I was full of my love and fear for little Connie, and my cheeks was wet with tears, the sound of Morgan's voice made my hair prickle on my neck. I felt sick all through me, like I was full of poison—and then I felt the murder comin, and everything in the room before my eyes got brighter than usual, and then the lights seemed to turn slightly reddish, the color of blood.

NOAH ADAMS

All of us was in bed asleep when there was a knock on the door. I rose up and yelled to find out who was there and what they wanted.

"Get out of bed and git your gun, Noah," a voice says. "Bull Hargis raped Clabe Turner's brother's kid, little Connie. Old Morgan Huff has blowed the whistle. She's on."

KELLER'S GENERAL STORE

My phone rang and I sat up in bed and said, "Goddam it, who's callin me at this time of the night?" and my wife Hattie sat up beside me and told me for heaven's sake stop cussin and go git it, somebody might be sick. So I run over in my bare feet to the store and answered and it was Clabe Turner. He was callin from the Hammond camp. He told me about Connie. He said Mr. and Mrs. Hammond were gone. They were in Frankfort. He said I was to call everybody on the telephone that we'd agreed on when Morgan made up the plan about what we was goin to do if we ever went after them cops. While Clabe was talkin I felt my legs begin to shake, and when he finished I couldn't speak for a second.

"Rod," he says. "Rod—you still there?"

I found my voice.

"I'm here," I said.

"You get right on them phone calls," Clabe said.

"That I will," I said. My lips was dry as paper and my mouth felt sticky when I begun goin through my list and makin the calls as fast as I could. The party lines was clear, since it was late at night, and I was able to complete the whole list in less than half an hour.

CLABE TURNER

As soon as I called Rod Keller and told him to pass the word by phone I ran up to the top of the tipple where we had a big searchlight rigged to light the area when we were workin a night shift. We hadn't been workin a night shift for a long time, so the light was off. I found the big sheet of red glass we'd brought up there for just such a time as this. I fastened it over the lens of the searchlight.

189

Then I flipped the switch and bathed the tipple with a blood-red glow. Nothin happened in the camp for maybe a minute or so. Then the lights begun to come on. Every man in the camp knowed what that signal meant. I begun to hear men yellin, and cars begin to start. Then I left the red searchlight and run down to the storeroom where Morgan Huff had said to meet him to pick up the dynamite.

BULL HARGIS

As soon as I got to the jail I tried to get Doc Callahan to come over, but he was gone. His wife said he'd gone out to the Hammond Coal Camp. I'd made up my mind in advance how to handle that and I said, "What's wrong out there?"

"I don't know," Mrs. Callahan said. "They didn't say. They just told Doc it was an emergency and to get right out."

"Well all right," I said. "Tell Doc to come over when he gets back. I got a bullet in my leg. Shot myself clean in my gun."

"I'll tell him," Mrs. Callahan said, "the minute he gets back."

When I hung up I reached over and got my bottle of whiskey and poured out a big slug and drunk her down. Then I poured me another. My leg was hurtin like hell but it wasn't my leg I was worryin about. I was wonderin if that girl had seen me, and now that I was back I remembered Strelli usin my name back there by the car, after the man shot me. That flash had

190

been in close. Whoever shot me must have heard what Strelli said. When I think about it—that ignorant dago sonofabitch—blattin out my name— Well, it's their word against ours if it comes to a showdown, and we got the law on our side. We wasn't within ten miles of that spot tonight. That's our story and we'll stick to it.

DOMINIC STRELLI

I've been around long enough to know when to throw in my hand and get out of the game. After I helped Hargis into the jail I went right down to the railroad station. The night train for Louisville was in the station, waiting for a local train to clear the bridge on its way up to the Fletcher mine. I bought a ticket and got on the train. I went into one of the men's rooms and locked the door. Then I took out my .38 and stood in the corner, in the dark, and prayed for that coal train to hurry up.

THE BATTLE OF BOONEVILLE
NOV. 28, 1933

The old Booneville and Ohio railroad bridge which spans Otter Creek into Booneville, was dynamited a little after midnight. The heavy blast shifted a sup-

191

porting pier off its moorings. It toppled into the creek. The bridge then buckled and sagged down on top of it. A coal train on its way up from Ohio, with a string of empty gons, had not reached the bridge when the explosion occurred. The Fletcher mines depended on that bridge to get coal to market.

The reaction of the Knight County Police Force to this act of sabotage was immediate. Four automobiles filled with heavily armed men immediately roared down the main street of Booneville and across the concrete highway bridge on Route 119, in the direction of the site of the explosion. When the lead car reached a curve in the road, where it passed around a low rock bluff, six rifles opened on it simultaneously. The riflemen, whoever they were, held their fire until the car was slowing down for the corner, and then all concentrated on the driver. Four of them hit him. The car went out of control and ran off the road and turned over. It did not burn. But the second car, trying to stop, must have been hit in the gas tank because it exploded and burned. The last two cars were able to stop and turn around and drive back into Booneville. When they roared up to the jail to spread the alarm, two men did not get out. One had a bullet hole in the back of his neck. The other had three bullet holes in his lower back. Both were dead.

A county-wide alarm was spread by telephone to Knight County Patrol cars that could be reached at check points and they were told to gather back in Booneville for what appeared to be a full-scale war. Some patrol cars were not reached quickly enough. In Josie's All-Night Restaurant, which is next to Keller's General Store on Route 119, two Knight County policemen who patronized the place regularly were there having coffee and doughnuts. A young hillbilly boy about seventeen years old, wearing an overcoat, walked in and sat down a stool away from the two

192

policemen. He knew them both well. He had watched them evicting his neighbors from their homes and he had seen them in this restaurant, eating Josie's coffee and doughnuts free, and he knew they came from Cincinnati. One of them turned to reach for the sugar and noticed the boy.

"Hand me the sugar, kid," the policeman said.

The boy smiled at him. "Yes sir," he said, and passed the sugar.

As the policeman spooned it into his cup the boy drew a .38 special from under his coat, and shot the man in the left temple, then slid off his stool and shot the second policeman three times in the stomach. Then he turned and ran out. Josie saw it all, and there were two miners in a booth having a cup of coffee who saw it. But nobody recognized the killer.

Shortly after the explosion which demolished the Booneville and Ohio bridge, the office of the Governor of the State of Kentucky got an emergency phone call. It was from Mr. Williard Fletcher, in Booneville. Mr. Fletcher told the Governor that a large-scale battle was in progress between the coal miners and the County Police Force and that help from the State Militia was needed urgently—that minutes counted if wholesale bloodshed was to be avoided. The Governor promised to send the troops at once.

A little after midnight a man carrying a bundle of dynamite with the fuse burning, left the safety of a brick building across the street from the jail and made a dash for the front door. He was hit before he had run twenty feet by a hailstorm of bullets from Thompson guns. He fell in the middle of the street and his bundle of dynamite skidded ahead of him against a parked car.

When the dynamite exploded it hurled the car over

the sidewalk onto the lawn of the jail and broke windows in stores two blocks away.

A man's voice shouted from the brick building. The man could be heard plainly inside the jail. He was asking that Sheriff McCabe, Bull Hargis and Dominic Strelli come out. If they did come out, he would stop the fighting. He said his name was Morgan Huff. His reply was a prolonged burst of machine gun firing from the barred windows of the jail. Morgan Huff said no more. He left his place behind the brick wall and ran up the back alley toward the Booneville Blacksmith Shop.

And then, about one o'clock, the decisive part of the battle began. It was not fought just in Booneville but on all of the county roads. The sides of the roads, all over the county, began to be peopled by men with rifles and pistols who crouched in the laurel, waiting for a target. Civilian traffic had long ceased. The only cars abroad belonged to Knight County forces. All cars were fired on wherever and whenever they appeared. The roads of the county became too dangerous to use. The Knight County forces abandoned their cars and took to the woods. When an abandoned car was found it was doused with gasoline and burned. If a man in a police uniform was seen he was instantly fired upon. The miners were silent. There were no angry yells or curses. Just silence, and then a gunshot and a bullet out of the dark.

The hillsides above Booneville began to wink. There would be a moment until the sound of the rifle reached the streets, then the spang of a bullet hitting something and zinging off, or a yell of agony, or the crash of breaking glass. When the winking lights in the hills began, the streets of Booneville suddenly emptied of all men in police uniforms.

About four o'clock in the morning a weird contraption appeared on the hillside above the jail. It pulled out from behind the Booneville Blacksmith Shop and was seen to be a large coal truck with a massive steel plate welded on the bumper. It approached the jail head-on. The machine guns at once began to fire upon it. But it came on. The plate covered the entire front of the truck, including the windshield and it was too thick to be penetrated by the bullets. It was improvised out of two bulldozer blades. The truck crossed the curb and the sidewalk into the jail yard and rammed its steel-plate shield up to the windows where the machine guns were. Then milk bottles full of gasoline with crude wicks were lit and lobbed over the shield against the side of the building. Presently after a dozen of these were thrown the heat got so intense that the machine gunners had to leave the windows. Then a huge bulky shape, about four feet square and five feet high was pushed off the truck. A hissing sound came from the bundle as the truck backed up, off the curb, and then down the street. Screams and yells were heard in the jail as the men in there realized that half a ton of dynamite was going to go off on their doorstep.

Then a man ran out with a white flag. Nobody shot him. But a voice yelled from down the street where the armored truck had backed. "You better hurry!"

The jail emptied out. Bull Hargis was one of the first, limping and running. All of the men got out and were well down the street out of danger when the explosion came. It blew the foundation loose on the front of the jail and caused the building to sag. The wooden interior of the jail began to burn. Buildings in the area sustained heavy blast damage. The men who had come out of the jail were surrounded by armed miners and taken prisoner. This was probably the point at which the resistance of the Knight County Police Force cracked and broke, and policemen who were not

195

wounded and free to do so plunged into the woods and headed for the Knight County Line. There were a few highlights to the battle which are worthy of mention . . .

NOAH ADAMS

It was close to one in the mornin when I got to Booneville, havin walked through the woods over the mountains, takin the shortcut. I had my 32-20 with me and two boxes of shells. I'm seventy-four years old and by the time I reached the outskirts of town I was too tuckered to go in. I set down on a rock in the dark and got my breath back. While I was settin there I heered gunshots and the whang of bullets and screams. The rifles made a big slammin sound. The .38's made a whipcrack. Gradually I got my wind back and rose up and crep out on top of a rock and I seen I was directly over the Thompson Brick Yard. They was four cops huddled in the yard inside the brick wall and I knowed they was scared for their lives and was hidin, and I smiled because I had em cold. I lifted my 32-20 and drawed a bead on one of the cops, restin my rifle on a rock to make sure of my aim, and when I got him cold turkey I thought, *Boy you dreamed about this moment for years, ever since they run you out of the orchard, and now she's come.*

But I didn't pull the trigger. I could of, easy enough. I wasn't paralyzed nor nothin. I stares over my sights at these huddlin cops for maybe a minute. Then I gets up and starts walkin.

After a while the sound of the screams and the guns got weaker and after I got over the ridge and was headin down to my cabin I couldn't hear anything but the shots, very small, like little firecrackers. Then I remembered the two boxes of shells. I took em out of my pocket and throwed them over the hill. And when my wife met me, all excited and asked me what I'd done over to Booneville I told her it was a hell of a fight, I didn't know how many I'd killed for sure, but I reckon it must of been at least four or five. And she said she was sure proud of me, by God I give it to em, I showed em what was what when I finally got my chance.

WARD THOMAS

When the shooting commenced I knew what it was about, of course, and I turned all the house lights out and locked the doors and got my gun and me and my wife went down in the cellar, and sat there in the dark.

"You don't really think they'll bother us, do you?" my wife said. "After all, you didn't do anything but raise the taxes."

"Shh," I said. "There may be somebody out there in the bushes listening right now."

We sat there most of the night and listened to the gunfire and the yells and screams and the big dynamite blasts, and nobody came. I was beginning to think nobody would come at all and then, about four in the morning, a gang of men came up the street and stopped out front. I heard them talking. They wanted to burn

197

my house. One of the men was arguing with them. I sat there and scarcely breathed and my wife the same. Finally the men went away without bothering us at all. I didn't speak to my wife for quite a while even after they were out of earshot. In a way I almost wished they had burned my house. The man who was arguing with them, who talked them out of it, was Anderson Webb, my old neighbor up in Mad Dog holler, one of the first people I raised the taxes on when Mr. Fletcher gave me that $1000 check.

CLABE TURNER

I touched off the dynamite that knocked down the Booneville Bridge. We used three hundred sticks and it sure made a hell of a boom. But I wasn't interested in no bridge. I run up on the bluff overlookin the highway bridge and when the cars full of cops showed up, I laid my sights on the driver of the first car, and when it come so close I knew I couldn't miss, I squeezed her down. Me and three other guys. I guess ever one of us hit that boy, because ever one of us was a good shot. The car rolled off the road and turned over . . .

Morgan Huff was givin us instructions when we went down to the car after the shootin was over—but I wasn't payin Morgan no heed. I knowed what I wanted, and I found it in the back of that wrecked car. It was one of them Thompson guns. I grabbed it up. It hadn't been fired.

"This here is mine," I said, and I looked around at the boys.

198

I guess I must of looked a little crazy, and I guess I was, because one feller said to Morgan, "Let him be. He's nuts."

Morgan didn't say nothin. He knowed how I felt about Connie. He knowed I worshiped the ground she walked on. He knowed all that. And he'd seed me kneelin beside her when he come into the storeroom. Morgan could understand a thing like that—how I'd want that submachine gun . . .

All he said was, "You know how to work her, Clabe?"

And I says, "Not yet, but I'll soon find out."

And one of the other guys, who's been diggin in the back of the wrecked car, comes up with a handful of stuff. "Here's some extra clips, Clabe," he said. "In case you run out of shells."

They say you aint goin to get killed until they make a bullet with your name on it, and I believe it. I put those clips in my pockets, and then I fired the gun and figured how she worked, and how to reload her, and then I started runnin across the highway bridge into Booneville. If a feller don't care a damn if he gets it or not, and if he's movin fast and firin at any son-ofabitch that moves, he sure can do a hell of a sight of damage. I know. I done it that night. The town was full of cops, roarin around the streets in their cars, when I got acrost the bridge. But after I emptied a clip into one of em and she run through the window of the Booneville bank and blew up, the boys quit joy ridin. And even the armed guys on foot wasn't too eager to meet me after I got the hang of that Thompson. Bullets come so close to me I could feel the wind. But none hit me. And by the time I'd run through the main street and up to the Booneville Blacksmith Shop, where we'd agreed to use as our headquarters, there wasn't a livin soul on the street—clean back to the highway bridge I'd crossed about three minutes ago . . .

SIM YATES

The only thing I know about the Battle of Booneville is what I been told. I sat on the dogleg up in Mad Dog holler all night with my rifle in my hands waitin for somebody to try to dynamite the rocks and turn the creek into the Hammond mine. There wasn't a sound up there except the wind sighin in the trees and the little tiny plinks of rifles over on the other side of the mountain, ceptin, of course, them two big explosions when our fellers blowed the bridge and the jail. Nary a chipmunk showed up to bother the creek.

DR. BOONE CALLAHAN

Every time I touched Connie Turner, even lightly, when I was examining her, she shivered and went tense. I washed the blood off and set her jaw, which had been broken by a blow. I examined her to see if she had been sexually molested and she had, so I took medical precautions to be sure she wouldn't be pregnant. Her mother stayed with me. Her daddy was gone. Connie didn't say anything. She just laid there and looked at me and her eyes were very dark, almost all pupil, which is the result of shock. I wanted to give her a sedative but I didn't dare and I told her mother if she needed me in the night for any reason to be sure to call me. Mrs. Turner nodded. She seemed to be dazed. When I left the house I heard Connie scream, *"Mother! Mother! Quick! A man's comin in the window!"*

I rushed back inside but there was no man. It was just a shadow. I stayed there then, until Connie calmed down and seemed to doze before I started back to Booneville. I'd just got in my car when the miners blew up the railroad bridge and the fight was on.

BULL HARGIS

After they drove us out of the jail with the dynamite some men took me to the Booneville Blacksmith Shop which was the headquarters of the miners. Old Morgan Huff was there. The forge was lit. Morgan was workin a set of bellows and the bed of coals got bright every time he blew on them. There was a man of medium build with Morgan. When they brought me in they pushed me out on the dirt floor where the horses are shoed, and Morgan looks at me.

"Well hello Bull," he says, real soft and easy. "I got a man here I'd like you to meet. Hit's Jim Turner. He's got him a little daughter, name of Connie.

I looked at Jim Turner.

Then I turned and made a rush for the door. There were too many of them. I cursed and fought and kicked at them but I didn't get out. They got me down and

201

held me. I heard old Morgan speak, soft and easy, as before. "Cut his pants off," Morgan said. "While I git this here poker heated up a little more."

Somebody took a knife and slashed my pants and hands ripped them off me. I began to scream and beg for them to let me go, I'd do anything they said, I was sorry, I was awful sorry, oh God believe me I was sorry. But the faces of them men never changed a bit, and then Morgan Huff brought over the poker, glarin white hot and givin off little sparklers, and hands it to Jim Turner.

"I reckon you're the boy to do this here job," old Morgan says.

Then I begun to scream for them to shoot me, but they didn't pay any attention. They just held me like a vise and Jim Turner pushed that white-hot poker down between my legs into my balls and it felt like I'd been shot with a 30-30 with a big red-hot explosion bullet, and I let out a scream and bit my tongue, and then I passed out. I wish to God they'd shot me through the head. I'd be better off dead than the way I am now. Old Morgan was right about one thing. Just before Jim Turner gave me the poker, Morgan said, "Well Jim, when you git this job done there aint nobody gonna have to worry about old Bull Hargis here botherin no young girls. No old girls, either."

DOMINIC STRELLI

When I heard them blow up the bridge within a quarter of a mile of me I knew I had to leave the train and I did it at once. I'm a mobster. I know that when the big heat is on you have to act cool and quick or you wind up face down on the street full of bullets. I didn't aim to do that. I slipped off the train on the dark side, next to the river, and hurried down through the brush to the stones. The air was full of powder smoke but there weren't any flames. I knew that if I followed the river downstream I'd get over the county line eventually, and that's exactly what I did. By morning I was many miles from Booneville. But I didn't take any chances. I holed up under a rock ledge all day and it was lucky I did. Twice I saw men going through the woods with guns and I knew they were looking for people like me. But they missed me, and that night I got over the county line and was safe. I didn't stop. I had some money with me and I talked a young man who owned a filling station into driving me to Lexington. I didn't haggle about it. He wanted twenty dollars and I gave it to him. I didn't really feel safe, though, until I was on the train pulling into good old Chicago. One thing I was sure of. I'd never go back to Knight County, Kentucky. I'd had my fill of that stinkhole, even without the trouble with the miners.

SHERIFF FRANK McCABE

They made me stand and watch in the blacksmith shop when they burned the nuts off Bull Hargis. I tried to shut my eyes but when I did they hit me across the face with a bullwhip they had.

"Take a good look, McCabe," they told me. "Watch it close. Don't miss nothin."

I began to beg and I got down on my knees in the dirt of the floor and begged and I could feel the tears rollin down my cheeks.

"Look at him," a man said. "Jesus, what a sight. I wish old Bob Evartz and Jim Sizemore was here to see this."

Finally they finished with Hargis, and Morgan Huff put the poker back in the fire. It got quiet and I could hear the sound the bellows made when Huff worked it on the coals and I could see the way they went from red to white under the air blast.

Then a man came in with a quart pail. I smelled it when he set it down beside me, and I knew they must have got it out of a privy near by. Morgan came over to me and patted me on the head, like I was a little baby. "We decided to give you a break, McCabe," he said. "We goin to give you your choice. You can eat that little pail of shit, or have your nuts burnt off. Take your choice."

I puked for about twenty minutes at first, and then the smell and the taste kind of went out of me I guess, and I held it all down, the whole pailful, and the men all sat around in a circle, watchin me, and then old Morgan Huff came over and told me I was free to go any time I liked and nobody would lay a finger on me. They didn't, either. I got back to my hotel before I puked again. Then I puked and puked and puked and drank a bottle of whiskey. By that time it was mornin and the State Militia was comin into town to take over. By that time there wasn't much need for them. There weren't but a few police around who'd been lucky enough to hide and escape, and the miners had all pulled out. When the commander of the militia came and asked me what had happened and what I wanted him to do I just said there'd been a fight and he could do whatever he wanted. I only wanted one favor. I wanted him to give me a safe escort through to the county line, so I could get a ticket for my home in the South. I hadn't been back in a long time, and I was goin now. The commander said he would be glad to help me in that way.

"When do you figure to be back, McCabe?" he said.

I didn't reply. I felt nausea comin on me again and I had to run in the toilet and puke. There wasn't no use in explainin it anyhow. Maybe you'd like to live your life bein pointed out as the man who eats shit, but I wouldn't.

BOOK THREE

1933–1963

CHARLES HAMMOND

When I returned to Booneville from Frankfort, where I had gone, ironically enough, to make a personal appeal to the Governor to use his influence to alleviate the abuses of the police state—as Knight County had become—the Battle of Booneville was over. The streets were littered with broken glass. Burnt-out cars lay on their sides. The fronts of buildings were smashed. The jail, in fact, was so severely damaged that it would have to be more or less completely rebuilt. The bridge, of course, was going to be a major problem to the town as well as to the Fletcher mines. Any goods Booneville received would have to be off-loaded on the other side of Otter Creek and transported across on some kind of temporary structure, either by hand or vehicle. I had dropped Lucy off at our camp upon our return from Frankfort. There was no longer any danger of violence from the Knight County Police Force. They had been crushed—either killed or driven out of the county in last night's bloody battle.

Militiamen, having arrived belatedly from the Bluegrass, stood about in groups with their weapons in hand—but nobody to contend with: no miners on the rampage, no company cops. Smoke from still-smoldering debris lay like pools of blue fog in the low streets. The smoke smelled of burnt rubber, clothes and chemicals. It had a harsh sinister smell, unlike the smell of pure woodsmoke. People walked about the streets staring at the destruction, speaking in low tones. A hush hung over the town, the shocked and weary hush that hangs over any battlefield after the fury has passed.

In the afternoon a high gray overcast moved in from the west, and toward evening it began to snow. The flakes appeared singly and softly in the gray freezing air, and gradually thickened until the sky was a seething mass of white. Snow covered the roofs and streets and piled up like frosting on the railings, limbs of trees and the tops of cars. With the coming of the snow and the night, a deeper silence fell over the town and the scars of last night's fury were bandaged and the people went to their houses and dim yellow squares of light began to show in the murk and darkness as they turned on their lights.

I walked out of Booneville, making my way with difficulty over the broken backbone of the ruined bridge, slippery with snow in the darkness. The wrecked bridge was a symbol of the brainlessness of our dilemma. The boom of dynamite and the buckling of this old but useful structure must have thrilled the hearts of the miners who set the charge and watched it go. They knew they were putting Fletcher Coal Company out of business for many months, bottling up the mine behind a bridgeless stream. But that thrill of destruction and revenge must have been short—at least compared to the wretchedness and inconvenience to which all the people in Booneville must now be subjected, not for moments, but for many long and weary months.

I had heard a story of a vicious monster who lived somewhere in the hills of Virginia, and who posed as a doctor who could cure cancer. People came to him with lesions on their body and he placed a concoction of beeswax and some kind of fiercely active acid on the cancer. The pain was incredible. The patient screamed in agony. But the lesion was eaten away before his

210

eyes, by the fierce action of the acid, burnt out of his living flesh—and he believed himself cured, paid the so-called doctor a staggering fee, and went home rejoicing in his cure. He was not cured, of course. The roots of the deadly affliction were still at work in his body, hidden from view, hatching another devil's crust which would erupt again, sooner or later. It seemed to me that Knight County, in the Battle of Booneville, had undergone a somewhat similar experience. They had burned out the hated lesion—but the basic roots of the disease were still deeply and firmly embedded in the citizens: ignorance, superstition, lack of vision when times and circumstances were good.

But perhaps I was wrong. Perhaps if, God willing, these people ever experienced another period of boom times they would recall the misery and despair of the Great Depression, and would be provident, foresighted and alert—would build schools, repair roads, elect intelligent responsible leaders, lay away money for their old age, for sickness, for educating their young. I did not see any such boom on the horizon. Perhaps one would never come again. But if it did . . . the bitter lessons learned here in Knight County before and during the Battle of Booneville, might pay magnificent dividends. . . .

As I neared Hammond Camp the snow thickened. It filled the air with a great slowly falling veil which somehow comforted me. Hidden in the thick, softly falling snow, muffled in the windless silence, I seemed to be freed from the complex net of desperations, fears and doubts which bind all men to some degree or other, as a silken snare might bind him. My mind seemed free to range out from the earth—to yearn and stretch toward the infinite. I wondered, as I walked along in the snow, if there really was some kind of God, some great eternal power which observed the sparrow's fall and the rising of the grass blades and the giant motion of the galaxies. I wondered if there was something beyond death . . .

This is the most portentous, important and exciting gambit of thought which I personally ever take: this conjecture about what happens to a man when he experiences our Earthly Death. There are two main alternatives, it seems to me. Either a man *does* have an Eternal Essence, capable of perfecting—or he does *not*.

And it seems to me that every man of any imagination—any man with concern for his own well-being—must grapple closely with this situation, and must, in fact, base his entire philosophy of life upon it. I have always been more or less conservative by nature, and so I have tried to fashion my own philosophy so as to be as well off as possible—right or wrong. I have based my actions upon the idea that there is, indeed, a life after death—perhaps many many lives, extending through centuries—and that I, Charles Hammond, will pass through them by some name or other, in some form or other. So I try to cultivate the things I feel will be most useful to me on the journey: intelligence, wisdom, courage, and concern for my fellows.

I do not turn up my nose at sensual pleasures, however. Not by a long shot! Whatever pleasures of food, sex, music, travel, power, thrills, and sensual joy are available to me I try to take. But within the framework of my first concept. In short, the tools I feel I can use on my soul's journey through the centuries I sharpen first, oil first, and arrange first on the bench. *Then* I go and have a ball. Man does not live by bread alone —and if I am wrong, and we do not go anywhere but into the dark of unbeing—I have coppered my bets, so to speak, and have done a fairly good job of having my cake and eating it too.

As I neared the coal camp which I had built, and the buildings began to loom up warmly in the snow, I thought of the foolishness of trying to play God—of trying to instill the philosophy of life I had just been considering on my snowy walk in the minds of these coal miners. It was impossible. One man's philosophy was another man's yawn—or chuckle. My financial help in this great depression had really not changed my friends the miners. It had merely sustained them better than their fellows, who had no God-player to lean upon. When I withdrew my subsidy, if I did, my people would sink as deeply as the rest of the plateau, and just as promptly. They were at the mercy of what transpired at the market place. And they would remain so until their ignorance was removed by education, their slipshod irresponsible habits by experience in independence. If these conditions were not fulfilled, my ministrations would not be as cruel as those of the quack cancer doctor in Virginia, but they would hardly be any more effective in the long run.

WILLIARD FLETCHER

Like everybody else, I am blessed with 20-20 hindsight. I can see now that we made a mistake. Instead of fighting the union we should have accepted it. Then all the operators would have had to hold the line on the price of coal. We didn't. We fought. And it cost us the ball game. We got into a suicide war among ourselves. We cut each other's throats every time we cut the price on a ton of coal. And then we took it out on the poor slobs in the mine. It could only end the way it did. I see that now, and I should have had the sense to see it then. You can push a man so far—even an ignorant coal miner—and finally he has nothing more to lose but his life. Then watch out. A man, pushed that far, will attack with his bare hands if he has to.

Thanks to my good friend, Charles Hammond, the Knight County miners did not have to. They were armed to the teeth. And again my 20-20 hindsight serves me well. Of course Hammond armed the men. We pushed him too far, too. I should have recalled how he dealt with that bullyboy, Big Son Evartz. Hammond shot that man dead with a .22 pistol. That is very indicative of character. I was a fool not to have recalled it before I let my men call Hammond and try to intimidate him.

Now my tipple had been burned, the bridge had been dynamited, and the expensive police force we hired has been smashed. I feel a strange emotion: relief. I won't say my police methods sickened me. They did not. I don't consider a miner a human being. He's an animal. He lives like an animal, and when you give him any kind of a break he acts like an animal. So you learn to treat him like one. You whip him, break his spirit, or kill him. Whatever is expedient. I am not regretting anything we did to the miners. I am merely sorry I was so foolish. I should have put my money into building a monopoly among the operators—a solid front, industry wide. Instead I let an insane price war rage without even trying to stop it or prevent it. When Charles Hammond's miners smashed my police force they did me a favor, really. I couldn't have won. And those goons and hoodlums were costing more than they were worth. Now I can collect insurance on my tipple, and I frankly don't care about the bridge. With coal prices so low, it doesn't pay me to ship anyhow.

I can see that the fight to keep the union out is already lost. That big beetle-browed son of a bitch, John Lewis, and his friend, that goddam cripple with the cigarette holder clamped in his grinning teeth and his hat turned up in front—they'll beat us. *My friends . . . and you are my friends . . .* When I hear that coming out of my radio set I want to puke.

Franklin D. Roosevelt is a traitor to his class. I'm not the only one who says it. Every man in this nation who believes in the sanctity of private property says so. Roosevelt is power mad. He sold out for the labor vote. And now he's got these insane make-work projects going. WPA. CCC. Just catchalls for no-good deadbeats.

And it was Roosevelt who put the gun in Lewis' hand. The gun is Section 7-A of the National Recovery Act, which says that a company has to bargain with a union the men organized themselves—not a company union. Lewis calls this Labor's Magna Carta, and for once in his life the man is right. When Roosevelt gave Lewis Section 7-A of the NRA, he handed him every one of us mine operators on a silver platter. And that big slob of a Lewis is tucking his napkin under his chin and bellying up to the table right now.

NELSON FEATHERS

A man asks me the other day—what do you think of Mr. Franklin Roosevelt, Nelse? And I thought it over for a minute and I said, "Let me put it this way. If Mr. Roosevelt was to come out here and say to me, 'Nelson boy, I want you to go down to the privy and jump in the honey hole,' I'd say, 'Mr. Roosevelt, sir, I'm on my way!' "

The man laughs.

"You wouldn't jump in no honey hole for nobody," he says.

I laughs too.

"No, of course I wouldn't," I says. "I was just talkin. But I'll tell you one thing. If it wasn't for Mr. Franklin D. Roosevelt a whole lot of folks around here would have plumb starved to death and that's the truth."

"Yes," the man says. "That's the truth and you aint lyin."

The WPA was funny, really, if a man could laugh in those days. I heered folks tellin jokes about Franklin Demented Roosevelt, as the rich folks called him. Them rich people sure was full of poison. But there's no use denyin we did have some pretty silly things goin on in Knight County. There was a big roadbuildin project. Gangs of men were out drillin blast holes by the thousands. But there was so much red tape in Washington or Frankfort or someplace that things were all fouled up. Nobody had any dynamite to blast with. So somebody got the idea of makin wooden pegs to stick in those blast holes so they wouldn't fill up with dirt and pebbles when it rained. Boy, you never seed so many pegs in your life. Whole armies of men and boys was out cuttin em. They was about a foot long and six inches thick. We called em stobs. Before we got through hewin stobs to plug dynamite holes we had a hundred for every hole. They laid around in big piles until finally folks come by and hauled them off for firewood.

But I wasn't laughin. Me and Sim Yates and about a hundred other fellers was put to work on a little bittie patch of clay outside a school house. This here little patch of clay had about two or three bushels of little stones layin around here and there on it. It took us men—a whole army of us—four days to get them three bushels of stones picked up and throwed over the bank.

216

Mr. Roosevelt was the man that paid for that. And I don't care what anybody says, I know what I'm talkin about: if Mr. Roosevelt hadn't put us men to hewin stobs and rakin stones and other foolish things like that, a lot of people in the Kentucky mountains would either have starved to death or grabbed their rifles and gone on a rampage.

I recall one day when I was workin alongside Sim Yates up on Mad Dog Creek and Sim says, "Remember the day when we was little kids and we was settin here waitin for school and we said what we was all gonna do when we growed up?"

I says, "Sure I remember that—just like it was yesterday."

Then we began to laugh.

"How'd that big old tree look when you seed it in California, Sim?" I asked. "Was she as purty as you expected?"

"Oh hell yes," Sim says. "Purtier. Finest goddam old tree I ever seed."

Then Sim looked at me. "How is the violin comin, Nelse boy?" he asked me. "You had any big concerts lately in New York?"

"New York?" I says. "Hell, I don't fool with New York. I just come back from London. Them people in London just went crazy over my playin. The Queen wanted to have me in for tea but I had to leave too soon. I was headed back home to give a command concert for the President."

Then we laughed so hard the foreman of the job come over and says, "Break it up, fellas. We got to get these here steppin stones laid in this creek afore winter comes."

ELIZA CLAY

After I killed Jim Webster and after my kids burnt up in the forest fire I hung around Booneville doin odd jobs. Judge Cooper left me work for him and his wife, doin the washin and cleanin, and I lived in a little shanty all by myself out on the edge of town. I was a mess by then. Every time I got any money I'd buy a jug. It was the only way I could stand to be alive. I took in a few men for a while, for a buck, but not many. I wasn't no bargain, not even at a buck when the man was drunk.

After a while, though, things got better for me. Everything gradually got blurred, even when I wasn't drunk. I got so I didn't know nobody and didn't hardly know what was goin on. Somebody would hand me a pail and a mop and show me the floor they wanted scrubbed. I'd get down and do her. That was that.

When old Hitler started raisin hell across the water and people begun to think a war was comin, the mines begun to pick up. On mine payday I would go and stand outside the bars and the miners would see me there and remember what had happened to me and give me loose change. A miner is a wonderful guy when he's half shot. He'll give you the shirt off his back. I used to make as much just standin outside bars as I did scrubbin floors, after old Hitler got to rollin good. . . .

CHARLES HAMMOND

Lucy was worried about that little clown with the Charlie Chaplin mustache but I wasn't. The Germans are too bright to be taken in by that hysterical nonsense, I said. They like to dress up in soldier suits and goose-step around and play war games. But when they pick a leader it will be somebody with dignity, like Paul von Hindenburg, who is more impressive in his dotage than that crazy little Hitler.

But when crazy little Hitler marched into the Rhineland I began to get worried like everybody else. We began to see newsreels of the new German Air Force. There were conflicting opinions. Some experts called the Luftwaffe the "German Air Farce." They claimed it was made up of glider pilots and old-fashioned training planes. But others, like Charles Lindbergh, were impressed. Lindbergh toured the Luftwaffe fields in Germany, and was toasted and feted, and returned to say that in his opinion they had a formidable and deadly machine.

The French weren't taking any chances. They had real foresight and built the Maginot Line, which was solid concrete four stories deep, bristling with high-powered guns, manned by tough French soldiers, and stretched all along the critical common border with the Reich. In an article I read, the Maginot Line was said to be impregnable. It had cost a fabulous number of francs, but it was worth it to have that impregnable

219

fortress holding off crazy little Hitler if he got any big ideas.

Then Hitler attacked Poland and we saw the German Air Farce in action, and it sent chills through us. Those black dragonfly planes called *Stukas* were shown dive-bombing Warsaw. They looked vicious with their stylized Nazi crosses and they flew in beautiful formation and dropped their bombs on the defenseless city with great precision, there being no anti-aircraft or Polish fighters around to bother them.

Some of the later Polish films which the Nazis took for our enjoyment and edification made me a little sick. Pictures of German machine-gun crews—big blond young men who looked like college football players, piling out of their attack vehicle, sprinting up to the emplacement site, setting up their portable machine gun and turning it on some Polish farmhouse. I guess the Nazis were proud of that stuff, or they wouldn't have released their own films of it. They also sent us a film of the shelling of a ship in the harbor at Danzig. This one showed closeups of the faces of the Nazi officers who were directing the shelling. There was a mixture of arrogance and what seemed to be almost sexual pleasure to be seen on those faces as the big guns poured those heavy shells into the ship. The German Patience, as Hitler had said, was exhausted.

Any school child, by this time, knew that America would be in the war sooner or later. There began to be a feverish build-up in the coal regions—and I took action in my own mine at once. The truth was, I was angry. I had been nurtured on anti-war propaganda all through college. But these newsreels the Nazis took of their young soldiers and officers killing people could be seen with my own eyes. There was no chance of being hoaxed. I saw the shells hit that ship. I saw the Nazis smile. I got my mine ready as fast as I could. . . .

ANDERSON WEBB

It took old Hitler and the Japs to get the mines really goin full blast. Drift mouths had caved in durin the depression but they was dug open. Old tunnels was cleaned out and re-timbered. Some of em was full of mushrooms and the timbers was holler shells of dry rot after years of standin there in the dark. Thousands of rotten ties was pulled out of spurs and inside tracks and sidings and new oak ties was shoved in their place. New rails was also installed if the old ones had rusted out too bad.

Then the old machines and cars that had laid rustin for years was cleaned up and overhauled and put into service. War gobbles coal like a starvin miner gettin after a big hamburger—and everbody knowed we'd have to put on full steam ahead to keep the coal rollin down to the war plants. Since Pearl Harbor there aint a miner that's under eighty that kin crawl out of the bed in the mornin who can't git work. The companies started in like gentlemen—but when labor begun to git scarce they took the kid gloves off and sent agents out in the hollers piratin men. You might come out of a drift mouth after work and start walkin home and some feller would ease up beside you and say, "How much they payin you in there, brother?" And you'd tell him. And he'd say, "Well look here, you come to work for us and we'll give you three bucks more a day." Or the man might even offer you five.

221

So you'd go. In the minin trade you got to git it when it's comin. If you don't, you might never git it atall.

DAVE SIZEMORE

The biggest disappointment of my life was when I was turned down by the draft for havin TB. I never knowed I had TB but they took some X-ray pictures of my lungs and they claimed they seed some kind of spots and I was no good for soldierin. They sent me home with a 4-F card. I was ashamed to show it to anybody at first, but later, after the mines got to hummin and I got me a good job, I wasn't ashamed of that little old 4-F card. No siree! In fact I used to take it out and look at it, just to make sure I wasn't dreamin—and I thanked the Good Lord for them spots on my lungs. Ma was real pleased. We was gettin reports, as the war went on and on, about Knight County boys gettin hurt or killed. They was one place called Anzio where it seemed like about half the kids I used to know in Knight County got killed. That Anzio sure must have been one hell of a hot spot.

Before the war I used to make a lot of talk about what I was agoin to do if I ever got any money. I was agoin to put Sis back in nursin school. I was goin to git ma a lectric refrigerator and washin machine. And I was goin to send away for one of them correspondence school courses and learn to be an auto mechanic. Well, after I started bringin in big money from my work in the mines, ma reminded me of them promises I'd made.

"When you goin to send away for that mechanic course?" ma asked me.

"Real soon," I said. "As soon as I get me a few little things I been needin."

I got a new suit, double-breasted, on account of I had seen Edward G. Robinson wearin one in some gangster picture. I got real pretty silk shirts in different colors. Then I started goin with a cute little gal up the holler and one day when we was walkin around Boone-ville together, waitin for the movies to start, we seed a great big shiny Cadillac car settin in one of them showrooms.

"Let's go in and take a look, Dave," my gal says. "We aint got nothin to do for about thirty minutes till the movie starts."

I have always been scared of them birds in their white shirts and fancy suits and a flower in their but-tonhole that stand around lookin high and mighty inside one of them auto showrooms, but I wasn't goin to let my gal see it, so I says sure we'll go in and look around.

Well, we done it, and this feller comes over and he's just as friendly as he can be and he tells us this big car we are lookin at is second hand—but she's really just like new. She was owned by an old maiden lady who kep it jacked up all the time to save the strain on the tires. Them little scratches on the left side was where the old maid run into the side of the garage tryin to park, and scared herself so bad she sold the car.

Well I says I couldn't see my way to buy no car, and we was just in here killin a little time before the movie —but this feller looks at my gal and he says if I really want to make her eyes shine, I'll just get her this won-derful Cadillac for only $200 down. And my gal looks at me, and says, "Oh, Dave—would you?"

Well what the hell can I do? I had $226.40 in the bank I was savin up for my schoolin and ma's stuff, but I couldn't stand to look like a piker in front of my gal, so I signs up for the car, and goes down to the bank and jerks out my savins for the down payment. Come to find out, after I signed the papers, this Cadillac wasn't ever owned by no old maid. She was a demonstrator from down in the Bluegrass and she'd been roaded the hell out of. But by that time it was too late, and I'll say this—demonstrator or not, that Cadillac had the sap. She run real good and she would get over 100 miles an hour on the straightaway goin up the valley toward Jenkins on 119. It did make my gal's eyes shine, too. And I guess it's just as well that I got me a good car and a good gal, because ma says I traded my whole future, and the chance to make somethin of myself, down there in Booneville that afternoon, while I was waitin for the movies to begin.

NELSON FEATHERS

I was in a bad jeep accident at Fort Dix, New Jersey, while I was waiting to ship out for overseas duty with the army. I broke my right leg and slipped a disc in my back and they had me in the hospital for several months before I could be up and around. Then my back gave me trouble and they put me on limited duty in the training department at Dix. I figured it was the worst break of my life. I was crazy to see London and Paris and those places, and I got a letter from Sim Yates telling me he was having a high old time in Merry Old England. Sim was a paratrooper and he said those paratrooper wings sure worked wonders with a British gal. I was half nuts with envy.

Well, as it worked out, that jeep smashup was the best break of my life, not the worst. After I'd been at Dix about five months they made me an instructor in the school and I took to it like a duck takes to water. I guess I was meant to be a teacher all my life and never had a chance to realize it. The Captain who was over my section took a liking to me and arranged to help me with my English, which was awful, so I could give better lectures to the recruits. The Captain gave me a list of books to read, starting out real easy, and gradually getting harder. Boy, I never dreamed a book could be so exciting. A book is like a ticket to another world. I had to look up a lot of words, of course, even in the easiest books. I'd come there without hardly a damned bit of background. But gradually I got so I knew more words, and of course the Captain helped me. He told the top brass that I was too valuable as an instructor to send overseas, and I guess he also told them a few little white lies about my back being worse than it was. Anyhow, they kept me at Dix all through the war, and I rose to be a Tech Sergeant in the Training Division. By the time the war ended I had read hundreds of books of all kinds, from detectives to real deep stuff. Those books actually changed me and made a different person out of me. I knew about the solar system and evolution and I even had a poor man's idea of the Einstein Theory. The Captain and I discussed that one for a long time, how Time depends on Speed. The faster you move the slower time moves. So that if a person got up to a speed of 186,000 miles a second, which is the speed of light, he wouldn't age at all. His body would have enormous Mass. His body functions would slow down to a dead stop. He would draw one breath for eternity. The Captain and I had fun kicking this idea around—you know what I mean, that stuff where a space traveler leaves the earth at terrific speed and goes all over the universe, and when he comes back all his friends are old and wrinkled or dead and gone, and he has barely aged at all.

I tried to explain this stuff to my barracks buddies but they laughed and kidded me so much I had to quit. It taught me a valuable lesson. If you want to convince a person of something, you have to keep it simple and easy as ABC. Because if you get the least bit fancy, so that the person loses the thread of what you are saying, he'll laugh. People always laugh to cover up when they can't understand. I know, because I used to do it a lot myself.

CLABE TURNER

Toward the end of the war me and my boys and Bood Morgan and his boys opened up a mine of our own up in Pity Me holler. It had got so the big mines couldn't keep up with the demand for coal. Little old dogholes was bein opened up all over. All a feller needed was a strong back and a weak mind, as we said, and a few bucks for dynamite, shovels and planks for a loadin bin. The profits was just unbelievable. People used to make jokes about us when they seed us flashin hundred dollar bills around. They ask us if we was diggin coal or gold up there in Pity Me holler.

"It don't make no difference," I said. "You kin trade em both for this green stuff." And we'd fan a sheaf of hundreds in their face, just to hear the lovely rustlin sound they made. Old Bood swears he can tell the difference between a stack of hundreds and a stack of singles, just by listenin to somebody riffle them. The hundreds makes a softer sound, Bood says. We tell him he's just a crazy old got-rich-too-quick hillbilly.

As time went by, Bood and me branched out. We had them big coal buyers eatin right out of our hand—and we recalled how they'd give it to us in the depression—and we give it right back. We went around the county shovelin up old abandoned piles of slate trash, and sprinklin a little good coal on top, and sellin it for the real stuff. Ever now and then a ramp owner would gripe, but we'd tell him if he didn't want our stuff we knew where we could take it—and he shut up might quick. My God, I never seed so much money. I was talkin to a man in Booneville the other day and he reaches in under his coat and drags out one of them big old wallets about a foot long that you can lace to your belt for safe keepin.

"Clabe old buddy," he says. "You want to see somethin?"

I said I did. He opens that big wallet and flashes a roll of bills. Not hundreds. Thousands. He let me count em. There was fifty-six in that old wallet.

"You better watch it," I said. "Flashin that money around—some income tax feller might see you and grab you right by the balls."

"Aint no smart sonofabitch of an income tax spector goin to grab me by no balls," the man says. "I got her figured out. I don't keep no records atall. Nothin. I pay cash for everything I get. Them income tax fellers kin bust a gut searchin and they'll never find a thing on me."

I had to laugh. "I guess we're all in the same boat," I said. "I don't keep no records neither—but for a different reason. I never learned to read or write."

Then we both laughed together, there on the street

in Booneville, thinkin how we were screwin that nosey old federal government and them little smart-assed fellers they send aroun to stick their nose in your business.

ANDERSON WEBB

Me and Angie had determined to save our money if we ever hit a real good streak of work—and when we made them high wages durin the war I stuck as much of it in the bank as I could. By the time the war was over I had about three thousand dollars saved up, and I tell you it sure felt good, particularly since most people we knew blew it as fast as they got it on shiny cars and fancy junk that wasn't worth a damn.

"We got her the hard way," I told Angie, "and we goin to hang on to her. No foolishness this time."

Angie says you bet. She had worked just as hard savin as I had. One of Angie's sisters is livin over in the Fletcher Coal Camp, and the other night she come over just about to bust with excitement. There was a man there by the name of Mr. Diamond. He was givin all the people a chance to buy the houses they was livin in. It was the chance of a lifetime, Angie's sister said. They could get the house they lived in for twenty-five hundred dollars.

"Well fine," Angie said. "Where are you goin to get the money?"

The sister started hemmin and hawin, and it soon come out where she hoped to get the money. She hoped to borrow it from me and Angie, out of our savins.

"I'm sorry, Berthe," I said to her, "but we worked too hard for that money to go handin it out for no damned second-hand house."

"We'll pay you back, Anse," Berthe said. "Herb is workin steady, and this here boom is goin to last for another twenty years anyhow."

"Nope," I said. "I can't do it, Berthe. I'd love to help you, but I done without too many things to get that money. You'll have to go borry from somebody else."

Well Berthe was just broke up. She had her heart set on ownin her own house, she said. Every real red-blooded American should own his own house, it was part of our heritage of freedom.

Well I didn't weaken. I told Berthe if she wanted to go and save up her own money for her American heritage of freedom, she had my blessin and my best wishes. But I didn't intend to get involved with my hard-earned savins. Berthe begun to cry. And soon after that she left.

Well Berthe is Angie's baby sister. Angie been lookin after her and fightin her battles and givin her stuff ever since they was little. Angie didn't say much for a little while after Berthe left, but after we got in bed she begun on it. We argued and fussed until nearly mornin. Finally I got into a coughin fit and had to go downstairs and sit. While I was down there I heered Angie upstairs cryin in the pilla. I got so goddam mad I couldn't see straight.

"Okay," I yells. "Lend her the money to buy the goddam house! Go ahead! Just stop blubberin!"

Then Angie comes down and says she wouldn't think of it, and we jabber and fuss and I cough, and it's nearly mornin before I got Angie convinced that I really want to let Berthe have the $2500 for the house they are livin in over in Fletcher's Camp. I tell you, when a woman starts in on you, you might just as well give up right off the bat. It saves you a lot of misery and a lot of yackity yack. And then, maybe Berthe is right. Maybe buyin that house really is a good investment, and they really will pay us back. Might as well look on the bright side. It doesn't cost any more, and it's a lot easier on the nerves and the peace of mind.

BILL DIAMOND

I had two or three drinks out of my bottle before I got on the train at Booneville and I was feeling no pain when the time came to go up to the dining car for dinner. I ordered the four-dollar sirloin steak, medium rare, the broccoli, a baked potato with sour cream and chives, and the deluxe head lettuce salad with anchovies. I felt like going first class. It was the first decent meal I'd had in God knows when. The head waiter brought a gray-headed man to my table and asked if I'd mind if he joined me, since the car was getting crowded. I said I'd be delighted. When I have a few drinks it makes me want to talk. I guess that's how it is with most salesmen.

"My name is Bill Diamond," I said, and stuck out my hand.

The gray-haired man took it and we shook, and he said his name was Charles Hammond.

"Don't tell me," I said. "Let me guess. You're from Boston."

He smiled a little. "I thought I had lost my accent by now."

"It's a better accent than this slobber that passes for

230

language in Kentucky," I said. "You heading back to Boston?"

He said no, he was going to Pittsburgh on business. He seemed to stiffen up a little when I made that crack about Kentucky. Maybe the guy has relatives here. Well, as I said, I'd had a few drinks, and the way they talk out here in Kentucky is about as sorry an excuse for human speech as I ever heard anywhere, so I'm not going to go into mourning over the man's precious feelings.

"I'm headed for New York," I said. "And let me tell you something. It was big money, this job, but you couldn't get me back in this country again for a million bucks."

Hammond is writing his order on the pad and he gives me the impression he's trying to upstage me. Nobody upstages Bill Diamond, particularly when I've had a few drinks. I looked out the window of the train. We were passing through one of those miserable coal camps like the one I'd just left.

"Some rathole," I said.

He looked at me. "Rathole?"

I nodded at the camp that was racing by the train window. "That place out there," I said. "It's even worse than the one I freed up."

"Freed up?" he said. "I don't know what you mean."

"I'm a real estate salesman," I said. "That's my line of work. And I've been out here freeing up the Fletcher Coal Camp. Those miners have been living on company property and in company homes too long. It's time they were free of it. It's time they owned their own homes, like all Americans should. It's part of our heritage."

"You sold the homes in the Fletcher camp to the tenants?" this Hammond said.

"That's right," I said. "And for nice hunks of dough, too."

"But this boom won't last forever," he said. "And when it's over, those homes won't be worth chopping up for firewood."

I suddenly felt a little respect for this guy. He was brighter than I thought. But I certainly didn't intend to tip my hand. I knew the boom wouldn't last, and so did Fletcher, and the other companies who were freeing their camps. The thing was, the miners didn't know it. They thought it would go on forever.

"Why Mr. Hammond," I said. "I'm surprised to hear you talk like that. Things have never been so good. The boom will go on for twenty years. We're giving those good folks a chance to own their homes at fair prices—before we get an inflation and the price we'd have to charge would go up so high they couldn't afford it."

Hammond didn't reply. In fact he didn't have much to say the rest of the meal. He sat and looked out the window at those horrible black hills flowing past in the night. I was glad when I finished eating and could leave. That guy gave me the creeps.

JUDGE FLOYD COOPER

They say that a man is what he constantly does, and I guess that's pretty close to the truth. Most of my life I've had the wish to do something for somebody—to stand up for what I knew to be right, and let the chips fall where they might. I hadn't had much success. After I accepted that coal boundary from Will Fletcher I kind of put myself in a box, and I never seemed to be able to crawl out of it.

But when the war came and went, and I saw money rolling in all over Knight County, I decided I would make a real attempt to do something I'd be proud of the rest of my life. I went down to Frankfort and went around and talked to the important people I know in state politics and urged them to set up a tax for school development in Knight County, and in Kentucky as a whole. The money was there. All they had to do was tap it—and use it—and the kids of Kentucky would thank them forever.

Well all my political friends were just as enthusiastic as they could be. They said it was a fine idea. They said they would certainly look into it just the first minute they got a little spare time. You bet you. That school tax was a fine idea.

So I went back to Booneville and waited to hear how the school tax was coming. But nobody ever mentioned it to me again, and I never saw anything about it in the paper. I guess none of those people I talked to really meant what they said. They were just brushing me off. I'm a politician myself, and I know how I act when I brush somebody off. I act just exactly the way they did. I haven't tried to push a school tax since then. There really isn't much point. It's like shoveling smoke.

NELSON FEATHERS

After the war, when the U. S. Government offered us GI's a college education, I jumped at it. I'd had very weak schooling before I got in the army, and even with all the hard work I'd put in while I was at Dix, it was touch and go—but I made it. I knew I was going to make it if I had to sit up and study all night every night. I wanted that AB degree more than I wanted anything in the world, because I had a dream. I knew what ailed Kentucky—and I had determined to go back and do something about it. I was going with a girl from Ohio, Frances Wilson, who was in college with me and I told her my plans.

"I'm a native son," I said. "It's up to me, and others like me, to help my home state. If we aren't willing to do it, who will be? I'll wage a war of my own—a war against ignorance—in the hollers of Knight County."

Frances said she couldn't think of a finer thing, and she was with me all the way, and when we got our degrees we were married and I returned to Knight County and got a job teaching in one of the high schools. The pay was poor and the house we lived in was awful. Frances was shocked. She had never been back in the hollers and she did not know how bad things could be. I saw, however, that I finally had a real chance to help and make things different. The people were making a great deal of money in the truck mines. Everybody was. Clabe Turner, who can't read or write, was making ten times what I was. I saw that now was the time to strike—when the money was flowing—and I went down to Booneville and had a talk with Mr. Carter Williams, who is superintendent of schools in Knight County. In fact he was superintendent when I was a kid. I don't remember we ever had another.

"Mr. Williams," I said, "I have worked hard to get an education so I could come back here and help the young kids who are coming out of these creeks and hollers. I want them to have a better chance than I had. Always before there was nothing we could do.

234

Nobody had any money. But now it's different. Everybody has money now. Lots of it. So now we must strike while the iron is hot. We must build schools—good ones—and give these kids a real chance. Ignorance is the sickness of Kentucky. Schools are the antidote. We must go to Frankfort and tell them, get them to act, before this boom ends and it's too late."

"Nelson," Mr. Williams said, "I am very glad you came in. You certainly have the right idea. I'll write a letter to the State Department of Education right away."

I had had some bitter experiences in the service with writing letters to big departments. I felt in my bones that this was not going to get anything accomplished. What was needed was a personal contact, face to face. I was very enthusiastic and I guess I failed to notice Mr. Williams' reaction as I spoke. I offered to go with him, at my own expense, and tell the State people what was going on up in my district of Knight County. Finally Mr. Williams said, "Nelson, I have been guiding education in this county for almost as many years as you have been alive. I think perhaps you had better let me decide how to handle it."

I stopped talking and looked at him. I wasn't prepared for the look of hostility in his eyes. It shocked me, and I tried to repair the damage I had done. "Mr. Williams," I said, "believe me, sir, I know of your long record. It isn't for myself I'm asking you to go to Frankfort. It's for the kids of Knight County—"

"I understand that, Nelson," he said. "Now I'm very busy. Unless you have something else to bring up, I'm going to have to ask to be excused."

"Yes sir," I said. "Thank you, sir."

I got up and left. I was still in awe of Mr. Williams. It was a holdover from my childhood. But when I got back and told Fran about it, she was furious. "His long record!" Fran cried. "His long record! His long record

235

of *what?* Why didn't you ask him that? If he's been in
office for a hundred years he ought to have something
to show for it, shouldn't he? Well what has he got?
The most miserable collection of old drafty firetraps
and outdated books in the United States of America!
That's what he's got! I don't know about you, Nelson,
but I'm not willing to rot up here in this miserable
holler, as you call it, while that lazy old politician who
is posing as a school man wastes your time and mine!"

I was aroused by this outburst. I saw that she was
right. And my diffidence turned to defiance. I went
back to see Mr. Williams and asked him how things
were coming with my request. Had he written to the
State? No, not yet. Well two weeks had passed, I said,
and why hadn't he?

"Young man," Mr. Williams said. "If you want to
continue to teach school in Knight County I would
advise you to go back and teach it, and let me run the
job of superintendent."

I blew up.

"Run it where?" I yelled. "Into the ground?"

"All right," he said. "I've had enough. A man has
just so much patience. You're fired."

"I can't be fired until the school year is over except
for incompetence," I said. "And by God if you cite me
for incompetence I'll go to Frankfort and spread this
whole thing over the front pages of every paper in the
state."

"I wouldn't advise you to do that," Mr. Williams
said.

"Well frankly," I said, "I don't think your advice
is worth a goddam penny."

And I walked out and didn't go back.

I worked doubly hard that year, trying to teach the
kids up in the back-county high school where I was
employed. We had some good results. We took field
trips down to the Bluegrass. I got hold of some books

236

and started a library. I had the kids over to our house and tried to get them interested in reading, the way that Captain back at Fort Dix had helped me get interested. A few of them seemed to react as I had done. But some of them did not. I had drop-outs and learned that my students had quit to get jobs in the mines. Later, when I met them, they were wearing flashy new clothes. Several of them were driving new cars, which had again become available. I was still driving an old third-hand Ford, which was all I could afford. My students were nervous in my presence, not anxious to talk to me. But I heard that behind my back they were saying I was a fool, and that they were making more money than I was.

When the school year ended I expected to be discharged, but I was not. I guess my threat to give the story to the newspapers had frightened Mr. Williams. No, I was not fired, but I was transferred to a school out on Pity Me Creek which was without doubt the worst I had ever seen. Both privies were full to overflowing, so the kids were going out in the woods. The place smelled like a cesspool for hundreds of yards around. The roof was leaking and the coal stove was cracked. They called it a High School, but in reality it was a sort of catchall for anybody who cared to come.

Naturally I was burned up. I stormed down to Booneville to see Mr. Williams and he was smooth as silk. He was sorry I didn't like my new assignment, he said. He had done it purposely, yes indeed, but not to punish me. He had understood that my mission in life was to help the underprivileged kids up in the hollers, and the school at Pity Me had seemed perfect to him. A man of my temperament ought to welcome it as a challenge. Well, he had me. I'd made my brag, and Mr. Williams had called it.

I stuck it out a year in Pity Me Creek. But the next summer my wife got pregnant, and she couldn't stand it any longer. She said I could take my choice. I could stay here in this hopeless place, in this shanty we were living in, and play Albert Schweitzer—or I could get out. If I stayed, I stayed alone. She did not intend to bear a child up here, and raise it here. She would get a job back in Ohio and raise it herself.

I hardly slept for two days, fighting with myself, but finally I reached my decision. They say Charity Begins at Home. I started looking around and I found a teaching position in Michigan which was too good to turn down. We moved at once. I didn't even go to see Mr. Williams to say good-bye. Fran says as far as she is concerned, she'll never go back to Knight County, even for a visit. I'm afraid I'm a little bitter. I doubt if I do myself.

ANDERSON WEBB

I seed John L. Lewis in person after the war when he come to Booneville to speak to us miners in a big outdoor rally. He was a big normous feller, must of weighed 250 pounds, and he told us he was borned and raised a miner and his daddy before him was a miner and so was his grandaddy before that. He knowed what it was to lay on his side in a wet seam and hack at it with a pick, Mr. Lewis said. He was one of us.

Well you could of heered the cheerin miles away, up in the hollers.

"You men had it rough before the union came to help," Mr. Lewis said. "There was a time when the
238

operators had it all their way. Well, that time is gone. The shoe is on the other foot!"

"You bet hit is!" some miner yells. "And we aim to pinch their goddam toes off!"

That got a laugh out of the crowd. But not out of Mr. Lewis. He seemed to have a permanent scowl under them big bushy eyebrows. He looks at the place in the crowd where that voice come from and it got quiet and we thought he was goin to bawl the man out for interruptin like that. But he didn't. He says, "Whoever said that—he's got the right idea! That's what I like to hear! Pinch their toes off, and I'll help you!"

The cheers almost blew him off the platform. Mr. Lewis was kind of like our daddy—the old daddy of every miner that ever lived. . . .

WILLIARD FLETCHER

We hated John L. Lewis. We hated him even more than we hated Roosevelt. Since the war, Lewis has bedeviled us continuously. Every year he had a strike. Every single year. It got so everybody expected it. The steel companies stockpiled huge tonnages of coal to get ready for Mr. Lewis's annual strike. They had to. You can't shut down a blast furnace, or even bank it, without enormous expense. We heard about it, too, from the steel people. They were getting disgusted with coal. As far as they were concerned, they had to have it—there is no substitute for coal in making steel. But other industries were not so vulnerable. They could switch to gas, or oil, or electricity. Sometimes the

cost was great, but those people were sore as a boil.
They had been bullied and inconvenienced and made
to accept dirty garbage of low BTU value for too long.
They didn't care how much it cost to get shut of Lewis.
They intended to pay it.

We tried to tell Lewis this, but he wouldn't pay any
attention. The truth was, he had begun to think of
himself as God. And the miners, of course, were willing to take anything he could get them. They were
greedy as a bunch of hogs. They had no limit. They finally got us up to $24 a day for 6 hours work, and we
had to shell out 40 cents on every ton of coal we mined
to the UMW Health and Welfare Fund. Poor down-
trodden miner? Who is kidding who? The poor down-
trodden miner was riding around in a big new car and
his wife was wearing a fur coat and John Lewis was
building him streamlined modern hospitals. And every
year the guy went on strike for more, while our customers fumed and cursed—and the oil companies
rushed in these big-inch pipelines between Texas and
the East Coast.

Well, finally we got a bellyful.

Then we got filled up to the eyebrows.

And we worked, brother. We knew there was only
one way to stop this big overbearing son of a bitch and
that was to find a miner that couldn't strike. A miner
made of steel, that could claw coal out of the hill with
its steel jaws when somebody pushed a button. It was
a complex and expensive thing to do, but we were
desperate. And we succeeded. We came up with a de-
vice called "The Continuous Miner" or, more com-
monly, "The Coal Mole." It didn't matter what you
called it. Push that brute up to a seam of coal, goose
the power to it, and it gobbled coal faster than fifty
men with picks.

So we just quietly fired the arrogant bastards who'd

been striking us every year: the drillers, the powder monkies, the coal heavers. We ran them off the place and put the Coal Mole in their place.

But we weren't through.

We invented a simple system of holding up the roof of a mine shaft. We did it by boring holes through the rotten slate into the solid rock and pinning that slate in place with steel pins called roof bolts. Almost overnight we did away with a whole big industry based on cutting mine timbers and collar poles and placing them in the mines. We fired thousands of men inside the mines, and we idled other thousands out in the forests.

Then we pulled our final play.

We tore out the steel tracks and wooden ties that had been used to carry mine cars into the working face. We did away with the cars and the motor that pulled them. We did away with the loaders and the track layers. We just put moving belts in their place. The Coal Mole gobbled coal and spit it on the moving belts. They ran it down to the main belt. The main belt ran it outside and threw the coal into a truck. So we fired more thousands of men. We were diplomatic about it, of course. We said we were sorry, and we hoped they could get another job in some other mine. "So long now," we'd say. "Good luck in that new job!"

New job my ass. Those men were finished. Most of them would never work again, except at slave wages in some doghole, and we knew it. It wasn't just inside mechanization. Big new methods were on the way. We knew about them. Coal would be mined by boring holes in the hillsides with huge augers—augers seven feet in diameter, which could fill a big coal truck in thirty seconds. Coal would be mined by giant shovels which stripped off the overburden of earth and gobbled the black seam underneath. We ourselves had al-

241

ready seen the handwriting on the wall. We had begun to invest our money in the new augers and the new
big stripping shovels.

And then, starting in 1948, the squeeze we had fore-
seen began. Oil, gas and electricity began to take great
bites out of our coal market. Buyers turned on us, as
we had known they would, and demanded clean coal,
on-time delivery, low price. The little doghole miners
went to the wall in droves, caught in the squeeze between lowering prices and higher costs. Hundreds of
them had never paid taxes on the big profits they had
made in the boom. They had paid cash for things they
bought, and never kept any records. They felt that
made them safe from income tax investigators—but it
didn't. The ramp operators had kept records of coal
they had bought. It was there in black and white when
the federal government agents finally got organized
and descended on the coal fields like a bunch of hungry locusts. Those poor devils who thought they were
getting away with murder were caught and grabbed by
the feet and held upside down and shaken until every
nickel they could beg, borrow or steal was lying on
the ground. Then the tax men picked it up and left.
They left a bunch of flat-broke hopeless broken-down
old miners. It would have been pitiful if those men
hadn't given us the shaft so unmercifully when they
were riding high. This time, they couldn't blame ex-
ploitation by outside interests. They couldn't blame
floods or acts of God. They had only one person to
blame: themselves.

BOOK FOUR

1964

DICK HUFF

Since early 1964, when President Lyndon Johnson declared war on poverty, Knight County has been a gathering place for newspaper people, magazine writers, TV crews, and would-be novelists. They come to see Ginny and me at the *Vigilante* office in Booneville and want us to give them the lowdown. We try to help them as much as we can, but the truth is, many of them don't want to stay here long enough to find out the real story. They want to hire a jeep and drive out into some woebegone hollow and shoot some pictures of the dilapidated shanties and the ragged children, and then hurry back to New York and do a story about the hard-pressed hills of Kentucky which the nation can look at and shudder and feel damned lucky they aren't in the same boat. Those stories do good. They do it in many ways. Some generous warm-hearted person will look at a picture of a dirty-faced child on the cover of a national magazine and say, "Oh that's terrible. I'll have to send those poor people some clothing, or food, or money." And maybe the warm generous feeling lasts long enough so that the clothing, food, or money actually gets sent. It gets to people in Knight County, or elsewhere, who are in desperate shape, and they accept it with real gratitude. It was a kindly act. It had a good intent, and served a good purpose.

But it didn't solve our problem.

It only alleviated it. And in some cases it might even

have aggravated it. There are deadbeats in Kentucky, just as there are deadbeats everywhere, who would rather sit back and wait for somebody else to support them than try to support themselves. I have seen sights back in our hollows you wouldn't believe. You would have to go back yourself, into the nightmare country, and see what has happened to some of our once-proud people. In fact I wish you would. I wish every person in America could come here and see what has happened. Then perhaps we wouldn't be so terribly concerned over little countries scattered all over the world that many of us never heard of until it was announced that we American taxpayers are sending them several millions of dollars. I am sorry for underprivileged countries overseas. I wish them well. But I cannot fail to notice that after we send those millions they very frequently storm and rage at us, repudiate us, and rush into the embrace of Red China or Russia. Just look at any magazine and you can see the bared teeth and curled lips of somebody like Sukarno, or some other little native dictator, shouting defiance and insults at old Uncle Sugar. Insults and defiance—in return for your tax dollars and mine.

I don't say we should turn around and give money to Kentucky. We should help Kentucky to help itself. We should care enough to find out what really ails this place—and then, by God, we should take steps to effect a permanent cure. Anything less is just playing games —silly, tragic little games.

246

PORTRAITS FROM A NIGHTMARE
Nestor Mazwell

Me and Vippie was double first cousins but we got
arter each other one time down in the medder and I
got her in a family way and she was only twelve or
thirteen I don't remember which but she was big fur
her age and she blossomed out with tits and a belly
like a full-blowed woman practical overnight. So there
warnt nothin to do but marry her. I was twenty-eight,
but that don't make nothin. I tell you Cousin Vippie
was the best screwin in the whole holler and everbody
kin tell you that cause everbody screwed her at one
time the other. But I was allus the one that could say
he got her cherry and also I was the father of mosta the
younguns. They all got my long nose n watery eyes,
Vippie says, and I guess hits true. But that's so many
years back I caint member when. We still got five of our
own younguns with us. The baby is forty-five or -six.
Alla em weak-minded, you might say. Couldn't go no
place and live by theirself for moren a couple days.
Plumb die a exposure. I like a close family anyhow.
Special little Boosie. Boosie is my favorite of em all and
she done likes me too, even though she don't know
me from a goddam ole hound. They got a sayin aroun
here that a hillbilly virgin is a little gal that kin run
fastern her pappy. Everbody laughs when they hear
that joke, but I never seed it was so funny. Little Boosie
never runs from me. When I got the old lady drunk
and went and got Boosie by the hand and pulled her

over to my bed she come real willin and I couldn hardly git rid of her, she kep grabbin at it and wantin it some more. The only bad thing was the baby she had aint ever got up from its bed and it's eighteen year old. He got a head as big as a punkin and great big dreamy eyes and his feet is little bittie tits, no biggern a minute. The old lady, that's Vippie, was real spicious of me and Boosie when the kid come, but I told her it was a goddam rovin miner that knocked Boosie up whilst we was out hoein the corn, and Vippie believed it. I just don't see how that big-headed baby lived so goddam long is the only thing that wonders me.

Redmond and Carrie Treeson

The Lord is Great. The Lord hath strength in All Things. Blessed is the Name of the Lord. Redmond and I have read the Bible through a hundred times. We know it by heart. We don't have anything to do except a little gardening and canning and look after mother and read the Bible. That was how it was, and how we spent our whole life. People never came to see us because they were afraid of us. Redmond wore a tall stovepipe hat that had belonged to pa. He was very careful with it and wore it all his life, except in the rain. Redmond read in the Bible that you could take up serpents and one day I found him out in the garden holding a big copperhead in his hand. He held it for a while and then put it down and told it to go away to God. It crawled away. After that I knew that Redmond had Powers. When he found a passage in the

Bible that said you could kill a person and bring them back to life, if you were absolutely pure and had faith, both Redmond and I were very excited. We talked it over, trying to decide if I would kill Redmond or he would kill me. We couldn't decide so we went and talked to mother, who is very old, and she said if it was in the Bible it must be so, and if we wanted to, we could kill her and bring her back to life. Well that sounded like a fine idea and Redmond and I spent a long time figuring out how we would do it. We looked all through the Bible for various ways, and finally Redmond decided that the best way was stoning. They always stoned people to death in the Bible, and we wanted to stay as close to the Bible as we could. So we took mother down to the creek and laid her on a big flat rock and began throwing stones at her. She couldn't help from yelling when they hit her and we was afraid of getting somebody around before we had her killed and brought her back to life, so Redmond went down and got a big stone about as big as a mushmellon and hit mother on the head with it. It stopped her screaming right then. And her face was all crooked and blood trickled out of her mouth and her eyes stopped seeing.

"I reckon she's dead," I said to Redmond. "Go ahead and bring her back to life."

Redmond tried. He tried so hard the sweat stood out on his face in big drops. But he couldn't. And he said, "Carrie, I thought I had enough faith, and I thought I was pure, but I guess I was wrong. You better bring her back."

So I tried. I almost broke my brains concentrating on bringing mother back to life. But she never moved a muscle. And flies was starting to get after her.

Redmond lifted up his eyes to Heaven and apologized to the Almighty for not having faith and being pure. And I did the same thing. Then Redmond said we'd better get a shovel and bury the old lady before somebody came and found her. So we did. And nobody gave us a speck of trouble. When Doc Callahan came by on his rounds and asked where mother was we told him she had died of noomonia and we had buried her. And Doc said we should of called the County Coroner and we said we didn't know that, and we were sorry. Doc left and nothing happened. Redmond and I read the Bible every day. It's about all we have to do up here except gardening and canning, now that we don't have mother to look after.

Eliza Webster

Ah, Ah foog hit. What the foog. The hollers is alla same. Look alla like. Big hill. Big shadder. Big hill or shadder. How the hell I know? Could tell one from other. Never makes no different nohow . . .

Mister . . .

Hey mister . . .

Hey mister yole sumbitch mister . . .

Ah foog it. Foog that ole sumbitch. Long as I'm drunk. That's hit. That's the way. Gimme a jug and I'm ready fur em. Ready fur em. Alla em. Foog em . . . foog alla em . . . Foog . . .

Jimmy Hagin

As I was comin up the holler just now I seen old Liza Webster that cut off her man's whang with a ole butcher knife when she was young. I seen her crawlin away from a garbage can with an old rotten hunk of meat in her han, just as drunk as a big stinkin ole skunk, and I walked up real close to her and yanked down my eyelids and shoved up my nose and blithered at her with my tongue. And she looks up at me and makes them sounds she is always makin that don't mean nothin. Foog hit, mister, yole sumbitch, and like that. She don't know if it's winter or summer. I guess she plumb don't care. One of these days they gonna find her layin in the creek with rats eaten on her. Crazy ole drunk bitch garbage eater . . .

ALICE MENEFEE

Sis is keeping the family now. She's been doin it ever since the machines took all the work away at the mines and Dave lost his job. Sis lives here at the house with her three kids. She's not married. She thinks she knows who the fathers are of those kids, but she isn't sayin. As long as a child has no father Sis can collect $26.50 from the welfare every month. Three kids raises it up to $79.50. Course we can't get by too well on just $79.50, but we don't have to. Sis has a room fixed up in what used to be the tool house. She's got it decorated real pretty, with curtains at the windows and a rug on the floor and a big bed with a Beautyrest mattress on it and a kewpie doll on the dresser and perfume and everything.

I know Sis brings men in there at night. I see them come and go. Sometimes they stay all night. Sometimes they leave early and maybe another man will

251

come, or a couple. I suppose I ought to speak to Sis about that. I ought to tell her to go to church and pray for her soul. But I don't say a word. I've learned a lot since I was a child picking chestnuts. Sis is doing the best she can. She's a good girl. She loves me and I love her. And as she says, if something slips and she has another baby, it's an extra $26.50 every month. Sis knows she won't keep her looks forever. She has to look after the permanent investment when she aint good-lookin enough to get all this easy Night Money . . .

UNCLE EB THOMAS

I'm ninety-six years old, or maybe ninety-eight, I'm not real sure, and I live with my youngest son Virgil up in the Mad Dog Creek holler. I love it there because it's the finest place in Kentucky and in the whole world, probably. The trees are so tall they like to touch the clouds and the woods are full of arbutus and honeysuckle that smells like I imagine it will smell in heaven if I ever get there. They's all kind of berries, just for the pickin. Them tiny little wild strawberries that grow in clusters. Them little fellers is about the size of a pea and they fall off the stem into your hand when they dead ripe, just by touchin the stem of the plant. They sweet as honey in your mouth.

Speakin of honey, I kin show you a big old bee tree not more'n half a mile from here and I'm goin up there and git me a tubful one of these days. I betcha there's a hundred pounds of wild honey in that tree. The bees come out like a cloud of smoke when you pound on the trunk. I aint too partial to wild honey, though. You have to smoke the bees out by buildin a fire in the bottom of the holler tree and that gives the honey a smoky taste. Bound to. Then they's always a lot of dead bees in the honey when you git her out, and little bits of bark, and you have to strain her. She's real dark. Some people claims they like it but I don't. I'd ruther have honey from a hive, particular if hit's made with clover blossoms. That wild honey is a mite too strong for my taste.

My daughter says I ramble a lot, and I suppose she's right, but I guess a man who lives in such a wonderful place as this has got a right to be proud of it. The other day, or maybe it was last year, my son Ward brung a bunch of big shots up from Booneville and they sat and talked to me. My daughter says they didn't do much of the talkin. I done most of it myself. When I'm around, my daughter says, nobody kin get a word in edgeways. But anyhow I took the opportunity of tellin them how fine we got it here. I told them to look at the big forest awavin up there in the clouds, and I invited them to come fishin with me any time they wanted. Mad Dog Creek is the best fishin of any creek in the whole county. It is clear as crystal and ice cold and full of fish. Down below our place there's a hole where a great big old grandaddy bass lives. I been after him for a long time. One of these days I'm goin to hook him. Boy it makes my mouth water to think of it. Way my wife cooks a big bass, she peppers and salts and butters the dickens outen him and then she wrops him up tight in beech leaves and buries him in the sand about a foot. Then we build a great big roarin fire over the spot and let her burn down into embers. Then we dig up that old grandaddy bass and unwrap him and boy—that beech flavor goes right into the meat and she's so tender she practically falls offen the bones. You'll hafta come over and see me again when I catch

253

that old bass, and I'll get my wife to cook it up for you like I just described.

Well, my daughter got into the conversation just then. "Grandaddy's a fine old man," I heered her say. "But he's right old now and his mind sometimes gits to wanderin—so don't you mind when he talks about his wife as if she was present. She's been gone now for almost forty years."

"Now that just aint true!" I yelled. "She just left here a minute ago to go down to the springhouse for some milk!"

"Yes grandaddy," my daughter says soothinly. "Sure grandaddy. I'm sorry I gotcha stirred up. You just set in your rocker now and rest. I've got to show these gentlemen out."

"All right," I says. "I am a mite tired. I'll just catch me a little nap, I reckon. Good-bye, mister. It was nice talkin to you."

But I didn't go to sleep right off. I heered them talkin out on the porch before they left to go back to Booneville, and I heered what my boy Ward said. "We don't tell grandaddy how things have changed," he said. "He's happier the way he is—thinkin the valley is full of big trees and fish—the way it was when he was a boy here."

"I suppose that's better," a voice said. "It's amazing to look at his eyes. You say he can't see at all?"

"He can see light," Ward said. "But he can't make out objects. We could have the cataracts taken off but he won't let us. He says if he had to go and stay in a hospital, even one night, it would kill him."

"Well I think you are wise to let him decide it," the voice of the visitor said. "As a matter of fact, if he could see how things really are around here it would probably upset him."

There was a pause, and then I heard them goin down the patch. I laid there in the chair for a while

studyin over what they said about things bein changed.
I couldn't rightly get it straight in my head. But I
didn't think about it too hard. I was tired and drowzy,
and I just shet my eyes and laid back and pretty soon
I was sound asleep.

SIM YATES

It makes me laugh when I hear these Bluegrass politicians makin their big speeches about all us proud free
upstandin people—how brave and independent we are
in the face of our troubles. I tell you that aint the case
no more—not for a lot of folks. They on relief. They
layin drunk in their shacks rollin in the bed with the
old lady. They lettin their kids go hungry and cold and
when anybody sends em clothes or stuff like that they
just take it as a matter of course. Proud upstandin
people? Who are them politicians tryin to kid? I tell
you some of the sorriest folks in the whole United
States are livin in these hollers around here.

Well, I says to myself, Sim you old son, if you don't
do nothin else, you aint goin on no relief. No state
relief. No federal relief. No miner's pension. When
them politicians talk about the proud fine upstandin
people in the hills of Knight County, by God and by
Jesus, you are goin to be the one feller that keeps em
from bein liars. Even if you starve. Hell, starvin is bad,
but hit's better than sloppin yourself with the hogs.

So I looked around all over the county until I found
me the exact spot I wanted. It is up on a hill right next
to the Virginia line. On the biggest hill in Kentucky,

255

to be exact: Pine Mountain. To git to it you have to come up a mile of real rough steep slope covered with rocks, nothin to hide a person, not even huckleberry bushes. I figured I'd do just like my old grandaddy done when he come to Kentucky. I'd build me a pole cabin with an axe and my own two hands. I done it. I daubed the cracks good, and I put me in a field-stone chimbly and finished off the floor with nice smooth slabs. They was great big rocks, big as my cabin, all around me on that hill. I planned it that way. Out the back of my cabin, through them big rocks, was the Virginia line, a couple hundred feet off.

When I had my pole cabin built I got me a great big old .270 rifle and the best telescope sight money can buy. I used to be a sniper in the war. I was rated one of the best snipers in my outfit. I used a high-power rifle and a telescope sight and brother there was some mighty surprised sons of bitches that thought they was perfectly safe until I hit em from way to hell and gone off in the distance. It took me almost a year to get the money together for that .270 rifle and that special sight. I didn't spend a nickel on nothin. I worked down in Booneville and I saved every bit I could lay my hands on. But boy, when I finally got that gun and that sight and a big supply of them big powerful .270 bullets, and got up on top of my mountain, I was king of the world. I practiced up with my new weapon. I could actually see little bugs awalkin on the limbs of trees way down at the foot of my long rock slope, usin that sight. And I had her shot in just perfect to a gnat's eyewinker. My eyesight is still keen as a razor for distance, even though I can't see stuff that's in my hand too good, like a newspaper. That don't bother me none. I kin read a little but not enough to bother with. I never fooled with it when I was little, so why should I start now.

Then I saved some more money and I got my still in. I got the best still I could lay my hands on. Copper tubing and a real fine thumpin keg and the works. And I lines up sources of corn and mash and starts makin moonshine. Good moonshine. Maybe not as good as that stuff the fancy distilleries down in the Bluegrass make—but nobody ever went blind on my stuff, and after the first couple drinks you couldn't tell if it was moonshine out of my still or spensive stuff out of one of them fancy bottles. And I start makin money. Good money. Not relief money. Honest moonshine money. And I don't have to go up and stand in line at some cruddy counter and git some damn little paper signed by some little snot-nosed govment clerk. I'm old Sim Yates, up on my mountain among the rocks, two hundred feet from the Virginny line.

Sure the revenooers will be after me. I know that. But I got a system. I got me a whole slew of durn good friends down there in the holler. Bill Ott and Clabe Turner and Bood Morgan and like that. Most of them fellers is takin some kind of relief. They adoptin their grand-kids, or pretendin they got back injuries, or some such goddam trick to git on the county rolls. That aint none of my affair. They still friends of mine, and if they see any stranger slinkin up the holler they go out and fire three blasts on their gun. I got good ears among my other valuable assets and there aint no noise up here to stop me from hearin those gunshots. Even if I'm sleepin. So I'm in good shape. I got my still fixed on special wheels so I can roll her over into Virginia and hide her in a cave over there. When I put the big log back in place over that cave you could walk right up and stare at it and not know there was a still behind it. When I got nothin else to do, I practice hidin my still. I can do it in less than ten minutes. And I'll have half an hour, easy, to get ready for the revenooers, after I hear the warnin shots.

Course those revenoo fellers is smart. They may find a way to get by my friends and sneak up to my field of rocks and make a rush for it. I already decided what I'm goin to do if that happens. I'm goin to shoot her out. That .270 is a beautiful rifle—about the finest invention of man except a little old gal pantin and heavin under a feller in the light of the moon. I aint as young as I was once, but I still manage to git me a little. When I stop turnin and lookin at a purty leg, I'm nearin the end.

I don't do much prayin to God, but ever now and then when I'm drinkin a little of my own stuff I git to feelin religious as hell and I'll git down on my knees and say me a prayer. You know what it is? I'll tell you.

"Dear God," I pray, "if You are goin to send me a bunch of revenooers for a shoot out, please God let there be a couple of them Bluegrass politicians with em. God, if I miss them hand-wringin sons of bitches I deserve to go to Hell."

ANGIE WEBB

Anse is goin to die. I've knowed it for a long time but I never mention it, because what he's got there aint no cure for. We call it miner's asme, but there's a big medical word that Doc Callahan uses, silicosis. It's a growth inside the lungs that comes from breathin rock dust. Quarry workers gits it. So does miners, but not from the coal dust. They got it from the rock dust that the companies used to use in the mines to lay the coal dust and keep it from formin an explosion mixture with the air. The rock dust was heavy. It laid on the coal dust and kep it down. Anse used to say it was like workin in a yella fog when they throwed that rock dust around. He had a mask but he didn't wear it. You couldn't git your breath right with that mask on, Anse said. It was a great big nuisance.

Well, he should of wore it, nuisance or not, because now the disease is closin in on him. He'll be fine in the daytime and in the early evenin, maybe only have a couple little short coughin spells. But after he gits to layin down in bed and sleepin for a couple of hours, and wakes up, the stuff has gone and collected in his throat and it tickles him and he has to cough. Once that starts it goes on the rest of the night.

Did you ever hear a man cough that's got a real bad case of miner's asme? Well it aint like no other kind of coughin in the world. It's mostly gaspin for breath, on account of them growths has took away almost all of the breathin surface inside the lungs, and then it goes into a chokin, and you feel your toes curl up in your bed, and your eyelids tighten down, even though your eyes is shut, waitin to see if he is ever gonna breathe again . . . and then, when he does, it turns into a retchin. Anse thinks about me and about Rufe and Annie Fugate, who are livin with us, and he'll git up out of bed and go outside, if its summer, and walk up in the holler by hisself where he can cough and not bother nobody. I would go up there and set with him, and I told him so, but he wouldn't listen to me.

Anse has him a little dog, a little Cheewawa, they call it, no bigger than a big old mouse. Anse calls his dog Tiny. Tiny loves Anse. As soon as Anse comes home from the doghole mine where he works (Anse won't quit work as long as he can stand up, and he never took a nickel in any kind of welfare) little old Tiny comes arunnin and jumps up in the chair beside Anse and snuggles in under his arm and sticks its little snubby nose up and stares at Anse with them big brown bulgy eyes, and Anse grins down at it, and says, "I'm

259

goin to give you a whuppin! I swear, I'm goin to give you a big whuppin!"

Tiny wiggles and snuggles and stares up at Anse like he was God, and Anse pats its head. Why he wouldn't no more whup that little dog than I'd whup a newborn baby. Tiny is a real comfort to Anse at night, when he gits up to cough. It'll stay right with him, starin up at him, wonderin what's the matter, from the time Anse starts in coughin around midnight until mornin comes and it's time for him to put on his work clothes and go to the mine. Anse gits work when others can't because he'll really give them a day—and he aint afeered to go in and cut under shaky roof.

Rufe Fugate is gettin worse. He always was moody and cranky, ever since he got his eyes blowed out, but lately he sets all day and never speaks. Me and Annie has tried to joke him out of it but it won't work. Me and Annie are lucky. We got us good jobs cookin down at the hot lunch where we feed the school kids stuff that the federal government is buyin for them. A job like that is rare, I can tell you. It's like findin a diamond on your plate in the mornin when you come down for breakfast.

Since Mr. Hammond closed the mine for good and him and Mrs. Hammond took off for Europe on a big tour, things have been pretty bad around here. This town is nothin but a ghost town now, and the people in it is gettin like ghosts, too. I don't blame Mr. Hammond and Mrs. Hammond for leavin. The mine is about worked out. They is still-coal in there but it's so deep in that you can't git at it without a great expense. And now they got these augers and strippin shovels that kin get coal about as cheap as pickin it up off the street. Mr. Hammond done the best he could for us. We aint mad at him for leavin. But of course we miss him. And we miss Lucy. They quit us—but they didn't have no choice. They had to give up.

There's one feller in this town beside Anse that hasn't give up. It's Billy Collins in the barber shop acrost the street. Billy is one of the hardest-workin men in Eastern Kentucky, and one of the nicest. He must of cut a million heads of hair in his life. He's been cuttin it all through the depression and the boom and now he's still cuttin it when it looks like Kentucky is finished. Billy Collins never took a nickel of relief in his life. And he sure never will. He just stands there behind his barber chair and cuts away from morning to night. I can tell you, Billy puts the heart into me when I look over and see him.

There's one man that didn't give up, I think. *If Billy Collins can make it, I can make it too!*

RUFE FUGATE

I can't sleep no more. It aint only that Anse coughs, although that bothers me. It's the fact that I been livin here with Anse and Angie—both me and my wife—for too goddam long. We been here for years. We come in on a mergency basis and we just stayed forever. That aint right, even if Anse and Angie was rich, which they aint.

I'm drawin my welfare from the state for total disability, and I'm puttin that in the kitty, so I suppose in a way I'm helpin out. But oh Jesus, that aint the way a man wants to help out. I'm a miner. I always been a miner. And I aint geared to lay in a chair, year after year, like a stinkin old wore-out dog. I'd be better off dead, and don't think I aint thought of it. In fact, lately, I don't think of much else. I could git hold of a knife and cut my throat, or Anse's shotgun, and blow my head off, but I couldn't do a thing like that to Annie. Comin in and findin my brains all over the woodwork. She'd never git her mind washed clean of a thing like that as long as she lived.

No. I got a better idea. I been playin with it in my mind for a long time now, and it's about the only joy I had. To me this dream is like the dream some folks have of goin to Florida and layin on the beach under a palm tree. It's just as exciting to me—hell, it's more excitin. I aint goin to tell nobody about that dream. But I been plannin her for a long time and just bidin my time and one of these days I'm goin to pull her off . . .

WILLIARD FLETCHER

Well, we've finally got things our own way. Hammond and his wife pulled out. John L. Lewis surprised us. He turned out to be just as interested in automation as the mine owners. In fact, the United Mine Workers *are* mine owners now. They have bought controlling interests in some of the biggest mines in the country. They have bought into the big equipment companies, too. And finally the UMW has tightened up its pension plan, and its health-and-welfare benefits, and have unloaded some of those big hospitals which Lewis built with the miner's 40-cents-a-ton royalty on UMW-mined coal. The UMW is rich. They've got over $200,000,000 in their kitty. And the way it looks, they intend to keep it right there. The miners are a little bitter when they get their pensions reduced, or their health-and-welfare cards are taken away, but there isn't a whole lot they can do about it. They just have to sit and grind their teeth and take it. Lewis and his gang are finally getting smart. They are starting to act like businessmen . . .

Of course the power of the United Mine Workers of America is waning, has been waning ever since we mechanized. The membership is way down. Those little dogholes can't afford to kick in the 40 cents a ton for health and welfare. If they tried to do it, they'd go broke. Even the big mechanized deep mines are having trouble with that 40 cents. It's going back to the way it was before the unions came in. The miners are working for starvation wages in dangerous conditions without safety regulations, pension plans, or compensation for injury or death on the job. They are turning back into slaves . . .

What's hurried this along, oddly enough, is the much-praised Tennessee Valley Authority.

I guess you've heard about the TVA and what a wonderful job it has done in rehabilitating the Tennessee Valley. True. TVA did that. They started out building these big dams and generating cheap electric power. But they didn't stop there. They began building these mammoth plants where you can burn coal, and generate electricity. Those plants look like something out of the space age. They have smoke stacks as high as skyscrapers and their furnaces burn trainloads of coal. TVA buys huge tonnages of coal routinely. They buy coal in the millions of tons.

And here's the joker.

TVA is required by law to generate power as cheaply as they possibly can. So they try to drive the cost of those millions of tons of coal right down to rock bottom. And they do it! They'll let it be known, for example, that they won't even look at your bid unless it's under $3 a ton. And then, if somebody bids $2.80—and that's low—TVA tells all bidders to meet $2.80 or forget it. Well, we are all hungry for those big million-ton contracts, and we try to get our bite out of them.

The little doghole fellow can't do it, no matter how tight he yanks in his belt. Even the big mechanized mine has trouble. The only fellows who can meet TVA's brass-knuckle rock-bottom price are the big strip-shovel operators and the big auger-operators. With a stripping shovel you can get coal cheaply. You just grub the dirt off the top and gobble up the seam that's lying there under it. Yes, it raises hell with the landscape. It throws up spoilbanks of sterile subsoil which slide down through the trees and shrubs and silt the streams and cause floods. People in Hazard, for example, are raising their houses on stilts in antici-pation of more floods like the one which ripped through the place a year or so ago. And strip mining also kills the fish. Rain water washes over the exposed coal seam and picks up sulphur. This causes a solution of sulphuric acid which kills the fish, the algae, even the plant life in a stream. It makes a stream as sterile as a chemical dump! The fishermen set up a howl, but what good does it do them? They can't even be heard against the giant voice of the coal interests. Politicians listen to the man with the money. We are those men. Our Kentucky politicians are like politicians anywhere. They want to get elected to office. They know they can't get elected unless the coal interests are behind them. So they go along with us. They make these speeches full of the same old southern bullshit we've been hearing for years—all about the rugged pride of the hill people, and how those brave folks insist on standing on their own feet, without any help from out-siders. And all the time our politicians are working for bigger and bigger federal handouts—which they use to sweeten up the voters and tighten their grip on them.

I don't blame the politicians. They are acting in their own self-interest, just as we are. It does make me laugh, when I sit behind my TV set and listen to their pious promises and their professions of love and loyalty to the voters. I don't know who screwed the people of Kentucky the worst—we coal operators or their duly-elected leaders. I would say it's about a toss-up. It is gotten so a hill voter just goes ahead and votes for the man who offers him the biggest handout—like a dog barking for his bone. So maybe, in a way, the hill voter has been screwing himself. If a leader with real guts was to rise in Kentucky and try to help the people I really doubt if they'd let him. They'd vote for the boy with the sugar-tit to hand them to suck. . . .

Myself, I'm doing as I always have done. If I can't lick a man, I join him. I'm getting in the auger business and the strip-mine business. I'm going to invest in the company that has the biggest strip shovel. It's that simple. Because that's the company that can get at the coal quickest, make the biggest profit, and meet those hard-boiled TVA coal prices . . .

FORTUNE MAGAZINE
(Page 96, October 1962)

"World's largest mobile land machine is this 12,000-horsepower stripping shovel . . . and assembled in western Kentucky. . . . This shovel is designed to uncover coal seams as much as 100 feet under ground; in fifty seconds its 115-yard dipper picks up 173 tons of over-burden, dumps it 464 feet away, and swings back for the next bite. High as a twenty-story building, and thrice as big as any previous shovel, the machine is controlled by one man, who ascends five stories to his pulpit in a special elevator. A major breakthrough in shovel design, it is undeniably a superlative example of how capital investment enables industry to use both capital and manpower more efficiently."

ANDERSON WEBB

I came home from the mine as usual, about five o'clock. Annie Fugate and my wife hadn't arrived yet. They cook the hot lunch at noon, then clean up the lunchroom and get ready for the next day's meal. They don't get in until around six.

Little Tiny come a-ragin and a-barkin inside the door, until it seed it was me, and then it wiggled itself silly and leaped agin my legs and I reached down and petted it afore I went in to see if Rufe needed somethin. Rufe usually sets in the bedroom that him and Annie shares, listenin to the radio, but the radio wasn't playin and when I went in there I couldn't find Rufe. It sure beat me. I run all over the house lookin and callin and Tiny runs with me, barkin with excitement, thinkin its a game.

So when I realized Rufe has somehow left the house I went acrost the street to Billy Collins' barber shop and asked Billy if he seed anybody come and git Rufe.

"No," Billy says. "I didn't see a soul. Aint he there?"

"You reckon Doc Callahan could of come and took him to the hospital?"

"He could of," Billy says.

"Well look," I says. "Will you give Doc a ring and see if he's got Rufe?"

Billy said he'd be glad to, and he done it, and Doc Callahan said no, said he hadn't been out here and he didn't have any idea where Rufe could be. Well then I begun to really worry. I knowed Rufe had been awful moody for a long spell. About that time little Jimmy Hagin comes into the barber shop and pipes up and says he saw old Rufe crawlin up the mountain a while ago.

"You did?" I yells. "Well, why didn't you run and tell somebody?"

"I was going to," Jimmy says, "but I had to do an errand for ma, and she said she'd give me a whuppin if I didn hurry—and I just now got back."

"Well all right," I says. "Show us where you seed him."

Jimmy takes us out and points up the side of the mountain, and we look and there's no sign of Rufe. Up near the top I seed the mouth of one of Mr. Hammond's shafts that wasn't bein worked, and suddenly I knowed where Rufe was.

"Look Billy," I says. "Rufe's in that doghole up there. And if we want to git him out alive we got to move fast."

"Are you crazy or somethin?" Billy says. "What would he be doin up in that old mine shaft?"

"Cuttin coal," I says.

"Cuttin coal?" Billy yells. "My God Anse, you plumb out of your mind! An old blind man in an old abandoned shaft, cuttin coal?"

But I wasn't listenin. I run across the road and began clawin my way up through the slate and brush toward that drift mouth. I done fine for about two minutes, and then my breath give out, and I had to set down. By that time Billy Collins and a whole bunch of guys come aswarmin up through the brush past me, toward the drift mouth.

They got there, but not in time. Billy Collins told me later he heard a choppin sound comin from deep inside the mine, and he knows there's a man in there usin an axe, and he yells to see if it's Rufe and the choppin stops and Rufe's voice comes, faint and fur in, but it's Rufe's voice all right, and tells Billy to stay out, the mine is about to cave in. Well naturally Billy and the other men aint about to stay out. They start up the shaft and the sound of the axe gits frantic, and after they are about a quarter of a mile inside one of them puts his hand up, the way any miner will, to feel the roof. And the roof is quiverin, and this man yells to everbody to run for their lives . . .

Them men got out of there about ten seconds before that whole big tunnel come crashin down. Rufe had chopped out some timbers and started the slate to fallin. The other timbers was so rotten that once she started, she run right out the tunnel to the drift mouth, and the solid rock overhead come right in on top of her, and plugged the whole shaft tight as a drum. There wasn't no hope of diggin Rufe out then. He'd lay there forever and ever, with that old mine shaft for his grave, and that great big old mountain for his tombstone. I didn't say anything to anybody, but I was sure glad of that cave-in, because I knowed Rufe pretty good, and I knowed why he went up there, and I knowed this was probably how he hoped it would happen.

Everbody was saying what a terrible shame it was. I wasn't sayin nothin.

But I was thinkin: *If they got a heaven for miners,*

old Rufe is settin in it right now with his golden pick and his silver shovel, tellin the boys about his last act on earth. And when I thought about that, I just had to grin.

CHARLES HAMMOND

When Lucy and I sold out and left Kentucky forever I heaved a sigh of relief. Lucy had always wanted to travel in Europe but what with the war and the depression and all our business troubles I could never get away. So now we went to Europe and we were like two little kids let out of school. We went to a place called Santa Margherita, in Italy, right up the coast from a little harbor called Portofino, which was like something out of a travel folder to heaven, as Lucy said, and lay in the sun until we looked like a couple of natives. Then we went up into the Italian Dolomites to a place called Cortina d'Ampezzo, and filled our lungs with that high mountain air. Then we went to Salzburg, which is a tiny little town out of Grimm's Fairy Tales, tucked in under a mountain, and stayed in an old inn called the Goldener Hirsch. From there we went to Paris. We became adept at cocktail conversation and we met people like ourselves, well-to-do Americans who had worked hard and were now playing. We saw a few famous people at a distance, movie stars and writers and so on, but we did not meet them. Perhaps we could have, but we really weren't interested. We were having too much fun, just the two of us.

"Charles," Lucy said one day, "Why did we wait so long? Why didn't we do this before?"

"I was playing God," I said, and laughed. "Remember?"

Lucy laughed too. The pain was gone from it now. It all seemed too far away. It seemed unreal, as if it had happened to other people.

From Paris we went to Spain. We wanted to see the bullfights. Spain was pleasant, as all places are pleasant when you have plenty of money and can stay at the best hotels and go first class. In all the countries we visited I bought those handy little books which give pictures and short sentences you are likely to need in the native language and also in English. I managed to master the pronunciation fairly well in most cases —at least well enough to order our meals, hire cabs, and perform the other necessary functions of travel without waving my hands and shouting the way quite a few American tourists we encountered were doing. They seemed to feel that it was a matter of volume. If they yelled loud enough, even though their pronunciation was wrong, they'd be understood.

I had had two years of Spanish long ago, in prep school, and I had liked it. In fact I had made friends with some of the Spanish boys who had been sent from South America by their rich parents and I played poker with them. In order to succeed at poker with a bunch of sharp Spanish boys, it was handy to be able to speak the language and understand it, and so when I got to Spain I brushed up and Lucy said she was very proud of me, the beautiful accent I had. I sounded almost like a Spaniard, she said.

One day we were walking along a street in Seville and we stopped to browse in one of those variety stores which tourists frequent. In this shop was a section devoted to old books. I was looking at the titles more or less idly when one of them popped out suddenly, and stung me like a wasp. I stared at it. *Los Quatros Jinetes del Apocalypse*. It was by Blasco Ibáñez. I recalled a session I had had in Kentucky with a reporter from a big magazine who was relating to me the many reasons why he thought the hill people of Eastern Kentucky were doomed. They had become little better than Indians on a reservation this man said. They had become so used to government handouts that rehabilitation was impossible. And their birth-rate, this writer said, was one of the highest in the nation. I had become tired of hearing that kind of talk and I had said that there wasn't any answer and we might as well forget it.

"Oh no Mr. Hammond," this reporter said. "There's an answer all right, if the sentimental American public had the guts to take it."

"Yes?" I said. "And what is it?"

"The Four Horsemen," this reporter said.

I felt a sudden sick emptiness, and stepped away from the book counter in that little Seville shop. But then I stopped. Don't be silly, I told myself. It's only a book. So I went back and deliberately took Señor Ibáñez's book from the rack and stared at it. The picture on the dust jacket was ratty with age and wear but it showed the Four Horsemen quite clearly—four skeleton figures in shrouds, Famine, Pestilence, War and Death, riding furiously through the sky on ghostly horses. I put the book back in the rack and returned to Lucy, who was buying a lace mantilla. She modeled it for me and asked me if I liked it and I said yes it was fine. So Lucy and the shopkeeper went through the usual happy haggling and she bought it and we left the shop.

I did not mention the book to Lucy. I forgot it, or thought I did. One evening a day or so before we planned to leave for Greece, we ran into an American couple in our hotel and got into one of those easy conversations which happen abroad between Ameri-

271

cans. These people were stimulating and friendly. The man was head of a big contracting firm in Ohio. We talked of one thing and another and of course we got around to automation, which is so much in the news. This man mentioned the closing of the Studebaker plant in South Bend—how he had seen pictures on TV of families of men who had been laid off getting government commodities in a long line. Some of these people had been interviewed and said they had tried everywhere to get a job, but there were no jobs. They said that without these government handouts they would be in real trouble—just to eat.

"It's all over the place," this man said. "Not just in autos. I heard that several thousand jobs are being lost to automation every week in various parts of the business community in America. Jobs that won't ever be regained."

"It's terrible," Lucy said. "But I guess there's no answer to it."

The man looked at her. "Mrs. Hammond," he said, "I don't want to offend you, but you have just said something which annoys me. You have said a thing which Americans are saying lately, about a lot of things. There's no answer to it. Well that's for the birds!"

Lucy's eyes snapped. Her Kentucky temper rose up and lay just below the surface.

"Well that's very interesting," she said. "I'd be mighty glad to know the answer to automation, if you've got one!"

The Ohio contractor grinned. "I can't take credit for being original," he said. "Mr. Willard Wirtz, our Secretary of Labor, was on TV one night and he just happened to drop the idea in passing. But I caught it. It hit me right between the eyes. Wirtz said there are enough bona-fide, urgently needed projects in America right now to cause a desperate labor shortage

272

overnight if we had the imagination and the guts to turn ourselves loose on them."

"What projects?" Lucy said.

"Well just take highways," the contractor said. "They put a second deck on the George Washington Bridge not long ago—and nobody even noticed any let-up in the traffic using the first deck. Both were jammed the minute the thing was opened. There isn't a better investment the U. S. could make than good roads. It puts thousands of men to work across the board—from the cement mills and the steel mills to the boy who handles a muck stick down in the riverbed—and when the road is in place, it stimulates thousands of more jobs in filling stations, automobile makers, and the transport industry in general. And while I'm on transport—how about adopting old Axel Wenner-Gren's dream of building a high-speed monorail up through British Columbia to Alaska? Alaska's our forty-ninth state—and it's dying on the vine due to the inability of people to get goods up there. Old Axel had the idea of shooting things in on his high rail at a hundred miles an hour—above the snowbanks. And he was right, you know. The only thing that prevents this being done is the timidity of our once-rugged chance-taker—the Poor Sorry American."

"Poor sorry American!" Lucy said. "That kind of talk makes me sick! It seems to me that all we Americans do any more is apologize. We didn't give somebody ten million dollars—we only gave them five! And it hurt their poor tender feelings to have to take our money! I don't think we're poor and sorry at all! Just maybe a little soft in the head!"

"You said you were from Kentucky?" the man said. "Right?"

"That's right!" Lucy snapped. "What of it?"

"Well nothing," the man said. "Except before we came over here we saw a Sunday afternoon television

273

show devoted to the plight of miners and their families in the hills of Kentucky. What was the name of the town?" He looked at his wife.

"Boonesburg," his wife said.

I felt a quick catch in my stomach.

"Yeah, Boonesburg," the contractor said. "Well Mrs. Hammond, if you are from Kentucky and as well off as you and your husband certainly seem to be, I would think you'd be interested in what happened on that program."

I saw Lucy was pale. She stared at the man without speaking.

"It showed a coal camp nearby that had turned into a ghost town," the contractor said. "And it told of a blind man there who was living with another couple who got so desperate he climbed up the hill and went into an abandoned mine shaft and chopped down timbers until the roof fell on him."

I shut my eyes. In the darkness behind my shut lids I saw the drift mouth above Billy Collins' barber shop and I saw Rufe Fugate fighting his way up the hillside, blind, holding an axe, and I stopped hearing the man's voice, even though it was still going on. And then I heard it again, and it was saying that he apologized to Lucy and me and that he had gotten carried away, and he hoped we would forgive him, but this was a subject that really got to him . . .

I don't know what Lucy and I said—some polite small talk about understanding how he felt and of course we accepted his apology and we knew people got carried away at times—and then we excused ourselves and went back to our room. We didn't say anything to each other. We just sat there and looked out the window into the soft starlit Spanish darkness. But I was thinking. I wasn't thinking of Rufe Fugate or Anse Webb or my other friends. I was thinking of all the people in East Kentucky—how I'd condemned

274

them for passing up that golden chance they'd had, during the boom, to save their money for schools, security, and old age. As I saw it now, they couldn't have done anything else. They'd never had the training in self-discipline. Never. The coal interests had kept them children—and who can blame a child if he acts like a child?

Lucy had been watching me, I guess, from across the room, and she said, "Don't think about it, Charles. Don't get all upset. There's nothing you can do."

I looked at her.

And then, inside me, a little spark that I'd thought had died out burned bright, and a fire began to roar up inside me until it raged like a furnace in my head. I felt, somehow, as if I was a young man again—full of fight, full of power.

"Nothing I can do?" I said softly, and I smiled at my wife. "I wouldn't count on that, if I were you. There might just be a few little things I can do. After all, I've got five million dollars in the bank . . ."

Lucy looked at me, quite pale, her eyes wide.

"Do you really want to go to Greece?" I said.

And then Lucy's eyes changed. They got very bright, almost fierce, and then they filled with tears.

"No," she said. "No Charles, I don't want to go to Greece."

"Then what the hell are we waiting for?" I said. "Get on the phone. Call that cotton-picking airline! Let's get back home and get with it!"

THE LION PIT

BY FRANK HARVEY

**The thundering novel
of men, women,
sex and steel.**